The Silent Partner
and
"The Tenth of January"

THE SILENT PARTNER
A Novel

and

The Tenth of January
A Short Story

by Elizabeth Stuart Phelps
with an Afterword by
Mari Jo Buhle and Florence Howe

The Feminist Press
at The City University of New York
New York

Library of Congress Cataloging in Publication Data

Phelps, Elizabeth Stuart, 1844–1911.
  The silent partner.

  Reprint. Originally published: Boston: J. R. Osgood, 1871.
  I. Title.
PS3142.S5 1983   813'.4   82–25306
ISBN 0-935312-08-0 (pbk.)

First Feminist Press edition

Cover illustration created by Pro Photo, Bayside, New York from: Winslow Homer, "The Morning Bell," reproduced with permission from the Merrimack Valley Textile Museum; and *Costume Reference: Volume 6, The Victorians*, by Marion Sichel, Copyright © 1978 by Plays, Inc., reprinted with permission from the publisher.

CONTENTS

The Silent Partner

NOTE.

—◆—

IN the compilation of the facts which go to
form this fiction, it seems desirable to say
that I believe I have neither overlooked nor
libelled those intelligent manufacturers who have
expended much Christian ingenuity, with much
remarkable success, in ameliorating the condition
of factory operatives, and in blunting the edge of
those misapprehensions and disaffections which
exist between labor and capital, between employer and employed, between ease and toil,
between millions and mills, the world over.

Had Christian ingenuity been generally sy-
nonymous with the conduct of manufacturing cor-
porations, I should have found no occasion for
the writing of this book.

I believe that a wide-spread ignorance exists
among us regarding the abuses of our factory
system, more especially, but not exclusively, as
exhibited in many of the country mills.

Note.

I desire it to be understood that every alarming sign and every painful statement which I have given in these pages concerning the condition of the manufacturing districts could be matched with far less cheerful reading, and with far more pungent perplexities, from the pages of the Reports of the Massachusetts Bureau of Statistics of Labor, to which, with other documents of a kindred nature, and to the personal assistance of friends who have " testified that they have seen," I am deeply in debt for the ribs of my story.

E. S. P.

ANDOVER, December, 1870.

THE SILENT PARTNER.

CHAPTER I.

ACROSS THE GULF.

THE rainiest nights, like the rainiest lives, are by no means the saddest.

This occurred to Miss Kelso one January night, not many winters ago. Though, to be exact, it was rather the weather than the simile which occurred to her. The weather may happen to anybody, and so serves a purpose like photography and weddings. Reflections upon life you run your chance of at twenty-three.

If, in addition to the circumstance of being twenty-three, you are the daughter of a gentleman manufacturer, and a resident of Boston, it would hardly appear that you require the ceremony of an introduction. A pansy-bed in the sun would be a difficult subject of classification. Undoubtedly, pages might with ease

be occupied in treating of Miss Kelso's gene-
alogy. Her descent from the Pilgrims could be
indisputably proved. It would be possible to
ascertain whether or not she cried at her mother's funeral. Thrilling details of her life in the
nursery are upon record. Her first composition
is still legible. Indeed, three chapters, at the
least, might be so profitably employed in con-
veying to the intelligence of the most far-sighted
reader the remotest intimation of Miss Kelso's
existence, that one feels compelled into an apol-
ogy to high art for presenting her in three lines
and a northeaster.

Perhaps it should be added that this young
lady was engaged to be married to her father's
junior partner, and that she was sitting in her
father's library, with her hands folded, at the
time when the weather occurred to her; sitting, as she had been sitting all the opaque, gray
afternoon, in a crimson chair by a crimson fire,
a creamy profile and a creamy hand lifted and
cut between the two foci of color. The profile
had a level, generous chin. The hand had —
rings.

There are people who never do anything that

is not worth watching ; they cannot eat an apple
or button a shoe in an unnoticeable, unsuggestive
manner.   If they undertake to be awkward, they
do it so symbolically that you feel in debt to
them for it.   Miss Kelso may have been one
of these indexical persons ; at any rate, there
was something in her simple act of sitting before a fire, in her manner of shielding her eyes
from the warmth to which her figure was languidly abandoned, which to a posture-fancier
would have been very expressive.

She had noticed in an idle way, swathed to
the brain in her folds of heat and color, that the
chromatic run of drops upon a window, duly
deadened by drawn damask, and adapted nicely
to certain conditions of a cannel blaze, had a
pleasant sound.   Accurately, she had not found
herself to be the possessor of another thought
since dinner ; she had dined at three.

It had been a long storm, but Miss Kelso had
found no occasion to dampen the sole of her
delicate sandals in the little puddles that dotted
the freestone steps and drained pavement.   It
had been a cold storm, but the library held, as
a library should, the tints and scents of June.

It had been a dismal storm ; but what of that ? Miss Kelso was young, well, in love, and — Miss Kelso. Given the problem, Be miserable, she would have folded her hands there by her fire, like a puzzled snow-flake in a gorgeous poppy, and sighed, " But I do not understand ! "

To be sure, her father was out of town, and she had mislaid the score of *La Grande Duchesse*, — undesirable circumstances, both, but not without their compensations. For the placid pleasantness of five o'clock paternal society, she had the rich, irregular delights of solitude in a handsome house, — a dream, a doubt, a daring fancy that human society would snap, an odd hope pellmell upon the heels of an extraordinary fear, snatches of things, the mental chaos of a liberated prisoner. Isolation in elegance is not apt to be productive of thought, however, as I intimated.

Opposed to the loss of *La Duchesse* would be the pleasure of making Maverick look for it. Miss Kelso took a keen, appreciative enjoyment in having a lazy lover ; he gave her something to do ; he was an occupation in himself. She had indeed a weakness for an occupation ; suffered passions of superfluous life ; at the Cape

she rebelled because Providence had not created her a bluefisher ; in Paris she would make
muslin flowers, and learn the *métier* to-morrow.

This was piquant in her; her plighted husband found himself entertained by it always ;
he folded her two hands like sheets of rice-
paper over his own, with an easy smile.

The weather occurred to the young lady
about six o'clock in the form of a query : Was
it worth while to go out to-night ? She cultivated an objection to *Don Giovanni* in the rain,
— and it always rained on *Giovanni;* Maverick
could talk Brignoli to Mrs. Silver, and hold a
fan for Fly, as well without her ; she happened
to find herself more interested in an arm-chair
than in anything else in the world, and slippers
were the solution of the problem of life. Was
it worth while ?

This was one of those vital questions which
require immediate motives for a settlement, and
of immediate motives Miss Kelso possessed very
few. Indeed, it was as yet unanswered in her
own mind, when the silver handle of her carriage-
door had shut with a little shine like a smile

upon her, and Fly's voice, like boiling candy, bubbled at her from the front seat.

Maverick had called ; there had been a whiff of pleasant wet air in her face ; and, after all, life and patent springs are much alike in doors or out.

Miss Kelso sank languidly back into the perfumed cushions ; the close doors and windows shut in their thick sweetness ; the broken lights of the street dropped in, and Maverick sat beside her.

"You have had your carriage re-scented, Perley, I'm sure," said Fly, who was just enough at home with Perley to say it.

"From Harris's, — yes."

" Santalina, unless I am quite mistaken ? "

This, softly, from Mrs. Silver ; Mrs. Silver was apt to speak very softly.

" I was tired to death of heliotrope," said Perley, with a weary motion of her well-shaped head ; " it clings so.   There was some trouble, I believe, to take it out ; new stuffing and covering.   But I think it pays."

" Indeed, yes, richly."

" It always pays to take trouble for *sachet*, I think," said Fly, sententiously.

"Perley never makes a mistake in a perfume,"
— that came, of course, from Maverick.

"Perley never did make a mistake in a perfume," observed Mrs. Silver, in the mild motherly manner which she had acquired from frequently matronizing Perley. "Never from the
day Burt made the blunder of tuberoses for
her poor mother. The child flung them out
of the casket herself. She was six years old
the day before. It was a gratification to me
when Burt went out of fashion."

Perley, it may be presumed, feeling always
some awkwardness at the mention of a dead
parent for whom propriety required her to
mourn, and in connection with whose faint memory she could not, do the best she might, acquire
an unhappiness, made no reply, and *sachet* and
Mrs. Silver dropped into silence together. Fly
broke it, in her ready way : "So kind in you
to send for us, Perley !"

"It was quite proper," said Perley.

She did not think of anything else to say,
and fell, as her santalina and her chaperone
had fallen, a little noticeably out of the conversation.

Fly and Maverick Hayle did the talking. Mrs. Silver dropped in now and then properly.

Perley listened lazily to the three voices; one sometimes hears very noticeable voices from very unnoticeable people; these were distinct of note as a triplet; idle, soft, and sweet — sweetly, softly idle. She played accompaniments with them to her amused fancy.

The triplet rounded into a chord presently, and made her a little sleepy. Sensitive only to an occasional flat or sharp of Brignoli or Kellogg, she fell with half-closed eyes into the luxury of her own thoughts.

What were they? What does any young lady think about on her way to the opera? One would like to know. A young lady, for instance, who is used to her gloves, and indifferent to her stone cameos; who has the score by heart, and is tired of the *prima donna;* who has had a season ticket every winter since she can remember, and will have one every winter till she dies?

The ride to the theatre was not a short one, and slow that night on account of the storm, which was thickening a little, half snow.

Perley, through the white curtains of her falling eyelids, looked out at it; she was fond of watching the streets when no one was watching her, especially on stormy nights, for no reason in particular that she knew of, except that she felt so dry and comfortable. So clean too! There were a great many muddy people out that night; the sleet did not wash them as fast as the mud spattered them; and the wind at the corners sprang on them sharply. From her carriage window she could look on and see it lying in wait for them, and see it crouch and bound and set teeth on them. She really followed with some interest, having nothing better to do, the manful struggles of a girl in a plaid dress, who battled with the gusts about a carriage-length ahead of her, for perhaps half a dozen blocks. This girl struck out with her hands as a boxer would; sometimes she pommelled with her elbows and knees like a desperate prize-fighter; she was rather small, but she kept her balance; when her straw hat blew off, she chased headlong after it, and Perley languidly smiled. She was apt to be amused by the world outside of her carriage. It conceived such original ways of holding its hands, and wearing its hats, and carrying its bundles. It had such a taste in colors, such disregard of clean linen, and was always in such a hurry. This last especially interested her; Miss Kelso had never been in a hurry in her life.

" There ! " said Fly.

" Where ? " said Perley, starting.

" I 've broken my fan ; made a perfect wreck of it ! What shall I do ? No, thank you. Mr. Hayle, I am in blue to-night. You know you could n't fail to get me a green one if you tried. You must bring me out — but it 's too wet to bring fans out. Mother, we must go in ourselves."

So it came about that in the land of fans, or in the region roundabout, Maverick and the Silvers disappeared in the flash of a fancy-store, and Perley, in the carriage, was left alone.

" Dear me ! " said Mrs. Silver, placidly, as the umbrella extinguished her, " we are making our friends a great deal of trouble, Fly, for a little thing."

Now Perley did not find it a trouble. She was rather glad to be alone for a few minutes.

In fact, she took it very kindly in Fly to break that fan, and, as she afterwards thought, with reason.

The carriage door was left open, by her orders. She found something pleasant in the wet wildness of the storm ; it came near enough almost to dampen her cheek as she leaned forward towards it ; and the street came into the frame that was left, in a sharp picture.

The sidewalk was very wet ; in spots the struggling snow drifted grayish white, and went out into black mud under a sudden foot ; the eaves and awnings dripped steadily, and there was a little puddle on the carriage step ; the colored lights of a druggist's window shimmered and broke against the pavement and the carriage and the sleet, leaving upon the fancy the surprise of a rainbow in a snow-storm ; people's faces dipped through it curiously ; here, a fellow with a waxed mustache struck into murderous red, and dripped so horridly that a policeman, in the confusion of the storm, eyed him for half a block ; there, a hale old man fell suddenly into the last stages of jaundice ; beyond, a girl straggling jealously behind a couple of very wet, but very happy lovers, turned deadly green ; a little this way, another stepped into a bar of lily white, and stood and shone in it for an instant, ' without spot or stain, or any such thing," but stepped out of it, quite out, shaking herself a little as she went, as if the lighted touch had scorched her.

Still another girl (Miss Kelso expressed to herself some languid wonder that the night should find so many young girls out, and alone, and noted how little difference the weather appeared to make with that class of people) — the girl in plaid, whom the storm had buffeted back for the last few moments — came up with the carriage, and stopped, full against the druggist's window, for breath. She looked taller, standing in the light, than she had done when boxing the wind at the corners, but still a little undersized ; she had no gloves, and her straw hat hung around her neck by the strings ; she must have been very cold, for her lips were blue, but she did not shiver.

Who has not noticed that fantastic fate of galleries, which will hang a saint and a Magdalene, a Lazarus and Dives, face to face ? And who has not felt, with those transfixed glances, doomed by sunlight, starlight, moonlight, twilight, in crowds and in hush, from year unto year, to struggle towards each other, — vain builders of a vain bridge across the fixed gulf of an irreparable lot, — a weariness of sympathy, which wellnigh extinguished the artistic fineness of the chance? Something of this feeling would have struck a keen observer of Miss Kelso and the little girl in plaid.

Their eyes had met, when the girl lifted her arms to tie on her hat. Against the burning globes of the druggist's window, which quivered and swam through the sheen of the fall of sleet, and just where the perfect prism broke about her, she made a miserably meagre figure. Miss Kelso, from the soft dry gloom of her carriage door, leaned out resplendent.

The girl's lips moved angrily, and she said something in a sharp voice which the wind must have carried the other way, for the druggist heard it, and sent a clerk out to order her off. Miss Kelso, obeying one of her whimsical impulses, — who had a better right, indeed, to be whimsical ? — beckoned to the girl, who, after swearing a little at the druggist's clerk, strode up rather roughly to the carriage.

"What do you want of me? and what were you staring at? Did n't you ever see anybody lose his hat in a sleet-storm before?"

"I beg your pardon," said Miss Kelso; "I did not mean to be rude."

She spoke on the instinct of a lady. She was nothing of a philanthropist, not much of a Christian. Let us be honest, even if inbred sin and courtesy, not justification by faith, and conscience, induced this rather remarkable reply. I call it remarkable, from the standpoint of girls in plaid. That particular girl, without doubt, found it so. She raised her eyes quickly and keenly to the young lady's face.

"I think I must have been sorry for you," observed Miss Kelso; "that was why I looked at you. You seemed cold and wet."

"*You*'re not cold and wet, at any rate."

This was raggedly said, and bitter. It made Miss Kelso feel singularly uncomfortable; as if she were to blame for *not* being cold and wet. She felt a curious impulse towards self-defence, and curiously enough she followed it by saying, "I cannot help that!"

" No," said the girl, after a moment's thought.
" N-no ; but I hate to be pitied by carriage-
folks. I won't be pitied by carriage-folks ! "

" Sit down on the steps," said Miss Kelso, "and
let me look at you. I do not often see people
just like you. What is your name ? "

" What 's yours ? "

" I am called Miss Kelso."

" And *I* am called Sip Garth."

That ragged bitterness was in the girl's voice
again, much refined, but distinct. Miss Kelso, to
whom it seemed quite natural that the small
minority of the world should feel at liberty to
use, at first sight, the Christian name of the large
remainder, took little or no notice of it.

But what could bring her out in such a
storm, asked Miss Kelso of Sip Garth.

" The Blue Plum brings out better than me.
Who cares for a little sleet ? See how wet I
am ! *I* don't care." She wrung out her thin
and dripping shawl, as she spoke, between her
bare, wet hands.

" The Blue Plum ? " Miss Kelso hesitated,
taking the thing daintily upon her lips. What
did she, or should she, know of the Blue Plum ?

"But the theatre is no place for you, my poor girl." She felt sure of as much as that. She had dimly understood as much from her father and the newspapers. No theatre patronized by the lower classes could be a place for a poor girl.

"It's no place for you," she said again. "You had so much better go home."

Sip Garth laughed. She swung herself upon the highest step of Miss Kelso's carriage, and laughed almost in Miss Kelso's fine, shocked face.

"How do *you* know whether I had so much better go home? Wait till *you*'ve been working on your feet all day, and wait till *you* live where *I* live, before you know whether I had so much better go home! Besides" — she broke off with a quick change of tone and countenance — "I don't go for the Plum. The Plum does n't make much odds to me. I go to see how much better I could do it."

"Could you?"

"*Could n't* I!"

"I don't quite understand."

"I don't suppose you do. Give me the music,

give me the lights, and the people, and the
poetry, and *I*'d do it.   I'd make 'em laugh,
would n't I ?   I'd make 'em cry, you may make
up your mind on that.   That's what I go to the
Plum for.   I do it over.   That's what you think
of in the mills, don't you see ?   That's so much
better than going home, — to do it over."

"You seem," said Miss Kelso, with some perplexed weariness in her expression, — perhaps
she had carried her whim quite far enough, —
"you seem to be a very singular girl."

Evidently Miss Kelso's coachman, whose hat-
brim appeared and peered uneasily over the box
at disgusted intervals, thought so too.   Evidently
the passers, such of them as had preserved their
eyesight from the ravages of the sleet, thought
so too.   Evidently it was quite time for the girl
in plaid to go.

"I wonder what *you* seem like," said Sip
Garth, thoughtfully.   She leaned, as she spoke,
into the sweet dimness of the carriage, and
gravely studied the sweet dimness of the young
lady's face.   Having done this, she nodded to
herself once or twice with a shrewd smile, but
said nothing.   Her wet shawl now almost brushed

2

Miss Kelso's dress ; the girl was not filthy, but the cleanliest poverty in a Boston tenement-house fails to acquire the perfumes of Arabia, and Perley sickened and shrank. Yet it struck her as odd, for the moment, if you will believe it, that she should have santalina in her carriage cushions ; not as ill-judged, not as undesirable, not as in any way the concern of girls from tenement-houses, not at all as something which she would not do again to-morrow, but only as odd.

She had thought no more than this, when the disgusted coachman, with an air of infinite personal relief, officially announced Mr. Hayle, and Fly came laughing sweetly back. It was quite time for Sip to go.

In the confusion she dripped away among the water-spouts like one of them, before Miss Kelso could speak to her again.

The street came into the frame that was left in a sharp picture. The sidewalk was once more very wet ; in spots the struggling snow drifted, grayish white, and went out into black mud under sudden feet ; the eaves and awnings dripped steadily, and there was a little puddle on the carriage steps.

Miss Kelso had a young, fresh imagination, a little highly colored, perhaps, by opera music, and it made these things a vivid background for the girl in plaid, into which and out of which she stepped with a fanciful significance.

With the exception of her servants, her seamstresses, and the very little members of a very little Sabbath-school class, which demanded of her very little thought and excited in her very little interest, Miss Kelso had never in her life before — I think I speak without exaggeration — had never in her life before exchanged a dozen words with an example of what Maverick Hayle was pleased to term the οἱ πολλοί, thereby evincing at once his keen appreciation of the finer distinctions both of life and letters, as well as the fact, that, though a successful manufacturer, he had received a collegiate education and had not yet forgotten it. And, indeed, as he was accustomed to observe, " Nothing gives a man such a *prestige* in society."

The girl in plaid then, to repeat, was a novelty to Perley Kelso. She fell back into her cushions again to think about her.

" Poor Perley ! I hope she found herself amused

while we were gone," sympathized Fly, fluttering in with her new fan. Perley thanked her, and had found herself amused, much amused.

Yet, in truth, she had found herself saddened, singularly saddened. She could scarcely have understood why. Nothing more definite than an uncomfortable consciousness that all the world had not an abundance of *sachet* and an appreciation of Brignoli struck her distinctly. But how it rained on that girl looking in at her from the carriage steps! It must rain on many girls while she sat in her sweet, warm, sheltered darkness. It must be a disagreeable thing, this being out in the rain. She did not fancy the thud of drops on her carriage-roof as much as usual; the wind waiting at corners to crouch and spring on people ceased to amuse her; it looked cruel and cold. She shivered and looked so chilly that Maverick folded her ermines like a wonderful warm snow-cloud tenderly about her, and drowned the storm from her hearing with his tender, lazy voice.

In the decorous rustle of the crowd winding down through the corridors, like a glittering snake, after *Giovanni* that night, Fly started

with a little faint scream, and touched Perley
on the arm.

"My *dear* Perley! — Mr. Hayle, there is a girl
annoying Perley."

At Perley's elbow, trying quietly but persist-
ently to attract her attention, Perley was startled
and not well pleased to see the girl in plaid. In
the heat and light and scent and soft babble of
the place, she cut a jagged outline. The crowd
broke in beautiful billows about her and away
from her. It seemed not unlike a radiant sea
out of which she had risen, black and warning as
a hidden reef. She might have been thought to be
not so much a foreign horror as a sunken danger
in the shining place. She seemed, indeed, rather
to have bounded native from its glitter, than to
have forced herself upon it. Her eyes were very
large and bright, and she drew Perley's beautiful,
disturbed face down to her own with one bare
hand.

"Look here, young lady, I want to speak to
you. I want to know why you tell *me* the Plum
is no place for *me?* What kind of a place is
this for you? — now say, what kind of a place?
You don't know; but I do. I followed you here

to see. I tell you it's the plating over that's
the difference ; the plating over. At the Plum
we say what we mean ; and we mean bad enough,
very like. We 're rough, and we 're out with it.
Up at this place they're in with it. They plate
over. The music plates over. The people plate
over. It's different from us, and it ain't different
from us. Don't you see ? No, you don't. I do.
But you'd ought to, — you'd ought to. You're
old enough and wise enough. I don't mean to
be saucy ; but I put it to you honest, if I have
n't seen and heard that in this grand place to-
night — all plated over — that's no more fit for a
lady like you seem to be to sit and see and hear,
than it's fit for me and the like of me to sit and
see and hear the Plum. I put it to you honest,
and that's all, and I'm sorry to plague you with
all your fine friends about, for I liked the looks
of you right well when I sat on your carriage
steps. But it ain't often you 'll have the chance
to hear truer words from a rough girl like me ;
and it ain't likely you hear no more words true
nor false from me ; so good by, young lady. I
put it to you honest ! "

"Hush ! " said Miss Kelso, somewhat pale, as

Maverick stepped up to drive the girl away. "Let her alone. It 's only a girl I — amused myself with when you went with Fly for the fan. Let her be. It was only a whim of mine, and, as it has proved, a foolish one. I am not used to such people. She was coarse and hurt me. But let her go."

"I should advise you to choose your amusements more wisely another time," said Maverick Hayle, looking angrily after Sip, who was edging her way, with a sharp motion, through the radiant sea. She disappeared from view on the stairway suddenly, and the waves of scent and light and heat and babble met and closed over her as merrily as waves are wont to meet and close over sunken reefs.

The ripple of Miss Kelso's disturbed thoughts closed over her no less thoroughly, after the momentary annoyance was past. She had done a foolish thing, and been severely punished for it. That was all. As Maverick said, the lower classes could not bear any unusual attention from their betters, without injury. Maverick in his business connection had occasion to know. He must be right.

Maverick in his business connection had occasion to know another thing that night. Maverick in his business connection was met by a telegram, on returning with Miss Kelso to her father's house. The senior partner held the despatch in his hand. He was sitting in Miss Kelso's parlor. His face was grave and disturbed.

" Losses, perhaps," thought Perley, and left father and son alone. They did not seem inclined to remain alone, however. She had not yet taken off her wraps in the hall, when she heard Maverick say in an agitated voice, " I can't ! I cannot do it ! " and Mr. Hayle the senior came out. The despatch was still in his hand.

" My dear Miss Perley," he said, with some hesitation.

" Yes, sir ? " said Perley, unfastening her corded fur.

" Your father — "

" Wait a minute ! " said Perley, speaking fast. She unfastened the fur, and folded the cape up into a white heap with much pains and precision.

She was struck with a childish dread of hear-

ing a horrible thing. She felt singularly confused. Snatches of *Giovanni* danced through
her brain. She thought that she saw the girl
in plaid sitting on her front stairs, with a world-
ful of rain upon her head. Her own thought
came curiously back to her, in words: "How
disagreeable it must be to sit out in the rain!"
Her youth and happiness shrank with a sudden
faint sickness at being disturbed. It was with as
much fright as grief that she took the paper from
her father's old friend and read:—

"*Crushed at six o'clock this afternoon, in the
freight depot at Five Falls. Instant death.*"

2 *   C

CHAPTER II.

THE SLIPPERY PATH.

NOTHING is more conducive to one's sense of personal comfort than to live in a factory town and not be obliged to answer factory bells. This is especially to be said of those misty morning bells, which lay a cloudy finger upon one's last lingering dream, and dip it and dimple it into shreds; of those six-o'clock winter bells, whose very tongues seem to have stiffened with the cold, and to move thickly and numbly against their frosted cheeks. One listens and dozes, and would dream again but for listening again, and draws one's silk and eider shoulder-robe closer to one's warm throat with a shiver of rare enjoyment. Iron voices follow, and pierce the shoulder-robe. They are distinct in spite of the eider, though a little hoarse. One turns and wraps one's self again. They are dulled, but inexorable. One listens and dozes, and would dream again

but for listening. The inexorable is the delightful. One has to take only the pleasure of listening. A dim consciousness of many steps of cold
people cutting the biting, sunless air, gives a
crispness to the blankets. The bells shiver in
sympathy with the steps, and the steps shiver in
response to the bells. The bells hurry, hurry,
hurry on the steps. The steps hurry, hurry,
hurry to the bells. The bells grow cross and
snappish, — it is so cold. The steps grow pert
and saucy, — it is so cold. Bells and steps, in a
convulsion of ill-temper, go out from hearing together, and only a sense of pillows and two hours
before breakfast fills the world.

Miss Kelso, waking to the six-o'clock bells of a
winter morning, appreciates this with uncommon
keenness ; with the more uncommon keenness
that she has never waked to the six-o'clock bells
of a winter morning before. She has experienced
the new sensation of spending, for the first time,
a February night in her July house, and is so
thoroughly convinced that she ought to be cold,
and so perfectly assured that she is n't, that the
dangerous consideration of the possible two hours
before mentioned, and the undeniable fact that

she has invited Maverick to breakfast at seven, incite between her delicate young flesh and her delicate young conscience one of those painful and prolonged struggles which it is impossible for any one who is obliged to get up in the morning to appreciate. Conscience conquering, after a protracted contest, the vanquished party slips reluctantly and slowly out of silk and eider into *crépins* and Persiana, just as Mr. Maverick Hayle's self-possessed ring plays leisurely through the house.

The ghastly death of the managing partner has had its effect upon his business and his daughter, without doubt. Upon his business — as might be assumed from the fact that Maverick Hayle should breakfast at seven o'clock — a confusing effect, requiring care and time to adjust with wisdom. Upon his daughter, — what, for instance ? If he slipped from her life, as he slips from her story, so heart slips away from heart, and love from love, with the slide of every hour. To cross the gap from life with a father to life without, very much as the February night descended upon the July house, were not unnatural. One must be warm, at all events.

Her grief was wrapped in swaddling-clothes. It was such a young grief, and she so young a griever ; and the sun shone, and the winter air was crisp.

Perley had been fond of her father, — of course ; and mourned him, — of course : but fondness is not friendship, and mourning is not desolation. Add to this a certain obstinate vein in this young woman, which suggested it to her fancy as a point of loyalty to her father's memory not to strain her sorrow beyond its honest altitude, and what follows? To be at first very sadly shocked, to be next very truly lonely ; to wish that she had never been cross to him (which she had), and to be sure that he had never been cross to her (which he had) ; to see, and love to see, the best of the departed life and the sweetest of the departed days ; and then to wander musing away, by sheer force of contrast, upon her own unfinished life, and into the sweetness of her own coming days, and repent of it next moment ; to forget one afternoon to notice the five-o'clock solitude because Maverick comes in ; to take very much to her Prayer-Book the first fortnight, and entirely to

Five Falls the second ; and to be pouring out her lover's coffee this morning, very lovely, a little quiet, and less unhappy.

" But pale ?" suggested Maverick, leaning back in his chair, with the raised eyebrow of a connoisseur, to pronounce upon the effect of her. The effect was good, very good. Her black dress, and the little silver *tête-à-tête* service over which she leaned, set one another off quaintly ; and a trifle more color in her face would have left the impression of a sketch finished by two artists who had failed of each other's idea.

Perley did not know that she was pale ; did not feel pale ; felt perhaps — and paused.

How did she feel ?

Apparently she did not feel like explaining to Maverick Hayle. Something in the delicate motion with which he raised the delicate napkin in his well-shaped hand to his delicately trimmed mustache acted perhaps as a counter-irritant to some delicate shading of her thought. It would not have been the first time that such a thing had happened. He was as necessary to Perley Kelso as her Axminster carpets ; he suited her in the same way ; in the same way he — sometimes — wearied her. But how did she feel?

"As nearly as I can make out," said Perley, "I feel like a large damask curtain taken down for the first time off its cornice," with a glance at the heavy walnut mouldings of her windows. "All in a heap, you know, and surprised. Or like a — what do you call it? that part of a plane that runs in a groove, when you stop the groove up. And I'm not used, you know, Maverick, to feeling at all; it's never been asked of me before."

She smiled and playfully shook her head; but her young eyes were perplexed and gently sad.

"It was coming to this cold house, under the circumstances," suggested Maverick.

No; Perley shook her head again; the house was not cold; never mind. Was his cup out? The milk was cold, at any rate; he must wait a minute; and so sat thoughtfully silent while she touched the bell, with the little silver service shining against her shoulder and the curve of her arm.

"What did you come down here for?" asked Maverick, over his second cup.

Perley did n't know.

"When shall you go back?"

Perley did n't know that.

"What are you going to do?"

Perley did n't know that, either. "Perhaps I shall not go back. I am tired of town. Perhaps I shall stay here and look after — things."

"Things? For instance?"

"The mills, for instance. My property, for instance."

Maverick lazily laughed; pushing back his chair, and raising the connoisseur's eyebrow again at the little shining service, and the black curve of the womanly, warm arm.

Perhaps she would take his place this morning; he was late, now; she could rake over a shoddy-heap, he was sure, or scold an overseer. He would agree to sit by the fire and order dinner, if she would just run over to father's for him and bring him his slippers.

"I 'll run over to the counting-room with you, and bring you to repentance," said Perley; "the air must be like wine this morning, and the sun like heaven."

The air was so much like wine and the sun like

heaven, that Perley, upon leaving the junior partner at the mill-gates, strolled on by a path on the river's brink through and beyond the town, finding herself loath to go back and sit by the fire and order dinner ; the more so, possibly, because she was a bit annoyed that Maverick should have hit with such exactness her typical morning ; it had, somehow, a useless, silly sound.

A useless, silly sound in this town of Five Falls was artistically out of place. She almost felt herself to be a superfluity in the cold, crisp air filled to the full with business noises ; and took a pleasure in following the river almost out of hearing of the mill machinery, and quite into the frozen silence of the upper stream.

Though the stream was large, the town was not ; neither had the mills, from that distance, an imposing air. Perley, with a sudden remembrance of the size of her income, wondered at this for the first time. " The business " had been a standing mystery in the young lady's careless fancy, the existence of which she had dimly understood from her father, as she had dimly understood the existence of " The Blue Plum " ; perhaps both had been about equally withheld from her comprehension. That there was some cotton in it she felt sure ; that it was a responsible business and a profitable business she understood ; that there were girls in little shawls, ragged men, and bad tobacco, an occasional strike, and a mission Sunday school connected with it, she remembered.

Upon the cool of her summer rest the hot whir of the thing had never breathed. Factory feet had trodden as lightly as dewdrops upon her early dreams.

She put on Five Falls for a few months every year as she put on a white dress, — a cool thing, which kept wash-people busy.

Five Falls in July agreed with her, and she fancied it. Five Falls in February entertained her, and she found it suggestive ; and indeed Five Falls in February was not a barren sight.

She had wandered, it might be, half a mile up stream, and had turned to look behind her, just at the spot from which the five cascades, which named the town, broke into view ; more accurately, there were four cascades — pretty, swift, slender things — and the dam. The stream was a deep one, with a powerful current, and Perley noticed the unusual strength of the bridge below the dam. It was a county bridge and well built ; its stone piers, freckled and fringed with heavy frost, had the sombre, opulent air of time-worn frescos, behind which arches of light and sky drew breath like living things, and palpitated in time to the irregular pulse of the water.

The pulse of the water was sluggish, half choked by swathings of beautiful ice ; the falls, caught in their tiny leap, hung, frozen to the heart, in mid-air; the open dam, swift, relentless, and free, mocked at them with peals of hollow laughter ; and great puffs and palls of smoke, which overhung the distant hum of the little town, made mouths, one fancied, at the shining whiteness of the fields and river bank.

Miss Kelso, turning to retrace her steps with her face set thoughtfully towards this sight, was disturbed by a quick, loud tread behind her ; it came abreast of her and passed her, and, in so doing, thrust the flutter of a dingy plaid dress against her in the narrow path.

Either some faded association with the faded dress or with the energetic tread, or both, puzzled Miss Kelso, and she stopped to consider it.

Apparently the girl stopped to consider something, but without turning her head. Miss Kelso, after a moment's hesitation, stepped up and touched her on the shoulder.

"I knew you," said the girl abruptly, still without turning her head. "I did n't suppose you'd know me. You need n't unless you want to."

"I *had* forgotten you," said Perley, frankly. "But I remember now. I remember very well. I am surprised to see you in Five Falls."

"You need n't never be surprised to see factory folks anywhere," said Sip Garth. "We're a restless set. Wanderers on the face of the earth."

"Are you in my father's — in the mills?"

"Yes," more gently, and with a glance at Perley's mourning, "in your mills, I suppose; the brick ones, — yes. I supposed they were yours when I heard the names. But folks told me you only come down here in summer-time. I did n't expect to see you. I've been here three weeks."

"You like it here?" asked Miss Kelso, somewhat at a loss how to pursue the art of conversation under what she found to be such original circumstances, — she and Sip were walking towards the town now, in the widening path, side by side.

" I hope you like it here ? " she repeated.

" Catty likes. It does n't make much odds to me."

" Who is Catty ? "

" That 's my sister ; we 're the last of us, she and I. Father got smashed up three weeks ago last Friday ; caught in the gearing by the arm. They would n't let Catty and me look at him, he was smashed so. But I looked when there was n't anybody round. I wanted to see the last of him. I never thought much of father, but I wanted to see the last of him."

In her controlled, well-bred way, Perley sickened and shrunk again, as she had sickened and shrunk from this girl before, but said quickly, " O, I am sorry ! "

" You need n't be," said Sip Garth. " Have n't I told you that I did n't think much of father ? I never did neither."

" But that is dreadful ! " exclaimed Miss Kelso. " Your own father ! and now he is dead ! "

Something in their kindred deprivation moved

Perley ; an emotion more like sympathy than recoil, and more like attraction than disgust, took possession of her as they walked slowly and more slowly, in the ever-widening path, side by side into the town.

"He beat Catty," said Sip, after a pause, in a low voice. "He beat me, but I did n't make so much of that. He used to take my wages. I had to hide 'em, but he used to find 'em. He spent it on drink. You never saw a man get drunker than my father could, Miss Kelso."

Miss Kelso presumed that she never had ; thinking swiftly how amused Maverick would be at that, but said nothing.

"Drunk as a beast," continued Sip, in an interested tone, as if she were explaining a problem in science, — "drunk as a fool. Why, so drunk, he 'd lie on a rummy's floor for twenty-four hours, dead as a door-nail. I 've seen them kick him out, down the steps, into the ditch, you know, when they could n't get rid of him no other way. Then " — lowering her voice again — "then he came home and beat Catty."

"You seem to be fond of your sister," observed Miss Kelso.

"Yes," said Sip, after some silence, — "yes, I love Catty."

"You have not been to work this morning?" asked Perley, for want of something better to say.

"No, I asked out to-day. Catty's sick. I've just been up river to Bijah's after some dockweed for her; he had some dock-weed, and he told me to come; he's a well-meaning old chap, Bijah Mudge."

Not having the pleasure of the acquaintance of Mr. Mudge, Perley was perplexed how to follow the topic, and did not try.

"I suppose you think I was saucy to you," said Sip, suddenly, "in the Opera House, I mean. I did n't expect you 'd ever notice me again."

"You 'put it to me honest,' certainly," said Miss Kelso, smiling. "But though, of course, you were quite mistaken, I did not think, as far as I thought at all about it, that you meant to be impertinent. The Opera question, Sip, is one which it takes a cultivated lover of music to understand."

"Oh!" said Sip with a puzzled face.

"Poetry, fiction, art, all are open to the same

objections which you found to *Giovanni.* People are affected by these things very differently. Superior music is purity itself; it clears the air; and only — "

Miss Kelso remembered suddenly that she was talking to an ignorant factory-girl; a girl who went to the Blue Plum, and had never heard of Mozart; wondered how she could have made such a blunder; collected her scattered pearls into a hasty change of subject, — something about the cold weather and mill-hours and Catty.

" Catty's deaf," said Sip again in her sudden way, after they had walked in silence for a few moments down the shining, slippery, broadening way. She lifted her little brown face sidewise to Perley's abstracted one, to watch the effect of this; hesitating, it seemed, whether it were worth while to bestow some lingering confidence upon her.

"Ah!" said Perley; "poor thing!"

The little brown face fell, and with it fell another pause. It had been a thoughtful pause for Miss Kelso, and she broke it in a thoughtful voice.

"Can you stop with your dock-weed long enough to sit down here a minute? It is warm in the sun just here on these rocks, and we are so close to town; and I want you to talk to me."

"I have n't got anything to say to you," said Sip a little sullenly, sitting down, however, upon a broad, dry rock, and spreading her hands, which were bare and purple, out upon her lap in the sun.

"Don't you earn enough to buy you gloves?" asked Miss Kelso.

"Catty had my gloves," said Sip, evasively. "What do you want of me? I can't stay long."

"Why, I hardly know," said Perley, slowly. "I want you to talk without being questioned. I don't like to question you all the time. But I want to hear more about you, and — you did n't speak of your mother; and where you live, and how; and many other things. I am not used to people who live as you do. I presume I do not understand how to treat you. I do not think it is curiosity. I think it is — I do not know what it is. I suppose I am sorry."

"You need n't trouble yourself to be sorry, as I 've said before," replied Sip, chafing her purple fingers. "Besides, I have n't much to tell.

There's folks in your mills has enough to tell, that would make stories in newspapers, I bet you ! Foreigners mostly. If you want stories to amuse you, you've come to the wrong place. I'm a Yankee, and my mother was a Yankee. Father was n't ; but I don't know what he was, and I don't believe he knew himself. There's been six of us, put together ; the rest died, babies mostly, of drink and abuse. I wish Catty and me'd been two of 'em ! Well, mother she died with one of 'em four years ago (it was born of a Tuesday, and Thursday morning she was to work, and Saturday noon she was dead), and father he died of the gearing, and Catty and me moved here where there was easy work for Catty. We was in a hoop-skirt factory before, at Waltham ; I used to come in nights to the Blue Plum, as you see me in your carriage. I guess that's all. I've worked to cotton-mills before the hoops ; so they put me right to weaving. I told you we're a restless lot. But we're always at factory jobs someways, from father to son and mother to daughter. It's in the blood. But I guess that's all.

"You have good prompt pay," said Miss Kelso,

properly. " I suppose that you could not have
a better or healthier occupation. You get so
much exercise and air."

She had heard her father say this, in times
long past.

Sip shrugged her shoulders with a suppressed
laugh ; the unmistakable, incorrigible, suppressed
laugh of " discontented labor," but said nothing.

" I should like to see your sister Catty," said
Perley, obliged to reintroduce conversation.

" We 're on the Company board. You can
come when she gets well."

" How long has she been deaf? "

" It may not please you to hear," said Sip,
reluctantly.

Miss Kelso was sure that it would not displease
her to hear.

" Well, they were running extra time," said
Sip, " in the town where we was at work before Catty was born. They were running fourteen hours a day. Mother she was at work,
you know. There was no two ways to that.
Father was on a spree, and we children were
little shavers, earning next to nothing. She
begged off from the extra ; but it was all, or

quit ; it 's always all or quit.   Quit she could n't.
I 'll say this for Jack Bench, — he was our boss,
— Jack, he had n't got it through his head what
condition she was in.   But she worked till a
Saturday night, and Catty was born on a Mon-
day morning.   Father came off his drunk Sunday, and Jack Bench he always laid it on to
that ; but Catty was born deaf.   Father did
fly round pretty well that Sunday night, and
maybe it helped.   But he did n't strike mother.
I was round all day to see to it that he should
n't strike.   But Catty was born deaf — and,"
half under her breath, " and — queer, and dumb,
you know ; but I 've taught her a little talk.
She talks on her fingers.   Sometimes she makes
sounds in her throat.   But I can always understand Catty.   Poor Catty !   It 's never her fault,
but she 's a world of care and wear."

"But such things," said Miss Kelso, rising
with a shocked face from the sunny stone, " do
not often happen in our New England factories ! "

" I only know what I know," said Sip, shortly ;
" I did n't blame anybody.   I never knew any
other woman as it turned out so bad to.   They

're mostly particular about women in that state ; fact is, they 're mostly more particular than the women themselves. I 've seen a boss threaten a woman with her notice to get her home, and she would n't stir. But it 's all or quit, in general."

"But these people cannot be in such need of money as that !" said Perley.

"Folks don't do such things for fun," said Sip, shortly.

"But in our mills —"

"Your own mills are your own affairs," interrupted Sip. "You 'd better find out for yourself. It ain't to complain to you that I talk to you."

They had come now quite into the town, and stopped, at the parting of their several ways. Miss Kelso held out her hand to the girl, with a troubled face. The mills were making a great noise and confused her, and she felt that it was of little use to say anything further than that she should try to come and see Catty, and that she thanked her for — but she was sure that she did not know for what, and so left the sentence unfinished, and bade her good morning instead.

Sip Garth stood still in a snow-drift, and rubbed her hands, which had grown pink and warm. Her brown little face was puzzled.

"It was n't all the sun, nor yet the touch. It was the newness, I think," she said.

She said it again to Catty, when she got home with the dock-weed.

"Eh!" said Catty. She made a little harsh sound like a croak.

"O, no matter," said Sip, talking upon her fingers, "you could n't understand! But I think it must have been the newness."

CHAPTER III.

A GAME OF CHESS.

" I BEG your pardon ? " said Maverick Hayle. He said it in simple bewilderment.

Perley repeated her remark.

" You wish — excuse me — *do* I understand you to wish — "

"' Partner ' was undoubtedly the word that she used, Maverick," said Mr. Hayle the senior, with an amused smile.

" I want to be a partner in the firm," reiterated Perley, with great distinctness ; " you 're very stupid this morning, Maverick, if you 'll excuse *me*. I thought I had expressed myself clearly. I want to be a partner in Hayle and Kelso."

They were sitting — the two gentlemen and the young lady — around a table in Miss Kelso's parlor : a little table which Perley had cleared to its pretty inlaid surface, with some indefinite idea, which vastly entertained Maverick, of having

room in which to "conduct business." Some
loose papers, a new glazed blank-book, and a little
gold pencil lay upon the table. The pattern of
the table was a chess-board of unusual beauty :
Miss Kelso's hand, slightly restless, traced the
little marble squares, sometimes with the pencil,
sometimes without, while she talked. The squares
were of veined gray and green.

"I sent for you this morning," said Perley,
turning to the elder gentleman, "because it
seemed to me quite time that I should understand
the state of my affairs as my father's death has
left them. I am very ignorant, of course. He
never talked to me about the business ; but I
suppose that I could learn. I should prefer to
learn to understand my own affairs. This is not
inconsistent, I am sure you will appreciate, with
that confidence which it is my delight to feel in
you and Maverick."

Maverick, at the sound of his own name, looked
up with a faint effort to recall what had preceded
it, having plunged suddenly and irretrievably into
the depths of a decision that Story, the next time
he was in the country, should make a study of a
hand upon squares of gray and green. In self-
defence he said so.

"Whatever responsibilities," said Perley, with a slight twitch of annoyance between her eyes, and speaking still to the elder gentleman,—"whatever responsibilities rest upon me, as sole heir to my father's property, I am anxious to fulfil in person. Whatever connection I have with the Hayle and Kelso Mills, I am anxious, I am exceedingly anxious, to meet in person. And I thought," added the young lady, innocently, "that the simplest way would be for me to become a partner."

"Now I don't know another woman," said Maverick, rousing, with an indulgent smile, "who could have originated that, father, if she had tried. Let us take her in. By all means take her in. As she says, what could be simpler?"

"Miss Perley will of course understand what would be in due time legally and suitably explained to her," observed Mr. Hayle, "that she has, and need have, no responsibilities as heir to her father's property ; that she has, and can have, no such connection with the Hayle and Kelso Mills as requires the least exertion or anxiety upon her part."

"But I don't understand at all," said Perley.

3 *

"I thought I fell heir to all that, with the money. At least I thought I could if I wished to."

"But we 're private, not corporate, don't you see ? " explained Maverick, carelessly. "You don't fall heir to a partnership in a company as you would to stock in a corporation, Perley. You must see that."

Probably Perley did not see that in the least. The little gold pencil traced a row of greens and skipped a row of grays in a sadly puzzled, un-business-like way.

"You could not fall heir to the partnership even if you were a man," continued Maverick, in his patronizing fashion. "The choice of a new partner, or whether, indeed, there shall be a new partner, is a matter resting wholly with the Senior and myself to settle. Do I make it clear ? "

"Quite clear," said Perley, brightening ; "so clear, that I do not see anything in the world to prevent your choosing me."

Both gentlemen laughed ; about as much as they seemed to think was expected of them. Maverick took up the pencil which Perley had laid down, and jotted green squares at his end of the table. Perley, at hers, slipped her empty

fingers musingly along a soft gray vein. She
was half vexed, and a little mortified. For the
first time in her life, she was inclined to feel
ashamed of being a woman. She was seriously
interested, — perhaps, again, for the first time in
her life, seriously interested — in this matter. A
faint sense of degradation at being so ignorant
that she could not command the respect of two
men sufficiently to the bare discussion of it possessed her.

"One need not be a child because one is a
woman!" she said, hotly.

"The case is just this, my dear," said the
Senior, kindly observant of her face and tone.
"Your father dies" — this with a slight, decorous
sadness in his voice, but mathematically withal, as
he would propound a sum for Perley's solution:
A man buys a bushel; or, A boy sold a yard —
"your father dies. Maverick and I reorganize
the firm in our own way: that is our affair. You
fall heir to a certain share of interest in the business: that is your affair. It is for you to say
what shall be done with your own property. You
are even quite at liberty to withdraw it entire
from the concern, or you can leave it in our

hands, which, I am free to say, we should, in the existing state of affairs, prefer — "

" And expect," interrupted Maverick, pleasantly, making little faces on Perley's pink, shell-like nails with the pencil.

" Which we prefer, and very naturally, under the circumstances, expect," continued the Senior. " You then receive certain dividends, which will be duly agreed upon, and have thus the advantage of at once investing your property in a safe, profitable, and familiar quarter, and of feeling no possible obligation or responsibility — business obligation and responsibility are always so trying to a lady — about it.   You thus become, in fact and in form, if you prefer, a silent partner.   Indeed, my dear," finished the Senior, cheerfully, " I do not see but this would meet your fancy perfectly."

" Especially as you are going to marry into the firm," observed Maverick.

" Has a silent partner a voice and vote in — questions that come up ? " asked Perley, hesitating, and rubbing off the little faces from her nails with a corner of her soft handkerchief.

" No," said Maverick ; " none at all.   An ordinary, unprivileged dummy, I mean. If you have your husband's, that's another matter. A woman's influence, you know; you've heard of it. What could be more suitable?"

"Then, if I understand," said Perley, "I invest my property in your mills. You call me a silent partner, to please me and to stop my asking questions. I have nothing to do with the mills or the people. I have nothing to do but to spend the money and let you manage it. That's all it amounts to."

"That's all," said Maverick.

Perley's light finger and the Junior's pencil skirmished across the chess-table for a few moments in silence; the finger from gray to gray; the pencil on green and green; the finger, by chance, it seemed, pursuing; the pencil, unconsciously, it seemed, retreating, as if pencil-mark and finger-touch had been in the first idle stages of a long game.

"Who will go into the firm if I can't?" asked Perley, suddenly.

"Father talks of our confidential clerk," said Maverick, languidly, "a fellow we've promoted from East Street, but smart. Smart as a trap.

Garrick by name. You 've seen him, perhaps, —
Stephen Garrick. But nothing is settled ; and
this is submitted," bowing, " to the close confidence of our silent partner."

Perley did not seem to be in a mood for gallan-
try ; did not smile, but only knitted her soft brows.

" Still, I do not see that there is anything to
prevent my becoming an active partner. There
is nothing the matter with the law, I suppose,
which forbids a woman becoming an active partner in anything ? "

Maverick assured her that there was nothing
the matter with the law ; that the matter was
entirely with the existing firm. Excepting, indeed, some technicality, about which he could
not, at the moment, be precise, which, he believed, would make formal partnerships impossible in the case of husband and wife.

" But that case we are not considering," said
Perley, quickly. " That case it will be time
enough to consider when it occurs. As long as
I am unmarried and independent, Maverick, I
am very much in earnest in my wish to manage
my mills myself. I do not like to think that a
great many people may be affected by the use

of my property in ways over which I can have no possible control. Of course, I don't know what else to do with my money, and if it must be, it must be," — Perley noticed with some wonder here an amused glance between father and son. "But I shall be very much disappointed; and I am much, I am very much, in earnest."

"I verily believe she is," said Maverick, with sudden conviction. "Now, I admire that! It is ingenuous and refreshing."

"Then why don't you take my part, Maverick, instead of laughing at me?" asked Perley, and was vexed at herself for asking immediately.

"O, that," said Maverick, "is another matter. I may find myself entertained to the last degree by the piquancy, originality, *esprit*, of a lady, when I may be the last man upon earth to consent to going into business with my wife. Seriously, Perley," for Perley did not bear this well, "I don't see what has given you this kink, nor why you have become so suddenly reluctant to intrust the management of your property to me."

"It is not my property," said Perley, in a low voice, "which I am reluctant to intrust to you."

"What, then, may it be?"

" My people, — the people. Perhaps I have thought of them suddenly. But it may be better to remember a thing suddenly than never to remember it at all."

" People ! O, the hands, the mill-people. A little Quixotic fancy there. Yes, I understand now ; and very pretty and feminine it is too. My dear Perley, you may set your kind heart at rest about the mill-people, — a well-paid, well-cared-for, happy set of laboring people as you could ask to see. You can go down into our mission school and take a class, if that is what you are troubled about."

" Suppose I were to withdraw my share of the business," suggested Perley, abruptly. " Suppose, upon being refused this partnership for which I have asked this morning, I should prefer to withdraw my interest in the mills ? "

" We should regret it," said Mr. Hayle, courteously ; " but we should have nothing to do but to make the best of circumstances."

" I see, I see now ! " Perley flushed as the eyes of the two gentlemen met again and again with suppressed amusement in them. " I ought to have said that before I told you that I did n't know

what else to do with the money. Of course!
I see, I 've made a bad business blunder. I see
that you think I should always make bad business blunders. Now, Maverick Hayle, I don't
believe I should!"

"My dear Perley," said Maverick, wearily,
"just listen to reason for reason's sake. A
lady's patience and a gentleman's time are too
valuable to throw away at this rate. Even if
you possessed any other qualification, which you
do not, or all other qualifications, which you cannot, for this ridiculous partnership, you lack an
absolutely essential one, — the acquaintance of
years with the business. Just reflect upon your
acquaintance with the business!"

"I will acquire an acquaintance of years with
the business," said Perley, firmly.

"Begin at the spools, for example?"

"I will begin at the spools."

"Or inspect the cotton?"

"Or inspect the cotton."

"Wear a calico dress, and keep the books
in a dingy office?"

"Wear a dozen calico dresses, and keep books
in the dingiest office you have. I repeat, I am in

E

earnest.   I ask for the vacant partnership, or
a chance to fit myself for a partnership, in Hayle
and Kelso.   Whatever my disqualifications, I am
ready to remove them, any and all.   If you refuse
it to me, while I suppose we shall all go on and
be very good-natured about it, I shall feel that
you refuse it to me because I *am* a young lady,
not because I do not stand ready to remove a
young lady's disqualifications."

"Really, Perley, this is becoming absurd, and
the morning is half gone.   If you won't take a
gallant dismissal of a foolish subject, then I *do*
refuse it to you because you *are* a young lady."

"We must refuse it to you certainly, on whatever grounds," remarked the Senior, with polite-
ness, "however unpleasant it may be to refuse
you even the gratification of an eccentric fancy."

Perley's pursuing finger on the little gray
squares thoughtfully traced the course of Maverick's retreating pencil on the green.   Pencil-
mark and finger-touch played faster now, as if in
the nervous stages of a shortening game.

"What do you do," asked the young lady, irrel-
evantly, and still with her light fingers thoughtfully tracking the chess-board, and still watching

the little gold pencil, which still retreated before it, " in your mills, when you have occasion to run extra time ? "

" Run it," said Maverick, laconically.

" But what do you do with the people, — the operatives, I mean ? "

" Pay them extra."

" But they are not obliged, unless they desire, to work more than eleven hours a day ? "

" No," said the Junior, nonchalantly ; " they can leave if they prefer."

Perley's face, bent over the squares of gray and green, changed color slightly. She would have spoken, it seemed, but thought better of it, and only played with her thoughtful finger silently along the board.

" Your remark will leave an unfortunate impression upon the young lady, my son," observed the elder Mr. Hayle, " unless you explain to her that in times of pressure it would be no more possible for a mill to thin out its hands in extra hours than it would be for her to dismiss her cook when she has a houseful of company. The state of the market is an inexorable fact, an inex-orable fact, Miss Perley, before which employer and *employé*, whose interests, of course, are one, have little liberty of choice. The wants of the market must be met. In fast times, we are all compelled to work pretty hard. In dull times, we rest and make up for it. I can assure you that we have almost universally found our hands willing and anxious to run an extra hour or so for the sake of extra pay."

"How long a day's work has the state of the market ever required of your mills?" asked Perley, still with her head bent and her finger moving.

"Perhaps thirteen hours and a half. We ran thirteen hours and a half for a week last July, was n't it, Maverick?"

"What is the use of talking business to a woman?" said Maverick, with such unusual animation that he said it almost impatiently.

"I understand then," said Perley, with the same abruptness which had characterized her words so often that morning, "that my application to look after my mills in an official capacity is refused?"

"Is refused."

"In any official capacity?"

"In any official capacity."

"But that," with a faint smile, "of silent partner."

"But that," with a bow, "of silent partner."

"It is quite impossible to gratify me in this respect?" pursued Perley, with her bent head inclined a little to the Senior.

"Quite impossible," replied the Junior.

"So, out of the question."

"And so, out of the question."

The finger-touch brought the pencil-mark abruptly to a stop upon a helpless square of green.

"Checkmate?" asked the young man, smiling.

"Checkmate," said the young lady, smiling too.

She closed the pencil-case with a snap, tossed the little glazed blank-book into the fire, and rang for luncheon, which the three ate upon the chess-table, — smiling.

CHAPTER IV.

THE STONE HOUSE.

I F you are one of " the hands " in the Hayle and
Kelso Mills, you go to your work, as is well
known, from the hour of half past six to seven,
according to the turn of the season. Time has
been when you went at half past four. The
Senior forgot this the other day in a little talk
which he had with his silent partner, — very naturally, the time having been so long past ; but the
time has been, is now, indeed, yet in places. Mr.
Hayle can tell you of mills he saw in New
Hampshire last vacation, where they ring them
up, if you 'll believe it, winter and summer, in
and out, at half past four in the morning. O no,
never let out before six, of course. Mr. Hayle
disapproves of this. Mr. Hayle thinks it not
humane. Mr. Hayle is confident that you would
find no mission Sunday school connected with
that concern.

If you are one of " the hands " in the Hayle
and Kelso Mills — and again, in Hayle and Kelso,
— you are so dully used to this classification, " the
hands," that you were never known to cultivate
an objection to it, are scarcely found to notice its
use or disuse.   Being surely neither head nor
heart, what else remains ?   Conscious scarcely,
from bell to bell, from sleep to sleep, from day to
dark, of either head or heart, there seems even a
singular appropriateness in the chance of the
word with which you are dimly struck.   Hayle
and Kelso label you.   There you are.   The world
thinks, aspires, creates, enjoys.   There you are.
You are the fingers of the world.   You take your
patient place.   The world may have need of you,
but only that it may think, aspire, create, enjoy.
It needs your patience as well as your place.
You take both, and you are used to both, and the
world is used to both, and so, having put the label
on for safety's sake, lest you be mistaken for a
thinking, aspiring, creating, enjoying compound,
and so some one be poisoned, shoves you into
your place upon its shelf, and shuts its cupboard
door upon you.

If you are one of " the hands," then, in Hayle

and Kelso, you have a breakfast of bread and
molasses probably ; you are apt to eat it while
you dress ; somebody is heating the kettle, but you
cannot wait for it ; somebody tells you that you
have forgotten your shawl, you throw it over one
shoulder, and step out, before it is fastened, into
the sudden raw air ; you left lamp-light in-doors ;
you find moonlight without ; the night seems to
have overslept itself ; you have a fancy for trying to wake it, would like to shout at it or cry
through it, but feel very cold, and leave that for
the bells to do by and by.   You and the bells are
the only waking things in life.   The great brain
of the world is in serene repose.   The great heart
of the world lies warm to the core with dreams.
The great hands of the world, the patient, perplexed, one almost fancies at times, just for the
fancy, seeing you here by the morning moon, the
dangerous hands, alone are stirring in the dark.

You hang up your shawl and your crinoline,
and understand, as you go shivering by gaslight
to your looms, that you are chilled to the heart,
and that you were careless about your shawl, but
do not consider carefulness worth your while by
nature or by habit ; a little less shawl means a

few less winters in which to require shawling.
You are a godless little creature, but you cherish
a stolid leaning, in these morning moons, towards
making an experiment of death and a wadded
coffin.

By the time that gas is out, you cease, perhaps,
though you cannot depend upon that, to shiver,
and incline less and less to the wadded coffin, and
more to a chat with your neighbor in the alley.
Your neighbor is of either sex and any description, as the case may be. In any event, warming a little with the warming day, you incline
more and more to chat. If you chance to be a
cotton-weaver, you are presently warm enough.
It is quite warm enough in the weaving-room.
The engines respire into the weaving-room ; with
every throb of their huge lungs you swallow
their breath. The weaving-room stifles with
steam. The window-sills of this room are gut-
tered to prevent the condensed steam from running in streams along the floor ; sometimes they
overflow, and water stands under the looms ; the
walls perspire profusely ; on a damp day, drops
will fall from the roof.

The windows of the weaving-room are closed ;

4

the windows must be closed ; a stir in the air
will break your threads.   There is no air to stir.
You inhale for a substitute motionless, hot moisture.   If you chance to be a cotton-weaver, it is
not in March that you think most about your
coffin.

Being " a hand " in Hayle and Kelso, you are
used to eating cold luncheon in the cold at noon,
or you walk, for the sake of a cup of soup or
coffee, half a mile, three quarters, a mile and a
half, and back.   You are allowed three quarters
of an hour in which to do this.   You come and
go upon the jog-trot.

You grow moody, being "a hand" at Hayle
and Kelso's, with the growing day ; are inclined
to quarrel or to confidence with your neighbor in
the alley ; find the overseer out of temper, and
the cotton full of flaws ; find pains in your feet,
your back, your eyes, your arms ; feel damp and
sticky lint in your hair, your neck, your ears,
your throat, your lungs ; discover a monotony
in the process of breathing hot moisture, lower
your window at your risk ; are bidden by somebody whose threads you have broken at the other
end of the room to put it up, and put it up ;

are conscious that your head swims, your eye-balls burn, your breath quickens ; yield your preference for a wadded coffin, and consider whether the river would not be the comfortable thing ; cough a little, cough a great deal, lose your balance in a coughing fit, snap a thread, and take to swearing roundly.

From swearing you take to singing ; both perhaps are equal relief, active and diverting. There is something curious about that singing of yours. The time, the place, the singers, characterize it sharply, — the waning light, the rival din, the girls with tired faces. You start some little thing with a refrain and a ring to it ; a hymn, it is not unlikely ; something of a River and of Waiting, and of Toil and Rest, or Sleep, or Crowns, or Harps, or Home, or Green Fields, or Flowers, or Sorrow, or Repose, or a dozen things, but always, it will be noticed, of simple, spot-less things, such as will surprise the listener who caught you at your oath of five minutes past. You have other songs, neither simple nor spot-less, it may be ; but you never sing them at your work, when the waning day is crawling out from spots between your looms, and the girls lift up their tired faces to catch and keep the chorus in the rival din.

You like to watch the contest between the chorus and the din ; to see — you seem almost to see — the struggle of the melody from alley to alley, from loom to loom, from darkening wall to darkening wall, from lifted face to lifted face ; to see — for you are very sure you see — the machinery fall into a fit of rage. That is a sight ! You would never guess, unless you had watched it just as many times as you have, how that machinery will rage. How it throws its arms about, what fists it can clench, how it shakes at the elbows and knees, what teeth it knows how to gnash, how it writhes and roars, how it clutches at the leaky, strangling gas-lights, and how it bends its impotent black head, always, at last, without fail, and your song sweeps triumphant, like an angel, over it ! With this you are very much pleased, though only "a hand," to be sure, in Hayle and Kelso.

You are singing when the bell strikes, and singing still when you clatter down the stairs. Something of the simple spotlessness of the little song is on your face, when you dip into

the wind and dusk. Perhaps you have only
pinned your shawl, or pulled your hat over your
face, or knocked against a stranger on the walk ;
but it passes ; it passes and is gone. It is cold
and you tremble, direct from the morbid heat in
which you have stood all day ; or you have been
cold all day, and it is colder, and you shrink ; or
you are from the weaving-room, and the wind
strikes you faint, or you stop to cough and the
girls go on without you. The town is lighted,
and people are out in their best clothes. You
pull your dingy veil about your eyes. You are
weak and heart-sick all at once. You don't
care to go home to supper. The pretty song
creeps, wounded, back for the engines in the
deserted dark to crunch. You are a miserable
little factory-girl with a dirty face.

A broken chatter falls in pieces about you ;
all the melody of the voices that you hear has
vanished with the vanquished song ; they are
hoarse and rough.

" Goin' to the dance to-night, Bet ? "

"Nynee Mell ! yer alway speerin' awa' after
some young mon. Can't yer keep yer een at
home like a decint lassie ? "

"An' who gave *you* lave to hoult a body's hand onasked an' onrequested, Pathrick Donnavon?"

"Sip Garth, give us 'Champagne Charley'; can't you?"

"Do you think the mules will strike?"

"More mules they, if they do. Did ye never see a mouse strike a cat?"

"There's Bub beggin' tobacco yet! How old is that little devil?"

"The Lord knows!"

"Pity the Lord don't know a few more things as one would suppose might fall in his line."

"A tract?"

"A tract. Bless you, four pages long. Says I, What in —— 's this? for I was just going in to the meetin' to see the fun. So he stuffs it into my hand, and I clears out."

"Sip, I say! Priscilla! Sip Garth —"

But Sip Garth breaks out of sight as the chatter breaks out of hearing; turns a corner; turns another; walks wearily fast, and wearily faster; pushes her stout way through a dirty street and a dirtier street; stops at shadowy corners to look for something which she does not find ; stops at lighted doors to call for something that does not answer ; hesitates a moment at the dismal gate of a dismal little stone house by the water, and, hesitating still and with a heavy sigh, goes in.

It is a damp house, and she rents the dampest room in it ; a tenement boasting of the width of the house, and a closet bedroom with a little cupboard window in it ; a low room with cellar smells and river smells about it, and with gutter smells and drain smells and with unclassified smells of years settled and settling in its walls and ceiling. Never a cheerful room ; never by any means a cheerful room, when she and Catty — or she without Catty — come home from work at night.

Something has happened to the forlorn little room to-night. Sip stops with the door-latch in her hand. A fire has happened, and the kerosene lamp has happened, and drawn curtains have happened ; and Miss Kelso has happened, — down on her knees on the bare floor, with her kid gloves off, and a poker in her hands.

So original in Perley! Maverick would say; Maverick not being there to say it, Perley spoke for herself, with the poker in her hand, and still upon her knees.

"I beg your pardon, Sip, but they told me, the other side of the house, that you would be in in five minutes, and the room was dark and so I took the liberty. If you would n't mind me, and would go right on as if I had n't come, I should take it very kindly."

"All right," said Sip.

"The fact is," said Miss Kelso, meditatively twirling her poker, "that that is the first fire I ever made in my life. Would you believe it, to look at it?"

"I certainly should n't," said Sip.

"And you 're quite sure that you would n't mind me?"

"No, not quite sure. But if you 'll stay awhile, I 'll find out and tell you."

"Very well," said Miss Kelso.

"See how dirty I am," said Sip, stopping in the full light on her way to the closet bedroom.

"I had n't seen," said Miss Kelso to the poker.

" O, well. No matter. I did n't know but *you*'d mind."

There was dust about Sip, and oil about her, and a consciousness of both about her, that gave her a more miserable aspect than either. In the full light she looked like some half-cleared Pompeian statue just dug against the face of day.

" We can't help it, you see," said poor Sip ; " mill-folks can't. Dust we are and to dust do we return. I 've got a dreadful sore-throat to-night."

" Have you taken cold ? "

" O no. I have it generally. It comes from sucking filling through the shuttle. But I don't think much of it. There 's girls I know, weavers, can't even talk beyond a whisper ; lost their voices some time ago."

Sip washed and dressed herself after this in silence. She washed herself in the sink ; there was no pump to the sink ; she went out bare-headed, and brought water in from a well in the yard ; the pail was heavy, and she walked wearily, with her head and body bent to balance it, over the slippery path. She coughed while she walked and when she came in, — a peculiar, dry, rasping cough, which Perley learned afterwards to recognize as the "cotton-cough." She washed herself in a tin basin, which she rinsed carefully and hung up against the wall. While she was dressing in the closet bedroom, Perley still knelt, thoughtfully playing with the poker beside the fire.

"I don't suppose," said Sip, coming out presently in her plaid dress, with her hair in a net, and speaking as if she had not been interrupted, — "I don't suppose you'd ever guess how much difference the dirt makes. I don't suppose you ever *could.* Cotton ain't so bad, though. Once I worked to a flax-mill. *That* was dirt."

"What difference?"

"Hush!" said Sip, abruptly, "I thought I heard —" She went to the window and looked out, raising her hands against her eyes, but came back with a disappointed face.

"Catty has n't come in," she said, nervously. "There's times she slips away from me; she works in the Old Stone, and I can't catch her. There's times she does n't come till late. Will you stay to tea?" with a quick change of voice.

"Thank you. I don't understand about Catty," with another.

Sip set her table before she spoke again ; bustled about, growing restless ; put the kettle on and off the hob ; broke one of her stone-china plates ; stopped to sweep the floor a little and to fill her coal-hod ; the brown tints of her rugged little face turning white and pinched in spots about the mouth.

She came, presently, and stood by the fire by Miss Kelso's side, in the full sweep of the light. "Miss Kelso," her hands folding and unfolding restlessly, "there's many things you don't understand. There's things you *could* n't understand."

"Why ? "

"I don't know why. I never did quite know why."

"You may be right ; you may be wrong. How can you tell till you try me ? "

"How can I tell whether I can skate on running water till I try it ? — I wish Catty would come ! "

Sip walked to the window again, and walked back again, and took a look at the teapot, and cut a slice or two of bread.

"So you 've left the Company board," observed Miss Kelso, quite as if they had been talking about the Company board. "You did n't like it?"

"I liked well enough."

"You left suddenly?"

"I left sudden." Sip threw her bread-knife down, with an aimless, passionate gesture. "I suppose it 's no good to shy off. I might as well tell o't first as last. They turned us off!"

"Turned you off?"

"On account of Catty."

Miss Kelso raised a confused face from the poker and the fire.

"You see," said Sip, "I *told* you there 's things you could n't understand. Now there ain't one of my own kind of folks, your age, would n't have understood half an hour ago, and saved me the trouble of telling. Catty 's queer, don't you see? She runs away, don't you see? Sometimes she drinks, don't you understand? Drinks herself the dead kind. That ain't so often. Most times she just runs away about streets. There 's sometimes she does — worse."

"Worse?" The young lady's pure, puzzled

face dropped suddenly. " O, I was very dull! I am sorry. I am not used — " And so broke off, with a sick look about the lips, — a look which did not escape the notice of the little brown, pinched face in the firelight, for it was curving into a bitter smile when the door opened, banging back against the wall as if the opener had either little consciousness or little care of the noise it made.

" There 's Catty," said Sip, doggedly. " Come and get warm, Catty." This in their silent language on her rapid, work-worn fingers.

" If you mind me now, I 'll go," said Miss Kelso, in a low voice.

" That 's for you to say, whether I shall mind you now."

" Poor Catty ! " said Perley, still in a very low voice. " Poor, poor Catty ! "

Sip flushed, — flushed very sweetly and suddenly all over her dogged face. " *Now* I don't mind you. Stay to supper. We 'll have supper right away. Come here a minute, Catty dear."

Catty dear would not come. Catty dear stood scowling in the middle of the room, a sullen, ill-tempered, ill-controlled, uncontrollable Catty dear as one could ask to see.

"For love's sake," said Sip, on her patient fingers ; "here a minute, for love's sake, Catty."

"For love's sake?" repeated Catty, in her pathetic language.

"Only for love's sake, dear," said Sip.

Catty came with this, and laid her head down with a singularly gentle motion on Sip's faded plaid lap. Miss Kelso could see her now, in the light in which they three were sitting. A girl possibly of fifteen years, — a girl with a low forehead, with wandering eyes, with a dull stoop to the head, with long, lithe, magnetic fingers, with a thick, dropping under lip, — a girl walled up and walled in from that labyrinth of sympathies, that difficult evolution of brain from beast, the gorgeous peril of that play at good and evil which we call life, except at the wandering eyes, and at the long, lithe, magnetic fingers. An ugly girl.

She lay, for an ugly girl, very still in her sister's lap. Sip softly stroked her face, talking now to the child and now to her visitor, wound about in a pretty net of soft sounds and softer emotions. A pleasant change had fallen upon her since the deaf-mute came in.

"See how pleasant it is to come home early, Catty." (She won't talk to-night, because you 're here.) " For love's sake, dear, you know." (That 's the way I get along with her. She likes that.) "For love's sake and my sake, and with the lamp and fire bright. So much better — " (It 's never her fault, poor dear! God knows, I never, never laid it up against her as it was her fault.) " Better than the dark street-corners, Catty — "

" There 's light in the shops," said Catty, on her long fingers, with a shrewd, unpleasant smile.

" And supper at home," said Sip, quickly, rising. " For love's sake, you know. And company to supper ! "

" For love's sake ? " asked Catty, rising too.

" *I* don't know for whose sake ! " said Sip, all the pleasantness gone in a minute from her.

The young lady and Catty were standing now, between the lamp-glow and the fire-glow, side by side. They were a startling pair to be standing side by side. They stood quite still, except that Catty passed her fingers curiously over Miss Kelso's dress, — it seemed that she saw quite as much with her fingers as with her eyes, — and that she nodded once or twice, as if she were talking to herself, in a stupid way. Perley's fine, fair, finished smile seemed to blot out this miserable figure, and to fill the room with a kind of dazzle.

"Good God!" cried Sip, sharply. "You asked me for the difference. Look at that! You asked what difference the dirt makes. *That*'s the difference! To be born in it, breathe it, swallow it, grow on it, live it, die and go back to it — bah! If you want to go the devil, work in the dirt. Look at her!"

"I look at her," said Perley, with a solemn, frightened look upon her young face, — "I look at her, Sip. For love's sake. Believe me if you can. Make her understand. I look for love's sake."

Is it possible? Is Miss Kelso sure? Not for a whim's sake? Not for fancy's sake? Not for the sake of an idle moment's curiosity? Not to gratify an eccentric taste, — playing my Lady Bountiful for a pretty change in a pretty life? Look at her; it is a very loathsome under lip. Look well at her; they are not pleasant eyes. An ugly girl, — a very ugly girl. For love's sake, Miss Kelso?

Catty sat down to supper without washing her face. This troubled Sip more than it did her visitor. Her visitor, indeed, scarcely noticed it. Her face wore yet something of the solemn fright which had descended on it with Catty's coming in.

She noticed, however, that she had bread and butter for her supper, and that she was eating from a stone-china plate, and with a steel fork and with a pewter spoon. She noticed that the bread was toasted, it seemed in deference to the presence of a guest, and that the toasting had feverishly flushed Sip's haggard face. She noticed that Sip and Catty ate no butter, but dipped their bread into a little blue bowl of thick black molasses. She noticed that there was a kind of coarse black tea upon the table, and noticed that she found a single pewter spoonful of it quite sufficient for her wants. She noticed that Sip made rather a form than a fact of playing with her toasted bread in the thick black molasses, and that she drained her dreadful teacup thirstily, and that she then leaned, with a sudden sick look, back into her chair.

Everything tasted of oil, she said. She could

not eat. There were times that she could not eat
day nor night for a long time. How long? She
was not sure. It had been often two days that
nothing passed her lips. Sometimes, with the
tea, it was longer. There were times that she
came home and got right into bed, dirt and
all. She could n't undress, no, not if it was to
save her soul, nor eat. But, generally, she managed to cook for Catty. Besides, there was the
work.

"What work?" asked Miss Kelso, innocently.

"Washing. Ironing. Baking. Sweeping.
Dusting. Sewing. Marketing. Pumping. Scrub-
bing. Scouring," said Sip, drumming out her
periods on a teaspoon with her hard, worn fingers.

"Oh!" said Miss Kelso.

"For two, you see," said Sip.

"But all this, — you cannot have all this to do
after you have stood eleven hours and a half at
your loom?"

"When should I have it to do! There's Sunday, to be sure; but I don't do so much now Sundays, except the washing and the brushing up.
I like," with a gentle, quick look at the deaf and
dumb girl, who still sat dipping bread crusts into

black molasses, absorbed and still, " to make it a kind of a comfortable day for Catty, Sunday. I don't bother Catty so much to help me, you know," added Sip, cheerfully. " I like," with another very pleasant look, " to make it comfortable for Catty."

" I went into the mills to-day," said Miss Kelso, in reply. It was not very much to the point as a reply, and was said with an interrogatory accent, which lessened its aptness.

" Yes ? " said Sip, in the same tone.

" I never was in a mill before."

" No ? "

" No."

There was a pause, in which the young lady seemed to be waiting for a leading question, like a puzzled scholar. If she were, she had none. Sip sat with her dogged smile, and snapped little paper balls into the fire.

" I thought it rather close in the mills."

" Yes ? "

" And — dirty. And — there was one very warm room ; the overseer advised me not to go in."

" It was very good advice."

" I went into the Company boarding-house too."

" For the first time ? "

" For the first time. I went to inquire after you. The landlady took me about. Now I think of it, she invited me to tea."

" Why did n't you stay ? "

" Why, to tell the truth, the — tablecloth was — rather dirty."

" Oh ! "

" And I saw her wipe her face on — the dish-towel. Do the girls often sleep six in a room ? They had no wash-stands. I saw some basins set on trunks. They carried all the water up and down stairs themselves ; there were two or three flights. There was n't a ventilator in the house. I saw a girl there sick."

" Sick ? O, Bert Bush. Yes. Pleurisy. She 's going to work her notice when she gets about again. Given out."

" She coughed while I was there. I thought her room was rather cold. I thought all the rooms were rather cold. I did n't seem to see any fire for anybody, except in the common sitting-room. But the bread was sweet."

" Yes, the bread was sweet."

" And the gingerbread."

" Very sweet."

" And, I suppose, the board —

" The board is quarter of a dollar cheaper than in other places."

Sip stopped snapping paper balls into the fire, and snapped instead one of her shrewd, sidewise glances at her visitor's face.

The fine, fair, finished face ! How puzzled it looked ! Sip smiled.

Catty had crept around while they were talking, and sat upon the floor by Miss Kelso's chair. She was still amusing herself with the young lady's dress, passing her wise fingers to and fro across its elegant surface, and nodding to herself in her dull way. Miss Kelso's hand, the one with the rings, lay upon her lap, and Catty, attracted suddenly by the blaze of the jewels, took it up. She took it up as she would a novel toy, examined it for a few moments with much pleasure, then removed the rings and dropped them carelessly, and laid her cheek down upon the soft flesh. It was such a dusty cheek, and such a beautiful, bare, clean hand, that Sip started anxiously to speak to Catty, but saw that Perley sat quite still, and that her earnest eyes were full of sudden tears.

"You will not let me say, you know, that I am sorry for you. I have been trying all the evening. I can't come any nearer than this." This she said smiling.

"Look here!" said Sip; her brown face worked and altered. She said, "Look here!" again, and stopped. "That's nigh enough. I'll take that. I like that. I like you. Look here! I never said that to one of your kind of folks before; I like you. Generally I hate your kind of folks."

"Now that," said Miss Kelso, musing, "perplexes me. We feel no such instinct of aversion to you. As far as I understand 'my kind of folks,' they have kindly hearts, and they have it in their hearts to feel very sorry for the poor."

"Who wants their pity? And who cares what's in their hearts?"

Sip had hardened again like a little growing prickly nut. The subject and her softer mood dropped away together.

"Sip," said Perley, fallen into another revery, "you see how little I know —"

Sip nodded.

"About — people who work and — have a hard time."

" They don't none of 'em know. That 's why I hate your kind of folks. It ain't because they don't care, it 's because they don't *know ;* nor they don't care enough *to* know."

" Now I have always been brought up to believe," urged Miss Kelso, " that our factory-people, for instance, had good wages."

" I never complained of the wages. Hayle and Kelso could n't get a cotton-weaver for three dollars a week, like a paper-factory I know about in Cincinnati. I knew a girl as worked to Cincinnati. Three dollars a week, and board to come out of it ! Cotton-weaving 's no play, and cotton-weavers are no fools."

" And I always thought," continued Miss Kelso, " that such people were — why, happy and comfortable, you know. Of course, I knew they must economize, and that, but — "

She looked vaguely over at the supper-table ; such uncertain conceptions as she might hitherto be said to have had of " economizing " acquiring suddenly the form of thick, black molasses, a little sticky, to be sure, but tangible.

Sip made no reply, and Perley, suddenly aware

of the lateness of the hour, started in dismay to take her leave. It occurred to her that the sticky stone-china dishes were yet to be washed, and that she had done a thoughtless thing in imposing, for a novel evening's entertainment, upon the scanty leisure of a worn-out factory-girl.

She turned, however, neither an entertained nor a thoughtless face upon Sip when she tried to rise from her chair. Catty had fallen asleep, with her dirty cheek upon the shining hand, from which the rings were gone. Her ugly lower lip protruded, and all the repulsive lines about her eyes came out. Her long fingers moved a little, as is often the way with the deaf and dumb in sleep, framing broken words. Even in her dreams, this miserable creature bore about her a dull sense of denial and distress. Even in her dreams she listened for what she never heard, and spoke that which no man understood.

"Mother used to say," said Sip, under her breath, "that it was the noise."

"The noise?"

"The noise of the wheels. She said they beat about in her head. She come home o' nights, and says to herself, 'The baby 'll never

hear in this world unless she hears the wheels';
and sure enough" (Sip lifted her face to Perlcy's,
with a look of awe), "it is true enough that
Catty hears the wheels; but never anything
besides."

CHAPTER V.

BUB MELL.

I T was a March night, and a gray night, and a
wild night ; Perley Kelso stepped out into
it, from the damp little stone house, with something of the confusion of the time upon her. Her
head and heart both ached.   She felt like a
stranger setting foot in a strange land.   Old,
home-like boundary lines of things to which her
smooth young life had rounded, wavered before
her.   It even occurred to her that she should
never be very happy again, for knowing that factory-girls ate black molasses and had the cotton-
cough.

She meant to tell Maverick about it.   She
might have meant many other things, but for
being so suddenly and violently jerked by the
elbow that she preserved herself with difficulty
from a smart fall into the slushy street. Striking
out with one hand to preserve her balance, she

found herself in the novel position of collaring either a very old young child or a very young old man, it was impossible at first sight to tell which. Whatever he was, it was easy at first sight to tell that he was filthy and ragged.

"Le' go!" yelled the old young creature, writhing. "Le' go, I say, dern yer! Le' me be!"

Perley concluded, as her eyes wonted to the dark street, that the old young creature was by right a child.

"If yer had n't le' go I 'd 'a' made yer, yer bet," said the boy, gallantly. "Pretty way to treat a cove as doin' yer a favor. You bet. Hi-igh!"

This, with a cross between a growl of defiance and a whine of injury.

"Guess what I 've got o' yourn? You could n't. You bet."

"But I don't bet," said Perley, with an amused face.

"Yer don't? *I* do. Hi-igh! Don't I though? *You* bet! Now what do you call that? Say!"

"I call that my glove. I did not miss it till this minute. Did you pick it up? Thank you."

"You need n't thank me till you 've got it, *you*

need n't," said the child. "*I* 'm a cove as knows
a thing or two. I want ten cents. You bet I do."

"Where do you live?" asked Perley.

He lived down to East Street. Fust Tenement. No. 6. What business was it of hern,
he 'd like to know.

"Have you a father and mother?"

Lor yes! Two of 'em. Why should n't he?

"I believe I will go home with you," said Perley, "it is so near by; and — I suppose you are
poor?"

Lor, yes. She might bet.

"And I can make it right about the recovery
of the glove when I get there?"

"N-n-oo you don't!" promptly, from the cove
as knew a thing or two. "You 'll sling over
to the old folks, I 'll bet. You don't come
that!"

"But," suggested Perley, "I can, perhaps,
give your father and mother a much larger
sum of money than I should think it best to
give you. If they are poor, I should think you
would be glad that they should have it. And
I can't walk in, you know, and give your father
and mother money for nothing."

"You give *me* ten cents," said this young old man, stoutly, "or what do you s'pose I'll do with this 'ere glove? Guess now!"

Perley failed to guess now.

"I'll cut 'n' run with it. I'll cut 'n' run like mad. *You* bet. I'll snip it up with a pair of shears I know about. I'll jab holes in it with a jackknife I've got. No, I won't. I'll swop it off with my sister, for a yáller yaggate I've got my eye on in the 'pothecarry's winder. My sister's a mill-gal. She'll wear it on one hand to meetin', an' stick the t'other in her muff. That's what I'll do. How'll you like that? Hi-igh! You bet!"

"At least, I can go home with you," said Perley, absently effecting an exchange between her glove and a fresh piece of ten-cent scrip, which the boy held up in the light from a shop-window, and tested with the air of a middle-aged counterfeiter; "you ought to have been at home an hour ago."

"Lor now," said this promising youth, "I was just thinkin' so ought you."

"What is your name?" asked Perley, as they turned their two faces (one would have been struck, seeing them together, with thinking how much younger the woman looked than the child), toward East Street, the First Tenement, and No. 6.

" My name's Bub.   Bub Mell.   They used to call me Bubby, for short, till I got so large they give it up."

" How old are you?"

" Eight last Febiverry."

" What do you do?"

" Work to the Old Stone."

" But I thought no children under ten years of age were allowed to work in the mills."

" You must be green!" said Bub.

" But you go to school?"

"I went to school till I got so large they give it up."

" But you go a part of the time, of course?"

" No, I don't neither.   Don't you s'pose I knows?"

" What is that you have in your mouth?" asked Perley, suddenly.

Bub relieved himself of a quid of fabulous size, making quite superfluous the concise reply, " Ter-baccer."

"I never saw such a little boy as you chew tobacco before," said Perley, gasping.

"You must be green! I took my fust swag a year and a half ago. We all does. I'm just out, it happens," said Bub, with a candid smile. "That's what I wanted your ten cents for. I smokes too," added Bub, with an air of having tried not to mention it, for modesty's sake, but of being tempted overmuch. "You bet I do! Sometimes it's pipes, and sometimes it's ends. As a gener'l thing, give me a pipe."

"What else do you do?" demanded Perley, faintly.

"What else?" Bub reflected, with his old, old head on one side. He bet on marbles. He knew a tip-top gin-sling, when he see it, well as most folks. He could pitch pennies. He could ketch a rat ag'in any cove on East Street. Lor! could n't he?

"But what else?" persisted Perley.

Bub was puzzled. He thought there warn't nothin' else. After that he had his supper.

"And after that?"

Lor. After that he went to bed.

"And after that?"

After that he got up and went in.

"Went in where?"

She must be green. Into the Old Stone. Spoolin', you know.

Did he go to church?

She might bet he did n't! Why, when should he ketch the rats?

Nor Sunday school?

He went to the Mission once. Had a card with a green boy onto it. Got so old he give it up.

What did he expect, asked Perley, in a sudden, severe burst of religious enthusiasm, would become of him when he died?

Eh?

When he died, what would become of him?

Lor.

Could he read?

Fust Primer. Never tried nothin' else.

Could he write?

No.

Was he going to school again?

Could n't say.

Why did n't his parents send him?

Could n't say that. Thought they was too old;

no, thought he was too old ; well, he did n't know ;
thought somebody was too old, and give it up.

Was this where he lived ?

She must be green ! Of course he did.
Comin' in ?

Perley was coming in. With hesitation she
came in.

She came into what struck her as a very
unpleasant place ; a narrow, crumbling place ;
a place with a peculiar odor ; a very dark place.
Bub cheerfully suggested that she 'd better look
out.

For what ?

Holes.

Where ?

Holes in the stairs. *He* used to step into 'em
and sprain his ankles, you bet, till he got so old
he give it up She 'd better look out for the
plaster too. She 'd bump her head. She never
saw nothin' break like that plaster did ; great
cakes of it. Here, this way. Keerful now !

By this way and that way, by being careful
now and patient then and quite persistent at
all times, Perley contrived to follow Bub in safety
up two flights of villanous stairs and into the

5*

sudden shine of a low, little room, into which he shot rather than introduced her, with the unembarrassing remark that he did n't know what she 'd come for, but there she was.

There were six children, a cooking-stove, a bed, a table, and a man with stooped shoulders in the room. There was an odor in the room like that upon the stairs. The man, the children, the cooking-stove, the bed, the table, and the odor quite filled the room.

The room opened into another room, in which there seemed to be a bureau, a bed, and a sick woman.

Miss Kelso met with but a cool reception in these rooms. The man, the children, the cooking-stove, the bed, the odor, and the woman thrust her at once, she could not have said how, into the position of an intruder. The sick woman, upon hearing her errand, flung herself over to the wall with an impatient motion. The man sullenly invited her to sit down ; gave her to understand — again she could hardly have told how — that he wanted no money of her ; no doubt the boy had had more than he deserved ; but that, if she felt inclined, she might sit down.

" To tell the truth," said Perley, in much confusion, " I did not come so much on account of the glove as on account of the boy."

What had the boy been up to now ? The sullen man darted so fierce a look at the boy, who sat with his old, old smile, lighting an old pipe behind the cooking-stove, that Perley hastened to explain that she did not blame the boy. Who could blame the boy ?

" But he was out so late about the streets, Mr. Mell. He uses tobacco as most children use candy. And a child of that age ought not to be in the mills, sir," said Perley, warming, " he ought to be at school !"

O, that was all, was it ? Mr. Mell pushed back his stooped shoulders into his chair with an air of relief, and Bub lighted his pipe in peace. But he had a frowning face, this Mr. Mell, and he turned its frown upon his visitor. He would like to know what business it was of hers what he did with his boy, and made no scruple of saying so.

" It ought to be some of my business," said the young lady, growing bolder, " when a child of eight years works all the year round in these mills. I have no doubt that I seem very rude, sir; but I have in fact come out, and come out alone as you see me, to see with my own eyes and to hear with my own ears how people live who work in these mills."

Had she? Mr. Mell smiled grimly. Not a pleasant job for a lady he should think; and uncommon.

"It's a job I mean to finish," said Miss Kelso, firmly. "The stairs in this house are in a shocking condition. What is — excuse me — the very peculiar odor which I notice on these premises? It must be poisonous to the sick woman, — your wife?"

It was his wife. Yes; consumption; took it weaving; had been abed this four month; could n't say how long she'd hold out. Doctor said, five month ago, as nothin' would save her but a change. So he sits and talks about Florida and the South sun, and the folks as had been saved down there. It was a sort of a fretful thing to hear him. Florida! Good God! How was the likes of him to get a dyin' wife to Florida?

She did n't like strangers overmuch; better not go nigh her; she was kind of fretful; the childern was kind of fretful too; sometimes they cried like as his head would split; he kept the gell

home to look after 'em ; not the first gell ; he
could n't keep her to home at all ; she made
seven ; he did n't know 's he blamed her ; it was
a kind of a fretful place, let alon' the stairs and
the smell. It come from the flood, the smell did.

" The flood ? "

Yes, the cellar flooded up every spring from the
river ; it might be drained, he should think ; but
it never was as he heard of. There was the
offal from the mills floated in ; it left a smell
pretty much the year round ; and a kind of chill.
Then they had n't any drain, you see. There was
that hole in the wall where they threw out dish-
water and such. So it fell into the yard under
the old woman's window, and made her kind of
fretful. It made her fretful to see the children
ragged too. She greeted over it odd times. She
had a clean way about her, when she was up and
about, the old woman had.

" Who owns this house ? " asked Miss Kelso,
with burning eyes.

The man seemed unaccountably reluctant to
reply ; he fixed the fire, scolded Bub, scolded a
few other children, and shook the baby, but was
evidently unwilling to reply.

Upon Perley's repeating her question, the sick woman, with another impatient fling against the wall, cried out sharply, What was the odds? Do tell the girl. It could n't harm her, could it? Her husband, very ill at ease, believed that young Mr. Hayle owned the house; though they dealt with his lessee; Mr. Hayle had never been down himself.

For a sullen man, with a stoop in the shoulders, a frown in the face, seven children, a sick wife, and no drain-spout, Mr. Mell did very well about this. He grew even communicative, when the blaze in Miss Kelso's eyes went out, paled by the sudden fire in her cheek.

He supposed he was the more riled up by this and that, he said, for being English; Scotch by breed, you know; they 'd named the first gell after her grandma, — Nynee; quite Scotch, ye see; she was a Hielander, grandma, — but married to England, and used to their ways. Now there was ways and ways, and *one* way was a ten-hour bill. There was no mistaking that, one way was a ten-hour bill, and it was a way they did well by in England, and it was a way they 'd have to walk in this side the water yet — *w-a-l-k in y-e-t!*

He 'd been turned out o' mills in this country twice for goin' into a ten-hour strike ; once to Lawrence and once up to New Hampshire. He 'd given it up. It did n't pay. Since the old woman was laid up, he must get steady work or starve.

He 'd been a factory operative * thirty-three years ; twenty-three years to home, and ten years to the United States, only one year as he was into the army ; he was forty-three years old. Why did n't he send that boy to school ? Why did n't he drive a span of grays ! He could n't send the boy to school, nor none of the other boys to school, except as mayhap they took their turn occasional. He made it a point to send them till they was eight if he could ; he did n't like to put a young un to spoolin' before he was eight, if he could help it. The law? O yes, there was a law, and there was ways of getting round a law, bless you ! Ways enough. There was parties as had it in their hands to make it none so easy, and again to make it none so hard.

"What parties ?"

* Mr. Mell's " testimony " may be found in the reports of the Massachusetts Bureau of Labor.

Parties as had an interest in spoolin in common with the parent.

" The child's employers ? "

Mr. Mell suddenly upon his guard. Mr. Mell trusted to the good feelin' of a young lady as would have a heart for the necessities of poverty, and changed the subject.

" But you cannot mean," persisted Perley, " that a healthy man like you, with his grown children earning, finds it impossible to support his family without the help of a poor baby like Bub over there ? "

Mr. Mell quite meant it. Did n't know what other folks could do ; he could n't ; not since the rise in prices, and the old woman givin' out. Why, look at here. There was the gell, twenty year old ; she worked to weaving ; there was the boy as was seventeen, him reading the picture paper over to the table there, he draws and twists ; there was another gell of fifteen, you might say, hander at the harnesses into the dressing-room ; then there was Bub, and the babies.

Counting in the old woman and the losses, he must have Bub. The old woman ate a power-

ful sight of meat. He went without himself when-
soever he could ; but his work was hard ; it made
him kind of deathly to the stomach if he went
without his meat.

What losses did he speak of ? Losses enough.
High water. Low water. Strikes. Machinery
under repair. Besides the deathly feelin' to the
stomach. He'd been out for sickness off and on,
first and last, a deal ; though he looked a healthy
man, as she said, and you would n't think it.
Fact was, he'd never worked but *one whole*
month in six year ; nor he'd never taken a
week's vacation at a time, of his own will an'
pleasure, for six year. Sometimes he lost two
days and a half a week, right along, for lack of
work.* Sometimes he give out just for the heat.
He'd often seen it from 110° to 116° Fahrenheit
in the dressing-room. He wished he was back
to England. He would n't deny but there was
advantages here, but he wished he was back.

(This man had worked in England from 6 A. M.
to 8 o'clock P. M., with no time allowed for dinner ;

* "We may here add that our inquiries will authorize us to
say that three out of every five laboring men were out of
employ." — *Statistics of Labor.*

H

he paid threepence a week to an old woman who brought hot water into the mills at noon, with which she filled the tin pot in which he had brought tea and sugar from home. He had, besides, a piece of bread. He ate with one hand and worked with the other.)

He warn't complainin' of nobody in particular, *to* nobody in particular, but he thought he had a kind of a fretful life. He had n't been able to lay by a penny, not by this way nor that, considerin' his family of nine and the old woman, and the feelin' to the stomach. Now that made him fretful sometimes. He was a temperate man, he 'd like to have it borne in mind. He was a member of a ten-hour society, of the Odd Fellows, Good Templars, and Orthodox Church.

Anything for him? No ; he did n't know of anything she could do for him. He 'd never taken charity from nobody's hands yet. He might, mayhap, come to it some day. He supposed it was fretful of him, but he 'd rather lay in his grave. The old woman she would n't never know nothing of that ; it was a kind of a comfort, that was. He was obliged to her for wishing him kindly. Sorry the old woman was so fretful to-night; she was oncommon noisy; and the childern. He'd ask her to call again, if the old woman was n't so fretful about strangers. Hold the door open for the lady, Bub. Put down your pipe, sir! Have n't ye no more manners than to smoke in a lady's face? There. Now, hold the door open wide.

Wide, very wide, the door flung that Bub opened to Perley Kelso. As wide it seemed to her as the gray, wild, March night itself. At the bottom of the stairs, she stood still to take its touch upon her burning face.

Bub crept down after her, and knocked the ashes out of his pipe against the door.

"Ain't used to the dark, be ye?"

No; not much used to the dark.

"Afraid?"

Not at all afraid.

Lor. He was goin' to offer to see her home,— for ten cents. *He* used to be afraid. Got so old he give it up.

Half-way home, Miss Kelso was touched upon the arm again; this time gently, and with some timidity. Sip Garth, with a basket on her arm, spoke as she turned; she had been out marketing, she said ; getting a little beef for to-morrow's dinner ; had recognized and watched her half up the street ; it was very late ; Miss Kelso was not so used to being out late as mill-girls were ; and if she cared for company —

" I do not know that there is any reason why I should not be out as late as mill-girls are," mused Miss Kelso, struck by the novelty of the idea. But she was glad of the company, certainly ; fell into step with the mill-girl upon the now crowded walk.

" This is very new to me," she said in a low voice, as they turned a corner where a gust of oaths met her like an east-wind and took away her breath.

" You 'll see strange sights," said Sip, with her dogged smile.

She saw strange sights, indeed ; strange sights for delicate, guarded, fine young eyes ; but so pitifully familiar to the little mill-girl with the dogged smile! As familiar, for instance, as Maverick and Axminster carpets to Miss Kelso, Miss Kelso wondered.

The lights of the little town were all ablaze ; shops and lounging-places full. Five Falls was as restless as the restless night.

"Always is," said Sip, " in a wind. Take a good storm, or even take the moon, and it 's different. When mill-folks have a man to hate, or a wife to beat, or a child to drown, or a sin to think of, or any ugly thing to do, you may notice, ten to one, they 'll take a windy night; a dark night like this, when you can't see what the gale is up to, when you 're blown along, when you run against things, when you can't help yourself, when nothing seems to be any-body's fault, when there 's noises in the world like the engines of ten thousand factories let loose. You can't keep still. You run about. You 're in and out. You 've got so used to a noise. You feel as if you were part and parcel of it. I do. Next morning, if you 've lost your soul, — why, the wind 's down, and you don't understand it."

Sip's dark face lighted fitfully, as if the gusty weather blew its meaning to and fro; she gestic-ulated with her hands like a little French woman. It struck Perley that the girl was not far wrong in fancying that she could " do it over " at the Blue Plum.

But Perley saw strange sights. Five Falls in

the gusty weather was full of them. Full of knots of girls in bright ribbons singing unpleasantly ; of knots of men at corners drinking heavily ; of tangles where the two knots met with discordant laughter ; of happy lovers that one sighed over ; of haggard sinners that one despaired of praying over ; of old young children with their pipes, like Bub; of fragments of murderous Irish threats ; of shattered bits of sweet Scotch songs ; of half-broken English brogue ; of German gutturals thick with lager ; only now and then the shrewd, dry Yankee twang.

It was to be noticed of these people that the girls swore, that the babies smoked, that the men, more especially the elder men, had frowns like Mr. Mell.

" One would think," said Miss Kelso, as she watched the growing crowd, " that they had no homes."

" They have houses," said Sip.

They passed a dark step where something lay curled up like a skulking dog.

" What's that ? " said Miss Kelso, stopping and stooping. It was a little girl, — a very little girl. She had a heavy bundle or a pail upon her arm ;

had been sent upon an errand, it seemed, and had dropped upon the step asleep; had been trodden on once or twice, for her clothes bore the mark of muddy feet.

"That 's Dib Docket," said Sip. "Go home, Dib!" Sip shook her, not ungently.

The little thing moved away uncertainly like a sleep-walker, jostled to and fro by people in the street. She seemed either too weak or too weary to sit or stand.

"That 's Dib Docket," repeated Sip. "That child walks, at her work in the mills, between twenty and thirty miles a day. I counted it up once. She lives three quarters of a mile from the factory besides. She 's not so bright as she might be. It 's a wicked little devil; knows more wickedness than you 've ever *thought* of, Miss Kelso. No, you 'd better not go after her; you would n't understand."

Women with peculiar bleached yellow faces passed by. They had bright eyes. They looked like beautiful moving corpses; as if they might be the skeletons among the statues that were dug against the face of day. Miss Kelso had noticed them since she first came out.

" What are they ? "

" Cotton-weavers.   You can tell a weaver by the skin."

Threading her way through a blockade of loud-speaking young people by the railroad station (there was always plenty going on at the station, Sip said), Miss Kelso caught a bit of talk about " the Lord's day."   Surprised at this evidence of religious feeling where she was not prepared to expect it, she expressed her surprise to Sip.

" O," said Sip, " we mean pay-day ; that 's all the Lord's day we know much about."

There was an old man in this crowd with very white hair.   He had a group of young fellows about him, and gesticulated at them while he talked.   The wind was blowing his hair about. He had a quavering voice, with a kind of mumble to it, like the voice of a man with a chronic toothache.

" Hear him ! " said Sip.

Perley could hear nothing but a jargon of " Eight hour," " Ten hour," " Labor reform," " Union," " Slaves and masters," " Next session," and " Put it through."   Some of the young fellows seemed to listen, more laughed.

"Poor old Bijah!" said Sip, walking on; "always in a row, — Bijah Mudge; can't outgrow it. He 's been turned out of half the mills in New England, folks say. He 'll be in hot water in Five Falls before long, if he don't look out. But he 's a lonesome old fellow, — Bijah."

Just beyond the station Sip suddenly stopped. They were in the face of a gay little shop, with candy and dry goods in the windows.

"And rum enough in the back room there to damn an angel!" said Sip, passionately, "and he will have her in there in five minutes! Hold on, will you?" She broke away from Miss Kelso, who "held on" in bewilderment.

A pretty girl was strolling up and down the platform of this place, with her hand upon the arm of a young fellow with a black mustache. The girl had a tint like that of pale gold about her hair and face, and large, vain, unhappy eyes. She wore blue ribbons, and looked like a Scotch picture.

Sip stopped at the foot of the platform, and called her. The girl came crossly, and yet with a certain air of relief too.

"What do you want, Sip Garth?"

6

" I want you to go home, Nynee Mell."

" Home ! " said Nynee, with weak bitterness.

" Yes, home ; it 's better than this."

" It frets me so, to go home ! " said Nynee, impatiently. " I hate to go home."

" It is better than this," repeated Sip, earnestly. " Come. I don't set up to be a preacher, Nynee, but I *do* set up that Jim 's no company fit for a decent girl."

" I 'm a decent girl," said poor Nynee, trying to toss her silly head, but looking about her with an expression of alarm. " Who said I was n't ? "

Sip's reply Miss Kelso lost. The two girls talked together for a few moments in low tones. Presently Nynee walked slowly away.

" Jim 'll be cross to-morrow, if I give him the slip," she said, pettishly, but still she walked away.

" There ! " exclaimed Sip, stopping where she stood, " that will do. Dirk ! Dirk, I say ! "

Dirk I say stopped too. He had been walking rapidly down the street when Sip spoke. He was a young man of perhaps twenty-five, with a strong hand and a kindly eye. He looked very kindly at Sip.

"I want you to go home with Nynee Mell," said Sip.

"I'd a sight rather go home with some others than Nynee Mell," said the kindly young man.

"I know what I'm about," said Sip. "I know who'll keep Nynee Mell out of mischief. Go quick, can't you?"

The kindly young man kindly went; not so quickly as he might, but he went.

"Who was that young man?" asked Miss Kelso, as they climbed the hill.

"Jim? A miserable Irishman, Jim is; hasn't been in Five Falls a month, but long enough to show his colors, and a devilish black mustache, as you see. You see, they put him to work next to Nynee; he must go somewhere; they put him where the work was; they didn't bother their heads about the girl; they're never bothered with such things. And there ain't much room in the alley. So she spends the day with him, pushing in and out. So she gets used to him and all that. She's a good girl, Nynee Mell; wildish, and spends her money on her ribbons, but a good girl. She'll go to the devil, sure as death, at this rate. Who wouldn't? Leastways, being Nynee Mell."

" But I meant the other young man," observed Miss Kelso.

" Him ? O, that 's Dirk Burdock ; watchman up at the Old Stone."

" A friend of yours ? "

" I never thought of it," said Sip, gravely. " Perhaps that 's what you 'd call him. I like Dirk first-rate."

Sip pointed out one other young man to Miss Kelso before they were quite at home. They were passing a dingy hall where the mission, Sip said, held a weekly prayer meeting. The young man came out with the worshippers. It was Mr. Garrick (said Sip), the new partner. He 'd been in the way of going since he was in the dressing-room himself; folks thought he 'd give it up now ; she guessed it was the first time you 'd ever caught the firm into the mission meeting ; meaning no offence, however.

He was a grave man, this Mr. Garrick ; a man with premature wrinkles on the forehead ; with a hard-worked, hard-working mouth ; with a hard hand, with a hard step ; a man, you would say, in a hard place, acquired by a hard process ; a man, perhaps, who would find it hard to hope, and harder to despair. But a man with a very bright, sweet, sudden smile. A man of whom Perley Kelso had seen or heard half her life; who had been in and out of the house on business; who had run on her errands, or her father's, — it made little difference — in either case she had never troubled herself about the messenger; but a man whose face she could no more have defined than she could, for instance, that of her coachman. Her eyes followed him, therefore, with some curiosity, as he lifted his hat in grave surprise at passing her, and went his way.

Perley counted the people that came out from the mission meeting. There were six in all.

"There must be sixty folks within sight," observed Sip, running her quick eye up and down the gaudy little street, "as many as sixty loafin', I mean."

Miss Kelso made no answer, and they reached and entered her own still, clean, elegantly trimmed lawn in silence.

"Now I've seen you safe home," said the mill-girl, "I shall feel better. The fact was, I did n't know but the boys would bother you; they're a rough set; and you ain't used to 'em."

" I never thought of such a thing ! " exclaimed the young lady. " They all know me, you know."

" Yes ; they all know you."

" I supposed they would feel a kind of interest, or respect — "

" What reason have you ever given them," said Sip in a low tone, " to feel any special interest or respect for you ? "

" You are right," said Miss Kelso, after a moment's thought. " They have no reason. I have given them none. I wish you would come in a minute."

" Have I been saucy ? "

" No ; you have been honest. Come in a minute ; come, I want you."

The lofty, luxurious house was lighted and still. Sip held her breath when the heavy front door shut her into it. Her feet fell on a carpet like thick, wild moss, as she crossed the warm wide hall. Miss Kelso took her, scarcely aware, it seemed, that she did so, into the parlors, and shut their oaken doors upon their novel guest. She motioned the girl to a chair, and flung herself upon another.

Now, for a young lady who had had a sea-

son ticket to the Opera every winter of her
life, it will be readily conjectured that she had
passed an exciting evening. In her way, even
the mill-girl felt this. But in her way, the mill-
girl was embarrassed and alarmed by the condition in which she found Miss Kelso.

The young lady sat, white to the lips, and
trembled violently; her hands covered and re-
covered each other, with a feeble motion, as they
lay upon her lap; the eyes had burned to a
still white heat; her breath came as if she were
in pain.

Suddenly she rose with a little crouch like a
beautiful leopardess and struck the gray and
green chess-table with her soft hand; the blow
snapped one of her rings.

"You do not understand," she cried, "you people who work and suffer, how it is with us! We
are born in a dream, I tell you! Look at these
rooms! Who would think — in such a room as
this — except he dreamed it, that the mothers
of very little children died for want of a few
hundreds and a change of climate? Why, the
curtains in this room cost six! See how it is!
You touch us — in such a room — but we dream;

we shake you off. If you cry out to us, we only dream that you cry. We are not cruel, we are only asleep. Sip Garth, when we have clear eyes and a kind heart, and perhaps a clear head, and are waked up, for instance, without much warning, it is *nature* to spring upon our wealth, to hate our wealth, to feel that we have no right to our wealth ; no more moral right to it than the opium-eater has to his drug !

" Why, Sip," rising to pick up the chess-table, " I never knew until to-night what it was like to be poor. It was n't that I did n't care, as you said. I did n't *know*. I thought it was a respectable thing, a comfortable thing ; a thing that could n't be helped ; a clean thing, or a dirty thing, a lazy thing, or a drunken thing ; a thing that must be, just as mud must be in April ; a thing to put on overshoes for."

And now what did she think ?

" Who knows what to think," said Perley Kelso, " that is just waked up ? "

" Miss Kelso ? " said Sip.

" Yes," said Miss Kelso.

" I never knew in all my life how grand a room could be till I come into this grand room to-night. Now, you see, if it was mine —"

" What would you do, if this grand room were yours ? " asked Miss Kelso, curiously.

" Just supposing it, you know, — am I very saucy ? "

" Not very, Sip."

" Why," said Sip, " the fact is, I 'd bring Nynee Mell in to spend an evening ! "

An engraving that lay against a rich easel in a corner of the room attracted the girl's attention presently. She went down on her knees to examine it. It chanced to be Lemude's dreaming Beethoven. Sip was very still about it.

" What is that fellow doing?" she asked, after a while, — " him with the stick in his hand."

She pointed to the leader of the shadowy orchestra, touching the *baton* through the glass, with her brown finger.

" I have always supposed," said Perley, " that he was only floating with the rest; you see the orchestra behind him."

"Floating after those women with their arms up ? No, he is n't ! "

" What is he doing ? "

" It 's riding over him, — the orchestra. He can't master it. Don't you see ? It sweeps him

6*   I

along. He can't help himself. They come and come. How fast they come! How he fights and falls! O, I know how they come. That's the way things come to me; things I could do, things I could say, things I could get rid of if I had the chance; they come in the mills mostly; they tumble over me just so; I never have the chance. How he fights! I did n't know there was any such picture as that in the world. I'd like to look at that picture day and night. See! O, I know how they come."

"Miss Kelso —" after another silence and still upon her knees before the driving Dream and the restless dreamer. "You see, that's it. That's like your pretty things. I'd keep your pretty things if I was you. It ain't that there should n't be music anywhere. It's only that the music should n't ride over the master. Seems to me it is like that."

CHAPTER VI.

MOULDINGS AND BRICKS.

" MAVERICK!"

" At your service."

" But Maverick — "

" What then ? "

" Last year, at Saratoga, I paid fifteen dollars apiece for having my dresses done up!"

" Thus supporting some pious and respectable widow for the winter, I have no doubt."

" Maverick! how much did *I* think about the widow ? "

" I should say, from a cursory examination of the subject, that your thoughts would be of less consequence — excuse me — to a pious and respectable widow, than — how many times fifteen ? Without doubt, a serious lack of taste on the part of a widow ; but, I fear, a fatal fact."

" But, Maverick! I know a man on East Street whom I never could make up my mind to look in the face again, if he should see the bill for santalina in those carriage cushions!"

The bill was on file, undoubtedly, suggested Maverick. Allow her friend an opportunity to see it, by all means.

"Maverick! do you see that shawl on the arm of the *tête-à-tête?* It cost me three thousand dollars."

Why not? Since she did the thing the honor to become it, she must in candor admit, amazingly.

"And there's lace up stairs in my bureau drawer for which I paid fifty dollars a yard. And, Maverick! I believe the contents of any single jewel-case in that same drawer would found a free bed in a hospital. And my bill for Farina cologne and kid gloves last year would supply a sick woman with beefsteak for this. And Maverick!"

"And what?" very languidly from Maverick.

"Nothing, only — why, Maverick! I am a member of a Christian church. It has just occurred to me."

"Maverick!" again, after a pause, in which Maverick had languished quite out of the conversation, and had entertained himself by draping Perley in the shawl from the *tête-à-tête*, as if she had been a lay-figure for some crude and gorgeous design which he failed to grasp. Now he made a Sibyl of her, now a Deborah, now a Maid of Orleans, a priestess, a princess, a Juno ; after some reflection, a Grace Darling ; after more, a prophetess at prayer.

" Maverick ! we must have a library in our mills."

" Must we ? " mused Maverick, extinguishing his prophetess in a gorgeous turban.

" There ; how will that do ? What a Nourmahal you are ! "

" And relief societies, and half-time schools, and lectures, and reading-rooms, and, I hope, a dozen better things. Those will only do to start with."

" A modest request — for Cophetua, for instance," said Maverick, dropping the shawl in a blazing heap at her feet.

" Maverick ! I 've been a lay-figure in life long enough, if you please. Maverick, Maverick ! I cannot play any longer. I think you will be sorry if you play with me any longer."

Cophetua said this with knitted brows. Maverick tossed the shawl away, and sat down beside her. The young man's face also had a wrinkle between the placid eyes.

" Those will only do to start with," repeated Perley, " but start with those we must. And, Maverick," with rising color, " some tenement-houses, if you please, that are fit for human beings to inhabit ; more particularly human beings who pay their rentals to Christian people."

" It seems to me, Perley," said her lover, pleasantly, " a great blunder in the political economy of Hayle and Kelso that you and I should quarrel over the business. Why *should* we quarrel over the business ? It is the last subject in the world that collectively, and as comfortable and amiable engaged people, *can* concern us. If you must amuse yourself with these people, and must run athwart the business, go to father. Have you been to father ? "

" I had a long talk with your father," said Perley, " yesterday."

" What did he say to you ? "

" He said something about Political Economy ; he said something else about Supply and Demand.

He said something, too, about the State of the Market."

" He said, in short, that we cannot afford any more experiments in philanthropy on this town of Five Falls ? "

" He said, in short, just that."

" He said, undoubtedly, the truth. It would be out of the question. Why, we ran the works at a dead loss half of last year ; kept the hands employed, and paid their wages regularly, when the stock was a drug in the market and lay like lead on our hands. Small thanks we get for that from the hands, or — you."

" Your machinery, I suppose, would not have been improved by lying unused ? " observed Perley, quietly.

" It would have been injured, I presume."

" And it *has* been found worth while, from a business point of view, to retain *employés* even at a loss, rather than to scatter them ? "

" It has been, perhaps," admitted Maverick, un-easily. " One would think, however, Perley, that you thought me destitute of common human-ity, just because you *cannot* understand the ins and outs of the thousand and one questions

which perplex a business man. I own that I do
not find these people as much of a diversion as
you do, but I protest that I do not abuse them.
They go about their business, and I go about
mine. Master and man meet on business grounds,
and business grounds alone. Bub Mell and a
young lady with nothing else to do may meet,
without doubt, upon religious grounds ; upon the
highest religious grounds."

"These improvements which I suggest," pursued Perley, waving Maverick's last words away
with her left hand (it was without ornament and
had a little bruise upon one finger), " have been
successful experiments, all of them, in other mills ;
most of them in the great Pacific. Look at the
great Pacific ! "

"The great Pacific can afford them," said
Maverick, shortly. " That 's the way with our
little country mills always. If we don't bankrupt
ourselves by reflecting every risk that the great
concerns choose to run, some soft-hearted and
soft-headed philanthropist pokes his finger into
our private affairs, and behold, there 's a hue and
cry over us directly."

" For a little country mill," observed Perley,

making certain figures in the air with her bruised white finger, " I think, if I may judge from my own income, that a library.and a reading-room would not bankrupt us, at least this year. However, if Hayle and Kelso cannot afford some few of these little alterations, I think their silent partner can."

" Very well," laughed Maverick ; " we 'll make the money and you may spend it."

" Maverick Hayle," said Perley, after a silence, " do you know that every law of this State which regulates the admission of children into factories is broken in your mills ? "

" Ah ? " said Maverick.

" I ask," insisted Perley, " if you know it ? "

" Why, no," said Maverick, with a smile ; " I cannot say that I know it exactly. I know that nobody not behind the scenes can conceive of the dodges these people invent to scrape and screw a few dollars, more or less, out of their children. As a rule, I believe the more they earn themselves the more they scrape and screw. I know how they can lie about a child's age. Turn a child out of one mill for his three months' schooling, and he 's in another before night, half the

time.   Get him fairly to school, and I've known
three months' certificates begged or bribed out
of a school-mistress at the end of three weeks.
Now, what can I do? You can't expect a mill-
master to have the time, or devote it to running
round the streets compelling a few Irish babies
to avail themselves of the educational privileges
of this great and glorious country!"

"That is a thing," observed Perley, "that I
can look after in some measure, having, as you
noticed, nothing else to do."

"That is a thing," said Maverick, sharply,
"which I desire, Perley, that you will let alone.
I must leave it to the overseers, or we shall
be plunged into confusion worse confounded.
That is a thing which I must insist upon it
that you do not meddle with."

Perley flushed vividly. The little scar upon
her finger flushed too. She raised it to her lips
as if it pained her.

"There is reason," urged Maverick, — "there
is reason in all things, even in a young lady's
fancies. Just look at it! You run all over Five
Falls alone on a dark night, very improperly,
to hear mill-people complain of their drains,

and — unrebuked by you — of their master. You come home and break your engagement ring and cut your finger. Forthwith you must needs turn my mill-hands into lap-dogs, and feed them on — what was it? roast beef? — out of your jewelry-box!"

" I do not think," said Perley, faintly smiling, " that you understand, Maverick."

" I do *not* think I understand," said Maverick.

" You do not understand," repeated Perley, firmly but faintly still. " Maverick! Maverick! if you cannot understand, I am afraid we shall both be very sorry!"

Perley got up and crossed the room two or three times. There was a beautiful restlessness about her which Maverick, leaning back upon the *tête-à-tête*, with his mustache between his fingers, noted and admired.

" I cannot tell you," pursued Perley in a low voice, " how the world has altered to me, nor how I have altered to myself, within the past few weeks. I have no words to say how these people seem to me to have been thrust upon my hands, — as empty, idle, foolish hands, God knows, as ever he filled with an unsought gift!"

" Now I thought," mentioned Maverick, grace-
fully, " that both the people and the hands did
well enough as they were."

Perley spread out the shining hands, as if in
appeal or pain, and cried out, as before, " Maverick ! Maverick ! " but hardly herself knowing,
it seemed, why she cried.

" One would think," pursued Maverick, with a
jerk at his mustache, " to hear and to see you,
Perley, that there were no evils in the country
but the evils of the factory system ; that there
was no poverty but among weavers earning ten
dollars a week. Questions which political econo-
mists spend life in disputing, you expect a mill-
master — "

" Who does n't care a fig about them," interrupted Perley.

" Who does n't care a fig about them," admitted
the mill-master, " you are right ; between you
and me, you are right ; who does n't care a fig
about them — to settle. Now there 's father ; he
is *au fait* in all these matters ; has a theory for
every case of whooping-cough, — and a mission
school. Once for all, I must beg to have it
understood that I turn you and the State com-

mittees over to father. You should hear him talk to a State committee!"

"And yet," said Perley, sadly, "your father and you tie my hands to precisely the same extent by different methods."

"No?" said Maverick, "really?"

"He with Adam Smith, and you with a *tête-à-tête.* He is too learned, and you are too lazy. I have not been educated to reason with him, and I suppose I am too fond of you to deal with you," said the young lady. "But, Maverick, there *is* something in this matter which neither of you touch. There is *something* about the relations of rich and poor, of master and man, with which the state of the market has nothing whatever to do. There is *something*, — a claim, a duty, a puzzle, it is all too new to me to know what to call it, — but I am convinced that there is *something* at which a man cannot lie and twirl his mustache forever."

Being a woman, and having no mustache to twirl, urged Maverick, nothing could well be more natural than that she should think so. An appropriate opinion, and very charmingly expressed. Should he order the horses at half past ten?

"Maverick!" cried Perley, thrusting out her hands as before, and as before hardly knowing, it seemed, why she cried,—"Maverick, Maverick!"

Possibly it was a week later that the new partner called one evening upon Miss Kelso.

He was there, he said, at the request of Mr. Hayle the junior; was sorry to introduce business into a lady's parlor; but there was a little matter about the plans—

"Ah, yes," said Miss Kelso, hastily, "plans of the new mill?"

"A plan for the new mill; yes. Mr. Hayle desired your opinion about some mouldings, I believe; and, as I go in town to-morrow to meet an appointment with the architect, it fell to my lot to confer with you. Mr. Hayle desired me to express to you our wish—I think he said our wish—that any preference you might have in the ornamentation of the building should be rigidly regarded."

"Very thoughtful in Mr. Hayle," said Perley, "and characteristic. Sit down, if you please, Mr. Garrick."

He was a grave man, this Mr. Garrick; if there

were a biting breath in the young lady's even voice, if a curl as light as a feather fell across her unsmiling mouth, one would suppose that Stephen Garrick, sitting gravely down with mill plans in his hand, beside her, was the last man upon earth to detect either.

"Now," said Miss Kelso, pulling towards her across the table a marvellous green mill on a gray landscape, with full-grown umber shade-trees where a sand heap rightfully belonged, and the architect's name on a sign above the counting-room, "what is this vital question concerning which Mr. Hayle desires my valuable opinion?"

"The question is, whether you would prefer that the mouldings — here is a section ; you can see the design better about this door — should be of Gloucester granite or not."

"Or what?" asked Perley.

"Or not," said Mr. Garrick, smiling.

"I never saw you smile before," said Miss Kelso, abruptly, tossing away the plans. "I did not know that you could. It is like — "

"What is it like?" asked Stephen Garrick, smiling again.

"It is like making a burning-glass out of a

cast-iron stove. Excuse me. That mill has tumbled over the edge of the table, Mr. Garrick. Thank you. Is Gloucester granite of a violet tint ? "

" Outside of an architect's privileged imagination, not exactly. What shall I tell Mr. Hayle ? "

" You may tell Mr. Hayle that I do not care whether the mouldings are of Gloucester granite or of green glass. No; on the whole, I will tell him myself.

" You see, Mr. Garrick," said Miss Kelso after an awkward pause, " when you are a woman and a silent partner, it is only the mouldings of a matter that fall to you."

Mr. Garrick saw.

" And so," piling up the plans upon the table thoughtfully, " you become a little sensitive upon the subject of mouldings. You would so much rather be a brick-maker ! "

" I suppose," said Stephen Garrick, " that I have been what you would call a brick-maker."

" I suppose you have," said Miss Kelso, still thoughtfully. " Mr. Garrick ? "

Mr. Garrick lifted his grave face inquiringly.

" I suppose you know what it is to be very poor ? "

" Very poor."

" And now you will be very rich. That must be a singular life ! "

" It is in some respects a dangerous life, Miss Kelso."

" It is in other respects a privileged life, Mr. Garrick."

" It is proverbial of men with my history," said Garrick, slowly,— " men who have crawled on their hands and knees from the very quagmires of life, — men who know, as no other men can know, that the odds are twenty to one when a poor man makes a throw in the world's play— "

" Are they ? " interrupted the lady.

" Twenty to one," said Stephen Garrick, in a dry statistical tone, " against poverty, always. It is proverbial, I say, that men who know as God knows that it is by ' him who hath no money ' that the upright, downright, unmistakable miseries of life are drained to the dregs, — that such men prove to be the hardest of masters and the most conservative of social reformers. It has been the fancy of my life, I may say that it has been more like a passion than a fancy," said the *parvenu* in Hayle and Kelso, laying his hard hand hardly clenched upon the colored plates that Perley had piled up beside him, " as fast and as far as I got out of the mud myself to bring other people with me. I cannot find any dainty words in which to put this, Miss Kelso, for it is a very muddy thing to be poor."

" I have thought it — but very lately — to be a hard thing," said Perley.

The hard lines about Stephen Garrick's mouth worked, but he said nothing. Perley, looking up suddenly, saw what hard lines they were ; and when he met her look he smiled, and she thought what a pleasant smile it was.

" Mr. Garrick, do you think it is possible, — this thing of which you speak ? Possible to be Hayle and Kelso, and yet to pick people out of the mud ? "

" I believe it to be *possible*."

" You are not in an easy position, it strikes me, Mr. Garrick."

" It strikes me — I beg your pardon — that you are not in another, Miss Kelso."

Stephen Garrick took his leave with this ; wisely, perhaps ; would have taken his leave with a gravely formal bow, but that Miss Kelso held out to him a sudden, warm, impulsive woman's hand.

Walking home with his pile of colored plans under his arm, Mr. Garrick fell in with two of the mill-people, the young watchman Burdock and a girl whom he did not recognize. He said, What a pleasant evening for a walk it was ! as he went by them, cheerily.

" It 's nothing to say ' A pleasant evening,' I know," said Dirk as he passed them ; " but it 's a way I like about Mr. Garrick. A man thinks better of himself for it ; feels as if he was some-body — almost. I mean to be somebody yet, Sip."

" Do you ? " said Sip, with a patient smile. He said it so often ! She had so little faith that he would ever do any more than say it.

" It 's a hard rut to wrench out of, Dirk, — the mills. How many folks I 've seen try to get out of the mills ! They always came back."

" But they don't always come back, Sip. Look at Stephen Garrick."

" Yes, yes," said Sip patiently, " I know they don't always come back, and I 've looked at Stephen Garrick ; but the folks as I knew came back. I 'd go back. I know I should."

"It would be never you that would go back,"
urged Dirk, anxiously. "You 're the last girl I
know for that."

Sip shook her head. "It 's in the blood, maybe. I know I should go back. What a kind of
a pleasantness there *is* about the night, Dirk ! "

There was somehow a great pleasantness to
Sip about the nights when she had a walk with
Dirk ; she neither understood nor questioned
how ; not a passion, only a pleasantness ; she noticed that the stars were out ; she was apt to hear
the tiny trail of music that the cascades made
above the dam ; she saw twice as many lighted
windows with the curtains up as she did when
she walked alone ; if the ground were wet, it did
did not trouble her ; if the ground were dry, it
had a cool touch upon her feet ; if there were a
geranium anywhere upon a window-sill, it pleased
her ; if a child laughed, she liked the sound ; if
Catty had been lost since supper, she felt sure that
they should find her at the next corner ; if she
had her week's ironing to do when she got home,
she forgot it ; if a rough word sprang to her lips,
it did not drop ; if her head ached, she smiled ;
if a boy twanged a jew's-harp, she could have

danced to it ; if poor little Nynee Mell flitted jealously by with Jim, in her blue ribbons, she could sit down and cry softly over her, — such a gentleness there was about the night.

It was only pleasantness and gentleness that ever lay between her and Dirk. Sip never flushed or frowned, never pouted or coquetted at her sparse happiness ; it might be said that she never hoped or dreamed about it ; it might even be that the doggedness of her little brown face came over it or into it, and that it was not without a purpose that she neither dreamed nor hoped. Miss Kelso sometimes wondered. Dirk dully perplexed himself about her now and then.

" I wish," said Sip, as they came into the yard of the damp stone house, " that you 'd look in at the window for me a minute, Dirk."

" What shall I look at ? " said Dirk, stepping up softly to the low sill, " *her ?* "

Catty was in view from the window ; sitting on the floor with her feet crossed, stringing very large yellow beads ; she did this slowly, and with some hesitation ; now and then a kind of ill-tempered fright seemed to fall upon her repulsive face ; once or twice she dropped the toys, and once she dashed them with a little snarl like an annoyed animal's upon her lap.

" I give them to her to try her," whispered Sip. " Do you see anything about her that is new ? anything, Dirk, that you never took a notice of before ? "

" Why, no," said Dirk, " I don't see nothin' uncommon.   What 's the matter ? "

" Nothing !   It 's nothing only a fear I had. Never mind ! "

Sip drew a sudden long breath, and turned away.

Now it was pleasant to Sip to share even a fear with Dirk.

" Look in again," she said, with a low laugh, " over on the wall beyond Catty.   Look what is hanging on the wall."

" O, that big picture over to the left of the chiny-closet ? "   Dirk pointed to the Beethoven dreaming wildly in the dingy little room.

" A little to the left of the cupboard, — yes. One night I walked in and found it, Dirk !   She hung it there for me to walk in and find.   I laid awake till three o'clock next morning, I laid and looked at it.   I don't know anybody but you,

Dirk, as could guess what a strangeness and a forgetting it makes about the room."

Now it was very new to Sip to have a "forgetting" that she could share with even Dirk.

"It looks like the Judgment Day," said Dirk, looking over Catty's head at the plunging dream and the solitary dreamer.

There chanced that night two uncommon occurrences; for one, the watchman at the Old Stone was sleepy; for another, Miss Kelso was not.

The regulations in Hayle and Kelso were inexorable at night. Two fires and three drunken watchmen within the limits of a year had put it out of the question to temper justice with mercy. To insure the fidelity of the watch, he was required to strike the hour with the factory bell from nine at night till four o'clock in the morning.

Now upon the night in question Miss Kelso's little silver clock struck twelve, but the great tongue of the Old Stone did not. In perhaps twenty minutes, Old Stone woke up with a jerk, and rang in the midnight stoutly.

To be exact, I should have said that there chanced that night three uncommon occurrences.

For that a young lady should get up on a chilly and very dark spring midnight, dress herself, steal down stairs, unlock the front door, and start off alone to walk a quarter of a mile, and save a sleepy young watchman from disgrace, is not, it must be allowed, so characteristic an event as naturally to escape note.

It happened, furthermore, that it did not escape the note of the new partner, coming out on precisely the same errand at the same time. They met at the lady's gate : she just passing through, he walking rapidly by ; she with a smile, he with a start.

" Miss Kelso ! "

" Mr. Garrick ? "

" Is anything wrong ? "

" With the watchman ? Yes, or will be. I had hoped I was the only person who knew that midnight came in at twenty minutes past twelve."

" And I had hoped that I was."

" It was very thoughtful in you, Mr. Garrick," said Perley, heartily,

He did not say that it was thoughtful in her. He turned and looked at her as she stood shivering and smiling, with her hand upon the gate, —

the bare hand on which the bruise had been. He would have liked to say what he thought it, but it struck him as a difficult thing to do. Graceful words came so hardly to him ; he felt this hardly at the moment.

" I suppose I must leave the boy to you then," said Perley, slowly,

" You are taking cold," said the mill-master, in his hard way. It was very dark where they stood, yet not so dark but that he could see, in bowing stiffly, how Miss Kelso, with her bruised hand upon the gate, shot after him a warm, sweet, impulsive woman's smile.

Dirk was sitting ruefully upon an old boiler in the mill-yard. He rubbed his eyes when Mr. Garrick came up. When he saw who it was, the boy went white to the lips.

" Burdock, the bell was not struck to-night at twelve o'clock."

" Certainly, sir," said Dirk, desperately making his last throw.

" Not at twelve o'clock."

" Punctually, sir, you may be sure ; I never missed a bell in Hayle and Kelso yet."

" The bell rang," observed Mr. Garrick, with

7*

quiet sternness, "at twenty-one minutes past midnight, exactly."

"Mr. Garrick — " begged the watchman, but stammered and stopped.

"Of course you know the consequences," said the master, more gently, sitting down upon the rusty boiler beside the man, "of a miss in the bell, — of a single miss in a bell."

"I should think I'd been in Hayle and Kelso long enough to know," said Dirk, with his head between his knees. "Mr. Garrick, upon my word and honor, I never slept on watch before. I was kind of beat out to-night." The truth was, that Dirk had been carrying in coal for Sip half the afternoon. "Had n't so much sleep as common to-day ; but that 's no excuse for me, I know." He thought he would not say anything about the coal. "I would n't ha' cared so much about keepin' the place," broke forth the young man, passionately, "but for a reason I had, — I worked so hard for the place ! and so long, sir ! And, God knows, sir, I had such a reason for lookin' on to keep the place !"

"Infidelity on the part of a watchman, you see, Burdock," urged the master, "is not a matter that his employer can dally with."

"I'm no fool, sir," said the man; "I see that. Of course I look to lose the place."

"Suppose I were to offer to you, with a reprimand and warning, the trial of the place again?"

"Sir!" Dirk's head came up like a diver's from between his knees. "You're — your 're good to me, sir! I — I did n't look for that, sir!"

Mr. Garrick made no reply, but got up and paced to and fro between the boiler and a little old, disused cotton-house that stood behind it, absorbed in thought.

"Mr. Garrick," said the watchman, suddenly, "did you get out of bed and come over here to save the place for me?"

"For some such reason, I believe."

"Mr. Garrick, I did n't look to be treated like that. I thank you, sir. Mr. Garrick —"

"Well?" said the master, stopping his walk between the boiler and the cotton-house.

"I told you the first lie, sir, that I've told any man since I lied sick to stay to home from the warping-room, when I was n't much above that boiler there in highness. I think I'd not have been such a sneak, sir, but for the reason that I had."

It seemed that the master said " Well ? " again, though in fact he said nothing, but only stood between the boiler and the cotton-house, gravely looking at the man.

" There 's a — girl I know," said Dirk, wiping rust from his hands upon his blue overalls, " I don't think, sir, there 's a many like her, I don't indeed."

" Ah ! " said Stephen Garrick, restlessly pacing to and fro again, in the narrow limit that the boiler and the cotton-house shut in.

" I don't indeed, sir.   And I 've always looked to being somebody, and pushin' in the mills on account of her.   And I should have took it very hard to lose the place, sir, — on account of her. There don't seem to be what you might call a fair chance for a man in the mills, Mr. Garrick."

" No, not what might be called a fair chance, I think," said Mr. Garrick.

" Not comparing with some other calls in life, it don't seem to me," urged Dirk, disconsolately. " The men to the top they stay to the top, and the men to the bottom they stay to the bottom. There is n't a many sifts up like yourself, sir. It 's like a strawberry-box packed for market, the factory trade is. And when there's a reason, — and a girl comes into the account, it's none so easy."

"No, it's not easy, I grant you, Burdock. What a place this is to spend a night in!"

"A kind of a churchly place," said the young watchman, glancing over the cotton-house at the purple shadow that the mill made against the purple sky; and at purple shadows that the silent village made, and the river, and the bridge. "Takin' in the screech of the dam, it's a solemn place; a place where if a man knows a reason, — or a girl, he thinks o' 't. It's a place where, if a man has ever any longin's for things 't he can call hisn, — wife, and home, and children, and right and might to make 'em comfortable, you know, — he'll consider of 'em. It is a kind of a surprising thing, sir, — the feelin's that a man will have for a good woman."

"A surprising thing," said Stephen Garrick

CHAPTER VII.

CHECKMATE!

" I DO not love you, Maverick Hayle."

May sweetness was in the breakfast-room ; broken, warm airs from the river ; a breath of yellow jonquils, and a shadow of a budding bough ; on a level with the low window-sill a narcissus with a red eye winked steadily. The little silver service was in the breakfast-room, in sharp *rilievo* against a mourning-dress and the curve of a womanly, warm arm. Maverick Hayle, struck dumb upon his feet, where he stood half pushing back his chair, was in the breakfast-room.

On either side of the tiny teapot the man's face and the woman's lay reflected ; it was a smooth, octagonal little teapot, and the two faces struck upon it without distortion ; hung, like delicate engraving, as if cut into the pretty toy. There was something very cosey and homelike about this senseless little teapot, and there was something very lonely and cold about the man's face and the woman's, fixed and separated by the wee width of the polished thing.

Both faces in the teapot were a trifle pale. Both faces out of the teapot were a trifle paler.

"It is not possible!" exclaimed the man, instinctively.

"It is quite possible," explained the woman, calmly.

His face in the teapot flushed now scorching red. Hers in the teapot only whitened visibly.

The young man flung himself back into his chair and ground his teeth. The young woman sat and looked at the teapot and trembled.

"I do not believe it, Perley!" said her plighted husband, fiercely.

"I do not love you, Maverick," repeated Perley, firmly. "I have been afraid of it for a long time. I am very certain of it now. Maverick, Maverick, I am very sorry! I told you we should both be very sorry! But you could not understand."

"If it was your foolish *furor* over a parcel of factory-girls that I could not understand —" began Maverick.

But Perley sternly stopped him.

" Never mind about the poor little factory-girls, Maverick.   It is *you* that I do not love."

This was a thrust which even Maverick Hayle could not lightly parry ; he was fond of Perley and fond of himself, and he writhed in his chair as if it actually hurt him.

" I do not know how it is nor why it is," said Perley, sadly, " but I feel as if there had been a growing away between us for a great while.   It may be that I went away and you stood still ; or that we both went away and both in different ways ; or that we had never, Maverick, been in the same way at all, and did not know it.   You kissed me, and I did not know it ! "

" And if I kiss you again, you will not know it," said Maverick, with an argument of smothered passion in his voice.

" I would rather," said the lady, evenly, " that you did not kiss me again."

Her face in the teapot shone as if a silver veil fell over it.   His face in the teapot clouded and dropped.

" We have loved each other for a long time, Perley," said the young man in a husky voice.

" A long time," said Perley, sorrowfully.

"And were very happy."

"Very happy."

"And should have had — I had thought we should have had such a pleasant life!"

"A miserable life, Maverick ; a most miserable life."

"What in Heaven's name has come over you, Perley!" expostulated the young man. "There is no other man — "

"No other man," said Perley, thoughtfully, "could come between you and me. I do not see, Maverick, how I could ever speak of love to any other man." This she said with her head bent, and with grave, far-reaching eyes. "A woman cannot do that thing. I mean there's nothing in me that understands how she can do it. I was very fond of you, Maverick."

"That is a comfort to me now," said Maverick, bitterly.

"I was fond of you, Maverick. I promised to be your wife. I do not think I could ever say that to another man. The power to say it has gone with the growing away. There was the love and the losing, and now there's only the sorrow. I gave you all I had to give. You used it up, I

K

think. But the growing-away came just the same. I do not love you."

"You women do not understand yourselves any better than you do the rest of the world!" exclaimed the rejected lover with a bewildered face. "Why *should* we grow away? You have n't thought how you will miss me."

"I shall miss you," said Perley. "Of course I shall miss you, Maverick. So I should miss the piano, if it were taken out of the parlor."

Maverick made no reply to this. He felt more humiliated than pained, as was natural. When a man becomes only an elegant piece of furniture in a woman's life, to be dusted at times, and admired at others, and shoved up garret at last by remorseless clean fingers that wipe the cobwebs of him off, it will be generally found that he endures the annoyance of neglected furniture — little more. The level that we strike in the soul that touches us most nearly is almost sure to be the high-water mark of our own.

Now Maverick, it will be seen, struck no tide-mark in Perley. It had never been possible for him to say to the woman, "Thus far shalt thou go." Men say that to women, and women to men. The flood mistakes a nilometer for a boundary line, placidly. It is one of the bitter-sweet blunders of love, that we can stunt ourselves irretrievably for the loved one's sake, and be only a little sadder, but never the wiser, for it.

Perley Kelso thus swept herself over and around her plighted husband ; and in her very fulness lay his content. He would probably have loved her without a question, and rested in her, without a jar, to his dying day. A man often so loves and so rests in a superior woman. He thinks himself to be the beach against which she frets herself ; he is the wreck which she has drowned.

Maverick Hayle, until this morning in the breakfast-room, had loved Perley in this unreasonable, unreasoning, and, I believe, irreclaimable masculine manner ; had accepted her as serenely as a child would accept the Venus de Milo for a ninepin. One day the ninepin will not roll. There is speculation in the beautiful dead eyes of the marble. The game is stopped. He gathers up his balls and sits down breathless.

" But you love me ! " cries the player. " It

must be that you love me at times. It must *be* that you will love me in moods and minutes, Perley. I cannot have gone forever out of all the moods and minutes of your life. I have filled it too long."

He filled it, forsooth! Perley slightly, slowly, sadly smiled.

"If there is any love in the world, Maverick, that ought to be independent of moods and master of all moods, it is the love that people marry on. Now I'm neither very old nor very wise, but I am old enough and wise enough to understand that it is only that part of me which gets tired, and has the blues, and minds an easterly storm, and has a toothache, and wants to be amused, and wants excitement, and — somebody the other side of a silver teapot — which loves you. *I* do not love you, Maverick Hayle!"

"In that case," said Maverick, after a pause, "it is rather awkward for me to be sitting here any longer."

"A little."

"And I might as well take your blessing — and my hat."

"Good by," said Perley, very sadly.

"Good by," said Maverick, very stiffly.

"You 'll tell your father ? " asked the young lady.

" We 're in an awkward fix all around," said the young man, shortly. " I suppose we shall have to make up our minds to that."

" But you and I need not be on awkward terms, — need we ? " asked Perley.

" Of course not. 'Mutual thing; and part excellent friends,'" bitingly from Maverick.

" But I shall always be — a little fond of you ! " urged the woman, with a woman's last clutch at the pleasantness of an old passion.

" Perley," said Maverick, suddenly holding out his hand, " I won't be cross about it. I 've never deserved that you should be any more than a little fond of me. You 've done the honorable thing by me, and I suppose I ought to thank you."

He shut the door of the breakfast-room upon a breath of yellow jonquils, and a shadow of a budding bough, and the narcissus winking steadily ; upon the little silver service, and the curving, womanly, warm arm, and the solitary face that hung engraved upon the senseless little teapot.

CHAPTER VIII.

A TROUBLESOME CHARACTER.

OLD Bijah Mudge stepped painfully over a tub of yellow ochre and crossed the print-room at the overseer's beck. There had been an order of some kind, but he was growing deaf, and the heavy engines were on. The overseer repeated it.

" *Sir ?* "

"I said your notice, did n't I? I say your notice, don't I? You 'll work your notice, *you* will."

"A-a-ah!" said Bijah, drawing a long breath. He stood and knotted his lean fingers together, watching the yellow dye drop off.

" Is there a reason given, sir ? "

" No reason."

" Folks my age ain't often ordered on notice without reason," said the old man, feebly.

" Folks your age should be more particular

how they give satisfaction," said the overseer, significantly.

"I 've known o' cases as where a boss has guessed at a reason, on his own hook, you know, Jim."

Irish Jim was in the print-rooms at Hayle and Kelso at that time. Some said the new partner had a finger in getting him out of the weaving-room. It was a sharp fellow, and belonged some-where. Here he would be brutal to old men and little boys; but there were no girls in the print-room.

"On his own hook and at a guess," said the "boss," "a man might ask who testified to Boston on a recent little hour-bill as we know of."

"*I* testified," cried the old man, shrilly, "be-fore a committee of the Legislature of the State of Massachusetts. I 'd do it ag'in, Jim! In the face of my notice, I 'd do it ag'in! At the risk o' the poor-us, I 'd do it ag'in! I call Hayle and Kelso to witness as I 'd do it ag'in! In the name of the State of Massachusetts, I 'd do it ag'in!"

"Do it again!" said Jim, with a brutal oath. "Who hinders you?"

"But there were no reasons!" added the overseer, sharply. "You fail to give satisfaction, that's all; there's no reasons."

"I am an old man to be turned out o' work sudden, sir." The thin defiance in Bijah's voice broke. He made an obsequious little bow to the Irishman, wringing his dyed hands dry, and lifting them weakly by turns to his mouth. "It's not always easy for an old man to get work, sir."

But Jim was at the other end of the print-room, having some trouble with the crippled tender, who always spilled the violet dye. The boy had cut himself upon a "doctor," it seemed, to-day. Bijah saw blood about, and felt faint, and slunk away.

"Can I have work?"

"What can you do?"

"Anything."

"Where from?"

"Five Falls."

"Hayle and Kelso?"

"Yes, sir."

"You talk like a man with a toothache."

"Ay? Folks has told me that before. An old habit, sir."

" You have been printing ? "

" Yes, sir."

" For three months ? "

" Just about, sir."

" There 's yellow ochre on your clothes, I see."

" I 've none better, sir. I — I 'd not have travelled in my working-close if I 'd had better ; I 'd not have done it once. But I 'm an old man, and out of work."

" Your name is Bijah Mudge ? "

" I 'd not told you my name, sir."

" No, you 'd not told your name ; but you 're Bijah Mudge. We 've got no work for you."

" I am an old man, sir."

" You 're a troublesome character, sir."

" I 'm quite out of work, sir."

" You 'll stay quite out as far as we 're concerned. We 've got no place for you, I say, on this corporation."

" Very well, sir," bowing with grim courtesy. " Good evening, sir. I can try elsewhere."

" O yes," with a slight laugh, " you can try elsewhere."

" It 's a free country, sir ! " cried the troublesome character, in a little spirit of his shrill defiance.

" O yes ; it 's a free country, without doubt ; quite right. You 'll see the door at your left, there. — Patrick ! the door.   Show the man the door."

" And this is the end on 't."

The old man said that to Perley Kelso three weeks later.   He said it in bed in the old men's ward of the almshouse at Five Falls.   There was a chair beside the bed.

The room was full of beds with chairs beside them.   These beds and chairs ran in a line along the wall, numbered nicely.   In general, when you had taken possession of your bed, your chair, and your number, and sat or lay with folded, thin hands and gazed about with weak, bleared eyes, and so sat or lay gazing till you died ; you commanded such variety and excitement as consist in being bounded on both sides by another bed, another chair, another pair of folded hands, and another set of gazing eyes.   Old Bijah's bed and chair stood the last in the line.   So he lay and looked at the wall, when he said, " This is the end on 't."

He liked to talk, they said ; talked a great deal ; talked to the doctor, the paupers, the cat ; talked to the chair and the wall ; talked to Miss Kelso now, because she came between the chair and the wall ; had talked since he was brought struggling in and put to bed with nobody knew what exactly the matter with him. He was dead beat out, he said.

He must have talked a great deal upon his journey ; especially in its later days, since the earnings of the last " Lord's day " were gone ; since he had travelled afoot and gone without his dinner ; since he had taken to sleeping in barns and under fences, and in meadow-places undisturbed and wet with ebbing floods ; since he had traversed the State, and ventured into New Hampshire, and come back into the State, and lost heart and gained it, and lost it again and never gained it again, and so begged his way back to his old shanty up the river, and been found there by Stephen Garrick, in a driving storm, dozing on the floor in a little pool of water, and with the door blown down upon him by the gale.

He had talked to the fences, the sky, the

Merrimack, the sea when he caught a glimpse of it, the dam at Lawrence, and the Lowell bells, and the wind that sprang up in an afternoon, and gray clouds, and red sunsets, and the cattle on the road, especially, he said, to trees ; but always rather to these things than to a human hearer.

" They listened to me," he said, turning shrewd eyes and a foolish smile upon his visitor. " They always listen to me. It 's a free country and I 'm a troublesome character, but they listen — they listen. It 's a free country and there 's room for them and me. I 'm an old man to be turned out o' work. One night I sat down on Lawrence Bridge and said so. It was coming dark, and all the little trees were green. No, marm, I 'm not out o' my head. I 'm only a troublesome character out of work in a free country. The mill-gals they went by, but I 'd rather tell the little trees. I had n't eat no dinner nor no supper. It was dark ag'in the water and ag'in the sky ; all the lights in the mills was blazin', and the streets was full ; if I 'd been a younger man I 'd not have took it quite so hard, mebbe. A younger man might set his hand to this and that ; but I 've worked to factories fifty-six years, and I was very old to get my notice unexpected. I'm sixty-six years old.

"'We know you,' says they to me, 'we don't want you!' says they. Here and there, up to New Hampshyre and back ag'in, this place and that and t'other, 'We know you,' says they.

"So I set on Lawrence Bridge; there was cars and ingines come screechin' by; 'We know you,' says they; and the little trees held up like as it was their hands to listen. 'They know me,' says I, 'I'm a troublesome character out o' work!' There was a little Irish gal come by that night and took me home to supper She lived in one o' them new little houses adown the road.

"There, there, there! Well, well, it's oncommon strange how much more cheery-like it is a talkin' to women-folks than it is to trees. And clearin' to the head. But you'd never guess, unless you was a troublesome character and out o' work, how them trees would listen —

"I like the looks of you setting up ag'in the chair; it makes a variety about the wall. You'd never know, onless you'd come to the end on 't, how little of what you may call variety there is about that wall.

"Now I remember what I had to say; I remember clear. I think I 've had a fever-turn about me, and a man gets muddled now and then from talking to so many trees and furrests. There 's a sameness about it. They 're good listeners, but there 's a sameness about 'em; and a lonesomeness.

"Now this is what I had to say; in the name of the State of Massachusetts, this is what I 've got to say: I 've worked to factories fifty-six years. I have n't got drunk not since I was fifteen year old. I 've been about as healthy, take it off and on, as most folks, and I guess about as smart. I 'm a moral man, and I used to be a Methodist class-leader. I 've worked to factories fifty-six years steady, and I 'm sixty-six year old, and in the poor-us.

"I don't know what the boys would say if they see me in the poor-us.

"I 've married a wife and buried her. I 've brought up six children and buried 'em all. Me and the bed and the chair and the wall are the end on 't.

"It kind o' bothers me, off and on, wonderin' what the boys would say.

" There was three as had the scarlet fever, and two as I lost in the war (three and two is five; and one —) there's one other, but I don't rightly remember what she died on. It was a gal, and kinder dropped away.

" I 've worked fifty-six years, and I 've earned my bread and butter and my shoes and hats, and I give the boys a trade, and I give 'em harnsome coffins ; and now I 'm sixty-six year old and in the poor-us.

" Once when I broke my leg, and the gal was sick, and the boys was in the tin-shop, and their mother she lay abed with that baby that kep' her down so long, I struck for higher wages, and they turned me off. There was other times as I struck for wages, I forget what for, and they turned me off. But I was a young man then, and so I sawed wood and waited my chances, and got to work ag'in, and bided my time, in the name of the State of Massachusetts.

" Now I 've testified afore the Legislature, and I 've got my notice ; and away up in New Hampshyre they knew the yellow ochre on my close, and I could n't get the toothache out o' my voice, and I would n't disown my honest name, — in the name of the State of Massachusetts, I would n't beg for honest work, unless I got it in my honest name, — and so I am sixty-six year old, and in the poor-us.

"Tell Hayle and Kelso, — will you ? — that I'm sixty-six year old, and an honest man, and dead beat out and in the poor-us ! Curse 'em !

" All the leaves o' the trees o' the State of Massachusetts knows it. All the fields and the rivers and the little clouds and the winds o' dark nights and the grasses knows it. I told 'em, I told 'em ! And you' d never know how they listened — See here, marm. I'm no fool, except for the fever on me. I knew when I set out what I'd got to say. I'm no fool, and I never asked no favors from the State of Massachusetts. See here ! A workingman, as is only a workingman, and as lives and dies a workingman, he 'll earn enough to get him vittels, and to get him close, and to get him a roof above his head, and he genrilly won't earn much more ; and I never asked it of the State of Massachusetts as he should. But now, look here ! When I was to Boston on my journey, I picked up a newspaper to the depot, and I read as how a man paid forty

thousand dollars for the plate-glass winders in
his house. Now, look here ! I say there's something out o' kilter in that Commonwealth, and in
that country, and in that lot of human creeturs,
and in them ways of rulin', and in them ways of
thinkin', and in God's world itself, when a man
ken spend forty thousand dollars on the plate-
glass winders of his house, and I ken work
industrious and honest all my life and be be-
holden to the State of Massachusetts for my
poor-us vittels when I'm sixty-six year old !

" Not but what I've had money in the bank in
my day, a many times. I had forty-six dollars
laid by to once. I went into the dye-rooms that
year, and my rubber boots was wore out. We
stand about in dye, and it's very sloppy work,
you know. I'd been off work and out o' cash,
and so I tried to get along without ; so I wet my
feet and wet my feet, standing round in the stuff.
So there was lung fever and doctors' bills enough
to eat that bank account out as close as famine.

" Why was n't I far-seein' enough to get my
boots to the first place and save my fever ? Now
that's jest sech a question as I'd look to get
from them as is them of property. That's jest a

specimen o' the kind of stoopidity as always seems to be a layin' atween property and poverty, atween capital and labor, atween you settin' thar with yer soft ways and yer soft dress ag'in you, and me, and the bed, and the chair, and the wall, and the end on 't.

" How was I a goin' to get into that thar bank account forty mile away in East Boston ? Say ! You 'd never thought on 't, would you ? No, nor none the rest of you as has yer thousands, and the trust as thousands brings, and as would make no more of buyin' a pair o' rubber boots than ye would o' the breath ye draws. I was a stranger to town then, and it 's not for the likes of me to get a pair of rubber boots on trust. So I 'd had my lung fever and lost my bank account afore I could lay finger on it.

" So with this and that and t'other, I 've come into my old age without a dollar, and I 'm a troublesome character, and my boys are dead, and I 'm in the poor-us, and I 'm sixty-six years old.

" I won't say but there 's those of us that lays up more than I did ; but I will say that there 's not a man of us that ever I knew to spend his life in

the mills, and lay by that as would begin to keep
him in his old age. If there's any such man, I'd
like to see him.

"I tell you, marm, there's a many men and women in Hayle and Kelso, and there's a many men
and women in a many factories of this here free
country, as don't dare to testify afore a Legislature. When their testimony tells ag'in the interest of their employers, they don't *dare*. There's
them as won't do it not for nobody. There's
them as does it on the sly, a holdin' back their
names onto the confidence o' the committee, out
o' dread and fear. We're poor folks. We can't
help ourselves, ye see. We're jest clutched up
into the claws o' capital tight, and capital knows
it, jest as well as we do. Capital says to us,
'Hold your tongue, or take your notice.' It
ain't a many poor men as can afford to say, 'I'll
take my notice, thankee!' *I* done it! And
I'd do it ag'in! I'd do it ag'in! In the name o'
the State of Massachusetts, I'd do it ag'in!"

Old Bijah lies for a while, with this, blankly
gazing at the wall and at the visitor with the
"soft dress ag'in her," and at the paupers, and at
the cat. Now and then he shrewdly nods, and

now and then he smiles quite foolishly, and now the rows of beds and chairs file into hickory-trees, he says, and lift up their leaves in the name of the State of Massachusetts, and listen — And now he sees the visitor again, and turns sharply on her, and the hickory-trees file off and wring their hands in going.

"I heerd the t'other day of a man as give thirty thousand dollars for a fancy mare!"

All the trees of the State of Massachusetts are filing out of the old men's ward of the almshouse at Five Falls now, and all in going wring their hands and listen —

" Thirty thousand dollars for a mare! Jest fur the fancy of the fancy creetur. Thirty thousand dollars for a mare!"

He lies quite still once more, till the last hickory hands have passed, wringing, out of the almshouse, and some one has shut the door upon them, and the visitor softly stirs in going after them. He notices that the visitor does not wring her hands, but holds them folded closely down before her as she stirs.

He cries out that he wonders what the boys would say, and that he give 'em harnsome coffins,

and that she is to tell Hayle and Kelso, curse 'em,
as he's sixty-six year old, and out o' work, and in
the poor-us; and when she opens the door in
passing out, half the forests of New England jostle
over her and jostle in, and fill the room, and stand
and listen —

The visitor unclasps her hands on stepping
into the heart of the southern storm; it may be
fancy, or it may be that she slightly wrings them,
as if she had mistaken herself for a hickory-tree.

"They are cold!" exclaims Stephen Garrick,
who waits for her with an umbrella and an enig-
matical face. He takes one of the hands upon
his arm, and folds the other for her in her cloak.
Apparently, neither the man nor the umbrella
nor the action attracts her attention pointedly, till
the man says: "It is a furious storm, and you
will get very wet. What have you been about?"

"Feeling my way."

"I am afraid that is all you will ever do."

"I presume that is all I can ever do."

"But that is something."

"Something."

"You are not expected to cut and carve a

quarry with tied hands. You have at least the advantage of not being responsible for the quarry."

" Who can hold you responsible for a case like this ? You are one of three, and, as you say, tied by the hands."

" That old man will hold me responsible to his dying day. Half our operatives will hold me responsible. Miss Kelso, I am one of those people of whom you will always find a few in the world, adjusted by fate or nature to a position of unavoidable and intolerable mistake and pain."

His face, through the gray of the growing storm, wears a peculiar and a patient smile which Perley notes ; there being always something noteworthy about Stephen Garrick's smile.

" A position," he repeats slowly, " in which a man must appear, from force of circumstances, to pass the — the wounded part of the world by upon the other side. And I believe, before God, that I would begin over again in East Street tomorrow, if I could help to bind it up, and set it healthily upon its way ! "

Perley believes he would, and says so, solemnly.

She says too, very earnestly, that she cannot
think it to be true that a man who holds to such
a purpose, and who holds it with — she falters —
with such a smile, can permanently and inevitably be misunderstood and pained. She cannot
think it.

Stephen Garrick shakes his head.

" I suspect there always are and always will
be a few rich men, Miss Kelso, who just because
they *are* rich men will be forever mistranslated
by the suffering poor, and I suspect that I am
one of them. I do not know that it matters.
Let us talk of something else."

" Of something else than suffering and poverty ?
Mr. Garrick," — Perley turns her young face
against the west, where the sultry storm is
crouching and springing, — " why, Mr. Garrick !
sometimes I do not see — in God's name I do not
see — what else there can *be* to talk about in
such a world as this ! I 've stepped into it, as we
have stepped out into this storm. It has wrapped
me in, — it has wrapped me in ! "

The sultry rain wraps them in, as they beat
against it, heavily. It is not until a little lurid
tongue of light eats its way through and over the

hill, and strikes low and sidewise against the wet clovers that brush against their feet, that Perley breaks a silence into which they fall, to say, in a changed tone, "It is not an uncommon case, this old man's?" and that Mr. Garrick tells her, "Not an uncommon case"; and that she leaves him, nodding, at the corner of the road, and climbs the hill alone; and that he stands in the breaking storm for a moment there to watch her, brushing gilded wet clovers down about her as she climbs.

CHAPTER IX.

A FANCY CASE.

THE oculist shut the door. For a popular oculist, with a specialty for fancy cases, he looked disturbed.

A patient in waiting — a mild, near-sighted case — asked what was the matter with the girl.

"Why, the creature's deaf and dumb!"

"Not growing blind, I hope?"

"Incurably blind. A factory-girl, a charity case of Miss Kelso's. You know of Miss Kelso, Mr. Blodgett?"

Mr. Blodgett knew, he thought. The young lady from whom Wiggins bought that new house on the Mill-Dam. An eccentric young lady, buried herself in Five Falls ever since the old gentleman's death, broke an engagement, and was interested in labor reform, or something of that description.

"The same. Enthusiastic, very; and odd. Would send the girl to me, for instance; naturally it would have been a hospital case, you see. I have to thank her for a hard morning's work. There was a sister in the matter. She would be told then and there; a sharp girl, and I could n't put her off."

Ah! Mr. Blodgett weakly sighs. Very sad! Worn out at the looms perhaps? He seemed to have heard that the gaslight is trying in factories.

"This is wool-picking, sir; a clear case, but a little extraordinary. There's a disease of the hands those people acquire from wool-picking sometimes; an ugly thing. The girl rubbed her eyes, I suppose. The mischief has been a long time in progress, or she might have stood a chance, which gaslight-work has killed, to be sure; but there's none for her here, none!"

Sip and Catty, in the entry, sat down upon the office stairs. Sip was dizzy, she said. She drew up her knees and put her face into her hands. She could hear the doctor through the door saying, "None for her!" and the near-sighted patient babbling pity, and the rumble of the street, as if it had been miles away, and a newsboy shrieking a New York wedding through it. A singular, painful, intense interest in that wedding took hold of her. She wondered what the bride wore, and how much her veil cost. Long bridal parties filed before her eyes, and flowers fell, and sweet scents were in the air. It seemed imperative to think about the wedding. The solid earth would reel if she did not think about the wedding. She clung to the banisters with both hands, lest she should not think about the wedding.

The newsboy shrieked the wedding out of hearing, and Catty touched her on the arm.

" Good God ! " cried Sip. A whirl of flowers and favors shot like a rocket by and beyond her, and a ragged newsboy chased them, and all the brides were blind, and she thrust out her hands ; and she was sitting in the entry on the stairs, and the wind blew up, and she had frightened Catty.

So she said, " There, there ! " as if Catty could hear her, and held by the banisters and stood up.

Catty wanted to know what had happened, very petulantly ; the more so because she could not see Sip's face. She had been very cross since the blur came over Sip's face.

" Nothing has happened," said Sip, — "nothing but a — pain I had."

" *I* 've got the pain," scowled Catty. She put her hand to her shrunken eyes and cowered on the stairs, whining a little, like a hurt brute.

" Well, well," said Sip, on her fingers, stiffly, " very well. Stop that noise and come away, Catty ! I cannot bear that noise, not for love's sake, I can't bear it. Come !"

They crept slowly down the stairs and out into the street. It was a bright day, and everybody laughed. This seemed to Sip very strange.

She tried to tie Catty's face up in a thick veil she had ; but Catty pulled it off ; and she took her hand upon her arm, but did it weakly, and Catty jerked away. She was quite worn out when they got to the depot and the cars, and sat with her head back and shut her eyes.

" What 's the matter with the girl ? Blind, ain't she ? "

A curious passenger somewhere behind her said this loudly, as the train swept out of the station dusk. Sip turned upon him like a tiger. She could not remember that Catty could not hear. The word was so horrible to her ; she had not said it herself yet. She put her arm about Catty, and said, " Don't you talk ! "

" Dear, dear ! " said the curious passenger, blandly, " I would n't harm ye."

" I had n't told her," said Sip, catching her breath ; " I had n't gone away — by ourselves with the doors locked — to tell her. Do you think I 'd have it said out loud before a carful of folks ? "

Miss Kelso met her when she got home ; looked at her once ; put a quick, strong arm about her, and got the two girls into the carriage with the scented cushions immediately. Catty was delighted with this, and talked rapidly about it on her fingers all the way to the stone house. Sip pulled her hat over her eyes like a man, and sat up straight.

The little stone house was lighted, and supper was ready. The windows were open, and the sweet spring night airs wandered in and out. The children in the streets were shouting. Sip shut the window hard. She stood uncertainly by the door, while Catty went to take off her things.

" If I can do anything for you — " said Perley, gently.

Sip held up her hands and her brown face.

" Do you suppose," she said, " that you could
— kiss me ? "

Perley sat down in the wooden rocking-chair
and held out her beautiful arms.

Sip crept in like a baby, and there she began to
cry.   She cried and cried.   Catty ate her supper,
and nobody said anything, and she cried and
cried.

" My *dear !* " said Perley, crying too.

" Let me be," sobbed Sip, — " let me be for a
minute.   I 'll bear it in a minute.   I only wanted
some women-folks to cry to !   I had n't anybody."

She sat down on the edge of the bed with
Catty as soon as they were alone.   She had
dried her eyes to bear it now.   Catty must
understand.   She was quite determined to have
it over.   She set her lips together, and knotted
her knuckles tightly.

The light was out, but a shaft of wan moonlight from the kitchen windows struck into the
closet bedroom, and lay across the floor and
across the patch counterpane.   Catty sat in it.
She was unusually quiet, and her face indicated

some alarm or uneasiness, when Sip held up her trembling hand in the strip of light to command her close attention, and touched her eyes. Catty put out her supple fingers and groped, poor thing, after Sip's silent words. Walled up and walled in now from that long mystery which we call life, except at the groping, lithe, magnetic fingers, she was an ugly girl.

Sip looked at her for a minute fiercely.

" I should like to know what God means ! " she said. But she did not say it to Catty. She would not speak to Catty till she had wiped her dry lips to wipe the words off. Whatever He meant, Catty should not hear the words.

She tried, instead, to tell her very gently, and quite as if He meant a gentle thing by Catty, how it was.

In the strip of unreal light, the two hands, the groping hand and the trembling hand, interchanging unreal, soundless words, seemed to hang with a pitiful significance. One might have thought, to see them, how the mystery of suffering and the mystery of love grope and tremble forever after one another, with no speech nor language but a sign.

"There's something I've got to tell you, dear," said the trembling hand.

"For love's sake?" asked the hand that groped.

"For love's sake," said the trembling hand.

"Yes," nodded Catty, with content.

"A long time ago," said Sip; "before we went to Waltham, Catty, when you picked the wool—"

"And hurt my hands," said Catty, scowling.

"Something went wrong," said the trembling hand, "with your poor eyes, Catty. O your poor, poor eyes, my dear! All that you had left,— the dear eyes that saw me and loved me, and that I taught to understand so much, and to be so happy for love's sake! The poor eyes that I tried to keep at home, and safe, and would have died for, if they need never, never have looked upon an evil thing! The dear eyes, Catty, that I would have hunted the world over, if I could, to find pretty things for, and pleasant things and good things, and that I never had anything for but such a miserable little room that they got so tired of! The poor dear eyes!"

The shrunken and disfigured eyes, that had been such wandering, wicked eyes, turned and strained painfully in the half-light. Sip had said some of this with her stiff lips, but the trembling hand had made it for the most part plain to the groping hand. Catty herself sat and trembled suddenly.

When should she see the supper-table plain again ? the groping hand made out to ask. And the picture by the china-closet ? And the flies upon the window-pane ?

"Never !" said the trembling hand.

But when should she see Sip's face again without the blur ?

"Never ! O Catty, never again ! "

The trembling hand caught the groping hand to sting it with quick kisses. Sip could not, would not, see what the poor hand might say. She held it up in the streak of light. God might see. She held it up, and pulled Catty down upon her knees, with her face in the patch counterpane.

When Catty was asleep that night, Sip went out and got down upon the floor in the kitchen.

She got down, with her hands around her knees, in the wan lightness that fell about the picture behind the china-closet door. The driving dream seemed to fill the room. The factory-girl on the kitchen floor felt herself swept into it. Her lips worked and she talked to it.

"I could ha' borne it if it had been me," she said. Did the pictured women, with their arms up, nod as they drove wailing by? Sip could have sworn to it.

"We could have borne, if it had been we," they said.

"What's the sense of it?" asked Sip, in her rough way, half aloud. She had such a foolish way about that picture, often talking to it by the hour, upon the kitchen floor.

But the women only waved their arms and nodded solemnly. That which they could not know nor consider nor understand was in the question. They drifted over it with the helplessness of hopeless human pain.

"You're good for nothing," said Sip, and turned the picture to the wall.

She stumbled over something in doing this, and stooped to see what it was. It was an abused old book that Catty had taken once from the Mission Sunday School, and had never returned, — a foolish thing, with rough prints.

Catty had thrown it under the table in ten minutes. It opened in Sip's hands now, by chance, at a coarse plate of the Crucifixion.

Sip threw it down, but picked it up again, lost the place, and hunted for it; bent over it for a few minutes with a puzzled face.

Somehow the driving dream and the restless dreamer hushed away before the little woodcut. In some way the girl herself felt quieted by the common thing. For some reason — the old, the unexplained, the inexplicable reason — the Cross with the Man upon it put finger on the bitter lips of Sip's trouble. She could not ask a Man upon a Cross, " What was the sense of it?" So she only said, " O my poor Catty! my poor, poor Catty!" and softly shut the foolish little book and went to bed.

Beethoven did not stay with his face to the wall, however. Sip took a world of curious comfort out of that picture; quite perplexed Perley, who had only thought in sending it to do a pleasant thing, who had at that time never guessed — how should she? — that a line engraving after Lemude could make a " forgetting " in the life of a factory-girl.

" Sometimes now, when Catty is so bad," said Sip one day, " there's music comes out of that picture all about the room. Sometimes in the night I hear 'em play. Sometimes when I sit and wait for her, they sit and play. Sometimes when the floor's all sloppy and I have to wash up after work, I hear 'em playing over all the dirt. It sounds so clean ! " said Sip.

" Is Catty still so troublesome ? " asked Perley. Sip's face dropped.

" Off and on a little worse, I think. The blinder she grows the harder it is to please her and to keep her still. I come home all beat out ; and she's gone. Or, I try so hard to make her happy after supper, and along by nine o'clock she's off. She's dreadful restless since she left off workin', and gets about the street a'most as easy, for aught I see, as ever. She's so used to the turns and all ; and everybody knows her, and turns out for her. I've heard of blind folks that was like her ; she wasn't stupid, Catty wasn't, if she'd been like other folks. There's nights I sit and look for her to be run over and brought in. There's nights she gets at liquor. There's nights I follow her round and round, and follow her home, and make as if I sat there and she'd just come in. That's the worst, you see. What was that you said? No; I'll not have Catty sent anywhere away from me. There's no kind folks in any good asylum that would make it comfortable for Catty away from me. You need n't think," — Sip set her tough little lips together — "you need n't think that you nor anybody could separate me and Catty. She's never to blame, Catty is n't. *I* know that. *I* can work. *I* 'll make her comfortable. It's only God in heaven that will separate me and Catty."

It was about this time that Miss Kelso attempted, in view of Sip's increasing care, a long-cherished plan of experiment in taking the girl out of the mills.

"It is not a girl to spend life in weaving cotton," said the young lady to Stephen Garrick. "That would be such exorbitant waste."

"There's waste enough at those looms," said Mr. Garrick, pointing to his mills, "to enrich a Commonwealth perceptibly. We live fast down there among the engines. It is hot-house growth. There's the difference between a man brought up at machinery and a man brought up at a hoe, for instance, that there is between forced fruit and frozen fruit. Few countries understand what possibilities they possess in their factory population. We are a fever in the national blood that it will not pay to neglect ; there 's kill or cure in us."

" What 's the use ? " said Sip, with sullen, unresponsive eyes. " You 'll have all your bother for nothing, Miss Kelso. If I get away from my loom, I shall come back to my loom. Look at the factory-folks in England ! From father to child, from children to children's children, — a whole race of 'em at their looms. It 's in the blood."

" Try it," urged Perley. " Try it for Catty's sake, at least. There are so many ways in which it would be better for Catty."

" I should like it," said Sip, slowly, " to get Catty among some other folks than mill-folks. It seems as if I could have done it once ; but it 's too late now."

Now Sip was barely twenty-one. She said this with the unconscious assurance of fifty.

" I 'd try anything for Catty ; and almost anything for you ; and almost anything to get out of the mills ; but I 'm afraid it 's too late."

But Perley was persistent in her fancy, and between them they managed to " try it " faithfully.

Sip went out as somebody's cook, and burned all the soup and made sour bread. She drew about a baby's carriage for a day and a half, and left because the baby cried and she was afraid that she should shake it. She undertook to be a hotel table-girl, and was saucy to the house-keeper before night. She took a specimen of her sewing to a dressmaker, and was told that the establishment did not find itself in need of another seamstress. She stood behind a dry goods counter, but it worried her to measure off calico for the old ladies. Finally, Perley put her at the printer's trade, and Sip had a headache and got inky for a fortnight.

Then she walked back to her overseer, and " asked in " for the next morning.

" I told you it was no use," she said, shaking her head at Miss Kelso, half whimsically, half sadly too. " It 's too late. What am I fit for ? Nothing. What do I know ? Nothing. I can weave ; that 's all. I 'm used to that. I 'm used to the noise and the running about. I 'm used to the dirt and the roughness. I can't sit still on a high stool all day. I don't know how to spell, if I do. They're too fussy for me in the shops. I hate babies. It's too late. I'm spoiled. I knew I should come back. My father and mother came back before me. It's in the blood."

Perley would have liked even then, had it seemed practicable, to educate the girl; but Sip shook her dogged head.

"It's too late for that, too. Once I would have liked *that*. There's things I think I could ha' done." Sip's sullen eyes wandered slowly to the plunging dream and the solitary dreamer behind the china-closet door, and, resting there, flashed suddenly. "There's things I seem to think I might ha' done with *that;* but I've lost 'em now. Nor that ain't the worst. I've lost the caring for 'em, — that's the thing I've lost. If I was to sit still and study at a grammar, I should scream. I must go back to the noise and the dirt. Catty and me must stay there. Sometimes I seem to think that I might have been a little different someways; if maybe I'd been helped or shown. There was an evening school to one place where I worked. I was running four

looms twelve hours and a half a day. You 're so
dull about the head, you see, when you get home
from work ; and you ache so ; and you don't feel
that interest in an education that you might."

" Sometimes," added Sip, with a working of
the face, " it comes over me as if I was like a —
a patchwork bed-quilt. I 'd like to have been
made out of one piece of cloth. It seems as if
your kind of folks got made first, and we down
here was put together out of what was left.

" Sometimes, though," continued the girl, " I
wonder how there came to be so much of me as
there is. I don't set up for much, but I wonder
why I was n't worse. I believe you would yourself, if you knew."

" Know what ? "

" Knew what ! " echoed the factory-girl. " Knew
that as you know no more of than you know of
hell ! Have n't I told you that you *can't* know ?
You can't *understand*. If I was to tell you, you
could n't understand. It ain't so much the
bringing up I got, as the smooch of it. That 's
the wonder of it. You may be ever so clean,
but you don't *feel* clean if you 're born in the
black. Why, look here ; there was my mother,

into the mills off and on between her babies. There's me, from the time I run alone, *running* alone. She comes home at night. I'm off about the street all day. I learned to swear when I learned to talk. Before I'd learned to talk I'd seen sights that *you*'ve never seen yet in all your fine life long. That's the crock of it. And the wonder. And the talk in the mills — for a little girl to hear! Only eight years old — such a little girl — and all sorts of women working round beside you. If ever I'd like to call curses down on anybody, it's on a woman that I used to know for the way she talked to little girls! Why did nobody stop it? Why, the boss was as bad himself, every whit and grain. The gentlemen who employed that boss were professors of religion, all of them.

"But I've tried to be good!" broke off Sip, with a little sudden tremor of her bitter lip. "I know I'm rough, but I've tried to be a good girl!"

CHAPTER X.

ECONOMICAL.

THERE is something very pleasant about the town of Five Falls early on a summer morning.

There was something *very* pleasant about the town of Five Falls on one summer morning when Bub Mell got up at five o'clock to catch a rat.

To pluck a Five Falls morning in the bud, one should be up and in it before the bells, — like Bub. Until the bells are awake, there is a stillness and a cleanliness about the place that are noticeable ; about the dew-laid dusty streets and damp sidewalks bare of busy feet ; about the massive muteness of the mills ; about the very tenements on East Street, washed and made shining by the quiet little summer shower that fell perhaps last night, like old sins washed out by tears ; about the smooth, round cheek of the sky before the chimneys begin to breathe upon it ;

about the little cascades at play like babies upon
the bosom of the upper stream ; about the arches
of the stone bridge, great veins, one thinks, for the
pulsing dam ; about the slopes of buttercups and
clover which kneel to the water's edge with a
reverent look, as if they knelt for baptism ; about
some groups of pines that stretch their arms out
like people gone wearily to sleep.   The pines, the
clover slopes, the dam, the streets and houses, the
very sky, everything, in fact, in Five Falls, except
those babies of cascades, wears, upon a summer
morning, that air of having gone or of having
been wearily to sleep, — an air of having been
upon its feet eleven hours and a half yesterday,
and of expecting to be upon its feet eleven hours
and a half to-day.

Bub has been awake for some fifteen minutes —
he sleeps upon a mat, like a puppy, behind the
door, — before he shakes himself a little in his
rags (the ceremony of a toilet is one of Bub's lost
arts ; he can, indeed, remember faintly having been
forcibly induced to take certain jerks at the street
pump on mild mornings, at some indefinite past
period of juvenile slavery, till his mother was
nicely laid up out of the way in the bedroom, and

he " got so old he give it up "), and trots down the wretched stairs, and out with the other puppies into the clean stillness of the early time.

The sick woman is troublesome this morning ; there is a great deal of coughing and confusion going on ; and the husband up since midnight. Bub finds it annoying to be broken of his sleep ; suffers from some chronic sensitiveness on the dangers of being at hand to be despatched for the doctor ; and finds in the rat at once an inspiration and a relief.

There is indeed peculiar inspiration in the case of that rat. Bub chuckles over his shoulder at himself as he trots out into the peaceful time ; there is a large three-cornered jagged rag among Bub's rags ; the rat bit it yesterday ; it hangs down from his little trousers behind and wags as he trots. He put the rat into a hogshead to pay for it ; and shut it down with that piece of board fence with which he provided himself last week (from Mr. Hayle's garden) for such emergencies. There is a richness about going to sleep over-night with the game for your morning's hunt in a hogshead, which is not generally appreciated by gentlemen of the chase. There is a kind of security of happiness, a lingering on the lips of a sure delight, a consciousness of duty done and pleasure in waiting, which have quite an individual flavor.

None the other coves know about that rat. You *bet.* Not much. Hi-igh.

Bub's right shoulder chuckles at his left shoulder, and his left shoulder chuckles at his right shoulder, and the jagged rag behind wags with delight. Won't he jab him now ! Hi-igh, there. Hi-igh ! See him ! He thinks he 's a goin' to cut 'n' run, does he ? He must be green.

Away goes Mr. Hayle's board fence into the bean patch, and down goes Bub into the hogshead. There 's a contest for you ! All Bub's poor little puzzling soul is in his eyes. All his old young face — the only old young thing in the dawning time — is filled and fired. Won't he have that rat ? Five hundred cascades might play upon the pure bosom of the river, and all the buttercups in Five Falls kneel for baptism, — but he 'll have that rat.

The smooth, round cheek of the sky seems to stoop to the very hogshead, and lay itself tenderly down to cover the child and the vermin from the sight of the restful time.

Presently it begins to be very doubtful who shall cut 'n' run. And by and by it begins to be more than doubtful who must be green.

At one fell swoop of anguish, Bub finds his dirty little finger bitten to the bone, and himself alone in the hogshead.

Hi-*igh* !

Bub sits down in the bottom of the hogshead and grits his teeth. He does n't cry, you understand. Not he. Used to cry when he got bit. And holler. But got so old he give it up. Lor. Ain't he glad none the other coves knows now. You bet. Hi-igh.

All the foreheads of the buttercups and clovers seem dripping with sacred water, when Bub lifts his little aged yellow face with the dirt and blood and tobacco upon it, over — just over — the edge of the hogshead to see what became of the rat. The cheek of the sky blushes a sadder red for shame. The sleepy pine-trees stretch their arms out solemnly towards the little fellow. The cascades are at play with each other's hands and feet. The great pulse of the dam, as sad as life, as inexorable as death, as mysterious as both, beats confused meanings into the quiet time.

" Lor," says Bub in the hogshead, looking out, half pausing for the instant with his gashed finger at his sly mouth, — " Lor, it 's goin' to be a boozier of a day. I 'll bet."

But the bells have waked, with a cross cry, and Five Falls starts, to stand for eleven hours and a half upon its feet. The peaceful time has slipped and gone. The pine-trees rub their eyes and sigh. The pulse of the dam throbs feverishly fast. The sun dries the baptismal drops from the heads of the buttercups and clovers. The dew-laid streets fill and throng ; the people have dirty clothes and hurried faces ; the dust flies about ; the East Street tenements darken to the sight in the creeping heat, like the habit of old sins returned to darken a sad and sorry life ; you see that there are villanous stairs and no drains ; you hear coughing and confusion from the woman's bedchamber overhead. You see, too, that the spotless cheek of the sky is blackened now by the chimneys all about, and how still and patiently it lies to take the breath of the toil-worn town.

Only those tiny cascades play — eternal children — upon a mother's bosom ; as if the heart of a little child, just for being the heart of a little child, must somehow, somewhere, play forever in the smile of an undying morning.

By means of stopping to have his finger bound, and of a search in the bean-patch for the rat, and of another search in the cellar for the rat, and of the delay occasioned by a vindictive kick or two at the hogshead, and by forgetting his breakfast and remembering it, and going back for it to find that it is all eaten, if indeed there has ever been any, which the confusion in the sick-room renders a probable theory, Bub is late this morning. Nynce was cross about the finger, too; pulled the thread and hurt him; wanted her own breakfast probably. Bub's little old face wears an extra shade of age and evil as he trots away to work, and he swears roundly by the way; swears loud enough to be heard across the street, for Mr. Garrick, on his way to the station, turns his head to look after the child. Bub shies away; has been a little skittish about Mr. Garrick, since they tried to put him to school and his father swore him off for ten years old. It is generally understood now in Háyle and Kelso that the firm occasionally pull in different ways; Mr. Mell knows where to trace any unusual disturbance of his family government which is calculated to arrest a child's steady stride to ruined manhood ; everybody knows ; Mr. Garrick is unpopular accordingly. He has his friends among his work-people, chiefly of the kind that do not easily come to the surface. The young watchman at the Old Stone is one of them, you may be sure. But he is not a popular master so far.

Bub, with his sly eyes, and tobacco-yellowed skin, and his pipe in his mouth, and the blood and dirt upon his clothes, and the little rag behind, and his old, old smile, trots away to the mills, whose open door has, to Mr. Garrick's fancy, an air of gaping after the child.

" As a prison-door will do in the end," muses Mr. Garrick.

He takes a note-book from his pocket, jotting something in it ; about the child, perhaps. He has been making an estimate this week of the suffering and profligate children in his mills. There is scarcely a vice on the statute-book which he has not found in existence among the little children in those mills.

The leaf of the note-book turns, in closing, to recent entries, which run like this : —

" Said the chaplain of an English prison, after showing the cost of ninety-eight juvenile criminals to the State, in six years, to have amounted, in various ways, to £ 6,063 ($ 30,315) : ' *They have cost a sum of money which would have kept them at a boarding-school the whole time.*'

" Said the Honorable, the late Clerk of the Police of Fall River, Mass., in answer to an inquiry as to the number of children in that town peculiarly exposed to a life of crime : . . . . ' I should say, after consulting the docket of our Police Court, and inquiring as to the subsequent expenses, that the cost of such juvenile offenders as ultimately reach the State Prison would average two hundred and fifty dollars. We have had some who have cost much more than this ; one as much as five hundred dollars.' "

Mr. Garrick glances over them with his peculiar smile, just as Bub and the little wagging rag disappear in the yawn of the mill-door.

There is another noticeable entry, by the way, in Mr. Garrick's note-book. It lies against little Dib Docket's name : —

" In H—— the Chief of the Police estimates the number of openly abandoned women at not less than seventy-five, besides an equal number of a less notorious and degraded class. 'They are,' said he, 'brought before the Police Court again and again. Most of them are under twenty years of age. They come from the country *and the manufacturing towns.* They are the children of drunken and vicious parents.'"

Bub dips into the mouth of the door and crawls up the stairs on "all fours," so much, so very much like a little puppy! He is a little afraid of his overseer, being so late. At the top of the stairs he loiters and looks down. In the blue distance beyond the windows, the cascades are just to be seen at their eternal play.

The machinery is making a great noise this morning. The girls are trying to sing, but the engines have got hold of the song, and crunch it well. Bub, on the threshold of the spooling-room, stops with a queer little chuckle like a sigh.

He wishes he need n't go in. It looks kinder jolly out. Lor! don't it? Would a'most go to school fur the sake uv gettin' out. But guesses he must be too old.

Won't that boss jaw this mornin'! He'll bet. Hi-igh!

The strain from down stairs struggles and faints as Bub goes in to work ; as if the engines had a mouthful of it, and were ready for more.

The " boss " does " jaw " this morning. Bub expects it, deserves it, bears it, hangs his head and holds his tongue, glad, on the whole, that it is no worse. A cuff or a kick would not surprise him. The overseer is a passionate man, of a race of passionate men ; an overseer by birthright ; comes from a family of them, modernized, in a measure, to be sure. He can remember when his father, being an overlooker in a Rhode Island mill, carried to work a leathern strap, with tacks inserted, for the flagellation of children. This man himself can tell you of children whom he has run, in some parts of the country, at night work, when the little creatures dropped asleep upon their feet, and he was obliged to throw water over them to keep them awake and at work.

The girls down· stairs are singing something this morning about a " Happy Day." Bub, dimly hearing, dimly wonders what ; having never had but one green boy at the Mission, does not know ; thinks it has a pretty sound, wishes the wheels would let it alone, hopes the boss is out of the way now, wishes he had a chew, finds himself out of tobacco, and recovers sufficiently from the mortification of the " jawing " to lift his little, wrinkled face — it seems as if it never before had borne such wrinkles — to see what he can do about it.

Another little wrinkled face, old, yellow, sly, and sad, works close beside him. It has mouth and pockets full of quids.

" Give us a chaw," says Bub.

" Not much," says the little face, with a wink.

" Seems as if I should choke ! " says Bub. " I must have a chaw, Bill."

" You don't do none of *my* chawin'," says Bill, " less 'n five cents down."

" Fact is," says Bub, ruefully, " I 'm out o' cash just now. Never you mind, though."

Bub minds, however. He goes to work again with one eye on Bill. Bill's pocket is torn down. He must be green. You could a'most get a quid out and he 'd never know it. Bub watches his chance. He must have tobacco at any chance. The child lives upon it, like an old toper on his dram. Every inch of his little body craves it. He is in a dry, feverish heat. He thinks he shall burn up, if he does not get it. To work till nooning without it is not to be thought of. He meant to have sold that rat to a chap he knew, and to have been supplied.

Think a cove of his size can work all day without it? You — bet — not —

There is a spring and a cry. Bub has pounced upon Bill's torn pocket. Bill has backed, and dragged him. The wagging rag on Bub's little trousers has caught in a belt.

All over the spooling-room there is a spring and a cry.

All up the stairs there seems to be a spring and a cry. They come from the song about the Happy, Happy Day. The engines close teeth on the song and the child together.

They stop the machinery ; they run to and fro ; they huddle together ; they pick up something here, and wipe up something there, and cover up something yonder, closely ; they look at one another with white faces ; they sit down sickly ; they ask what is to do next.

There is nothing to do. Bub has saved the State his two hundred and fifty dollars, and has Bill's quid of tobacco in his mangled hand. There is nothing to do. Life, like everything

else, was quite too young for Bub. He has got
so old, he has given it up.

There is nothing to do but to carry the news
now ; nobody likes to carry the news to the sick
woman ; nobody offers ; the overseer, half wishing that there had been an oath or two less in
the " jawing," volunteers to help about the — the
— *pieces*, if they 'll find somebody to go on ahead.
That 's all he objects to ; goin' on ahead.

Mr. Hayle the senior, who has been summoned
from the counting-room, takes his hat to go in
search of some one ; would go himself, but the
fact is, he has never seen the woman, nor the
father to know him by name, and feels a delicacy
about obtruding his services. He mentions the
matter to his son, but Maverick succinctly re-
fuses ; remembers just now, for the first time
since it happened, some long-past allusion of
Miss Kelso's to a drain, and concludes that his
personal sympathy can hardly be the most
desirable to offer to Mr. Mell.

Just without the mill-yard, bent upon some
early errand of her own, the two gentlemen
chance upon Perley.

"Ask *her*," says the younger man, in a low voice ; "*she* would do to break ill news to the mother of the Maccabees."

They pause to tell her what has happened ; their shocked faces speak faster than their slow words ; she understands quite what is needed of her ; has turned the corner to East Street, while their unfinished explanation hangs upon their decorous lips.

The young man stands for a moment looking after her swift, strong, helpful figure, as it vanishes from view, with a sense of puzzled loss upon his handsome face, but shrugs his shoulders, and back in the counting-room shrugs them again.

Perley is none too soon at the First Tenement and No. 6.

The overlooker and his covered burden, and the little crowd that trails whispering after it, are just in sight, as she climbs the villanous stairs.

The overlooker, and the covered burden, and the whispering crowd, are none too late at the First Tenement and No. 6.

Mr. Mell comes out from the sick-room on

tiptoe ; the children crouch and hide their faces behind the door ; the doctor, who has been, has gone, and the coughing and confusion are quite over.

Mr. Mell stands still in the middle of the kitchen, with his hand at his ear.   Whether he is listening to a thing which Perley says, — a gentle, awful thing, said in a gentle, awful voice, — or whether he is listening to certain sounds of feet upon the stairs, it were difficult to say.

He stands still in the middle of the kitchen, with his hand behind his ear.

The feet upon the stairs have climbed the stairs, have passed the stairs, have passed the door, have paused.

The overlooker, with his hat in his hand, has laid the covered burden softly down upon the mat behind the door, where the little burden, like a little puppy, slept last night.

Mr. Mell sits down then in the nearest chair. He points at the open bedroom door.   He seems to be weak from watching, and the hand with which he points trembles badly.

"Do you see?" he says.   "Look there.   See, don't ye?   I'm glad ye did n't come ten minute sooner. It would ha' ben such a fretful thing for *her*. She would ha' greeted sair, I'm feared. Keep the laddie well covered, will ye? I wald na' like so much as her dead een to seem to see it. It would ha' ben sae fretful for her; I wald na' likit to see her greetin' ower the laddie. I wald na' likit yon; keep him covered, will ye?"

It is very touching to hear the man mourn in the old long-disused Scotch words of his youth, and very touching to hear what a cry there is in the words themselves.

But it is not heart-breaking, like the thing which he says in broad English, next. It is after the overlooker has gone, and the covered burden is laid decently upon a bed, and Perley has been busied in and out of the bedroom, and the chil dren have been washed a little, and the "fust gell," crying bitterly over a cup of coffee which she is trying to make, has been comforted, and a cleanly silence has fallen upon the two rooms, and upon the two beds with their mute occupants. It is after he has sat stupidly still with his face in his hands. It is just as Perley, seeing nothing more that she can do for him, is softly shutting the door to go and find flowers for little Bub.

Look a here.   Say !   What damages do you think the mills 'll give me ?   I 'd ought to have damages on the loss of the boy's wages.   He was earnin' reglar, and growin' too.

At the foot of the stairs Perley finds a girl with large eyes, and soiled blue ribbons on her hair, sitting and sobbing in her mill-dress, rubbing the dust about her pretty face.

" I would n't sit here, Nynee," suggests Perley gently ; " go up and help your sister, and do not cry."

" It seems as if everything fretful happened to me," sobs Nynee, pettishly. " The mills was bad enough.   Then it was mother, and then it was somebody comin' in to tell me about Bub, and now it 's both of 'em.   I wish I 'd tied up Bub's finger pleasant this morning.   It 'll be fretfuller than ever to home now.   I wish I was dead like them two ; yes, I do.   I had other things that bothered me besides.   I did n't want no more ! "

" What other things ? " asks Perley, very gently sitting down on the stairs, and very wisely taking no heed just now of the little miserable, selfish sobs.

" O, different things.   Things about somebody that I — like, and somebody that I don't like, and some folks that like some folks better than me. I was bothered to death before ! " cries Nynee.

"Some time," says Perley, "you shall tell me all about them. Run up to your sister, now."

Nynee runs up, and Perley, in going for Bub's flowers, thinks that she would rather gain the hearing of that little love-story, sitting on the dirty stairs, than to get the girl to church with her for a year to come.

CHAPTER XI.

GOING INTO SOCIETY.

" DELIGHTED, Perley, I am sure, and shall be sure to come. Nothing could give us greater pleasure than a day with you in your lovely, Quixotic, queer venture of a home. Mamma begs me, with her love and acceptance, to assure you that she appreciates," etc., etc.

" As for my friends, the Van Doozles of New York, you know, (it is Kenna Van Doozle who is engaged to Mr. Blodgett,) they are charmed. It was just like you to remember them in your kind," etc.

" And actually to see for ourselves one of your dear, benevolent, democratic, strong-minded *ré-unions*, of which we have heard so much! What could be more?" etc.

" I promise you that I will be very good and considerate of your *protégés*. I will wear nothing gayer than a walking-suit, and I will inform myself beforehand upon the ten-hour question, and I will be as charming as I know how, so that you shall not regret having honored me by," etc.

" And now, my dear Perley, I cannot come to Five Falls without telling you myself what I should break my heart if you should hear from anybody but myself.

" I know that you must have guessed my little secret before now. But Maverick and I thought that we should like at least to *pretend* that it was a secret for a little while.

" Ah, Perley, I see your great wise eyes smile ! Do you know, I suspect that you were *too* wise for him, dear boy ! He seems to think a little, foolish, good-for-nothing girl like me would make him happy.

" And I know he wants me to say, dear Perley, how we have neither of us ever had any hardness in our hearts towards you, or ever can. How *can* we now ? We are so very happy ! And I know *how* wise he thinks you still, and how good. So very good ! A great deal better than his ridiculous little Fly, I have no doubt ; but then, you see, we don't either of us mind that," etc., etc., etc.

Fly's note preceded Fly by but a few hours, it so chanced. That evening Miss Kelso's parlors presented what Fly perhaps was justified in calling " such a dear, delightful, uncommon appearance."

Kenna Van Doozle called it *outré.* She was sitting on a sofa by Nynee Mell when she said so.

It was a stifling July night, and closed a stifling day. Mrs. Silver, in the cars, on the Shore Line, and swept by sea breezes, had " suffered agonies," so she said. Even in the close green dark of Miss Kelso's lofty rooms, life had ceased to be desirable, and the grasshopper had been a burden, until dusk and dew-fall.

" In the houses from which my guests are coming to-night," she had said at supper, " the mercury has not been below 90°, day nor night, for a week."

Her guests seemed to appreciate the fact ; shunned the hot lawn and garden, where a pretty show of Chinese lanterns and a Niobe at a fountain (new upon the grounds, this year) usually attracted them, and grouped in the preserved coolness of the parlor.

Her guests, in those parlors, were worth a ride from town in the glare to meet.

There were some thirty, perhaps, in all ; families, for the most part, just as they came. Mr.
Mell, for instance, in decent clothes ; the "fust
gell," with one of the children ; Nynee, in light
muslin and bright ribbons ; old Bijah Mudge in
a corner with little Dib Docket, — they sent Dib
to the poorhouse by especial permit to bring
him, always ; Catty, closely following the crisp
rustle of the hostess's plain white dress (Sip was
delayed, nobody knew just why) ; and Dirk Burdock, apart from the other young fellows, drift-
ing restlessly in and out of the hot, bright lawn ;
little knots of young people chattering over pic-
ture-racks ; a sound of elections and the evening
news in other knots where their fathers stood with
hands behind them ; the elder women easily
seated in easy-chairs ; a tangle about the piano,
where a young weaver was doing a young waltz
very well.

Now there was one very remarkable thing
about these thirty people. With the exception
of a little plainness about their dress (plainness
rather than roughness, since in America we will
die of bad drainage, but we will manage to have
a "best suit" when occasion requires) and an air

10 *   o

of really enjoying themselves, they did not, after all, leave a very different impression upon the superficial spectator from that of any thirty people whom Fly Silver might collect at a *musicale*.

The same faces at their looms to-morrow you could not identify.

"I suppose they 're on their best behavior," suggested Fly, in an opportunity.

"What have you and I been on all our lives ?" asked Perley, smiling. "One does not behave till one has a chance."

"And not in the least afraid of us," observed Fly, with some surprise. "I was afraid we should make it awkward for them."

"But how," asked Miss Van Doozle, with her pale eyes full of a pale perplexity, — "you are exceedingly original, I know, — but *how*, for instance, have you ever brought this about ? I had some such people once, in a mission class ; I could do nothing with them ; they pulled the fur out of my muff, and got up and left in the middle of the second prayer."

"*I* have brought nothing about," said Perley, "They have brought themselves about. All that

I do is to treat these people precisely as I treat you, Miss Van Doozle."

" Ah ? " blankly from Miss Van Doozle.

" For instance," said the hostess in moving away, " I get up thirty or so of those every fort-night. I don't know how this came here. Put it in your pocket, please."

She tossed from the card-basket a delicate French envelope, of the latest mode of monogram and tint, enclosing a defective invitation in her own generous hand, running : —

" Miss Kelso requests the pleasure of Mr. Mell's company at half past seven o'clock on Friday evening next.

"July 15."

" Perley," observed Mrs. Silver, pensively, " *ought* to have been a literary character. I have always said so ; have n't I, Fly ? "

" Why, mamma ? " asked Fly.

" That excuses so much always, my dear," softly said Mrs. Silver.

There seemed to be some stir and stop in Miss Kelso's " evening," that hot Friday. Dirk Burdock, restlessly diving in and out of the lawn, finally found his hat, and, apparently at the hostess's request, excused himself and disappeared. The young weaver played the young waltz out, and politics in corners lulled.

" It is a Victor Hugo evening," explained Miss Kelso to her friends from town, " and our reader has not come. We always manage to accomplish something. I wish you could have heard an essay on Burns from a Scotchman out of the printing-rooms, a fortnight ago. Or some of our Dickens readings. Something of that or this kind takes better with the men than a musical night ; though we have some fine voices, I assure you. I wish, Fly, you would play to us a little, while we are waiting."

Fly, not quite knowing what clse to do, but feeling surprisingly ill at ease, accomplished a sweet little thin thing, and was prettily thanked by somebody somewhere ; but still the reader had not come.

It has been said, upon authority, that the next thing which happened was the *Andante* from the Seventh Symphony, Miss Kelso herself at the keys.

Mrs. Silver looked at Miss Van Doozle. Miss Van Doozle looked at Mrs. Silver.

" She has made a mistake," said Mrs. Silver's look.

" The people can*not* apprcciate Beethoven," was Miss Van Doozle's look.

Now, in truth, Beethoven could not have asked a stiller hearing than he and Miss Kelso commanded out of those thirty work-worn factory faces.

The blind-mute Catty stood beside Miss Kelso while she played. She passed the tips of her fingers like feathers over the motion of Perley's hands. It was a privilege she had. She bent her head forward, with her lip dropped and dull.

" When she plays," she often said to Sip, "there 's wings of things goes by."

" What, wings ? " asked Sip.

" I don't know — wings. When I catch, they fly."

Miss Kelso's elegant white, without flaw or pucker of trimming, presented a broad and shining background to the poor creature's puzzled figure. Catty seemed to borrow a glory from it, as a lean Byzantine Madonna will, from her gilded sky. Mrs. Silver fairly wiped her eyes.

After Beethoven there was Nynee Mell, with a

song or two in Scotch ; and then another stop
and stir.   The reader, they said, was coming.

Fly Silver, in the pauses, had done very well.
She was a good-hearted little lady, and nobody
succeeded in being afraid of her.   She had cate-
chised Dib Docket a little, and effected a timid
acquaintance with Bijah Mudge.   The old man
was in a wise dotage peculiarly his own.   He
came, however, regularly to Miss Kelso's " evenings " ; enjoyed his saucer of ice-cream as much
as any other child there ; and yet always managed
to gather about him a little audience of men with
frowns in their foreheads, who listened to his
wild ravings with a kind of instinctive respect,
which pleased the old fellow amazingly.

He had a paper in his hand which he showed
to Fly.   He always had a paper in his hand.   It
was a petition to the Legislature of the State of
Massachusetts, with illustrated margins of etch-
ings in pen and ink.   The designs ran all to foli-
age, — indiscriminate underbrush at first glance ;
upon examination, forests came out in rows ; upon
study, hands came out from the forests, hundreds
of them, from bough, from twig, from stem, from
leaf.   The forest on the left margin wrung its

hands, it seemed. The forest on the right margin clapped them smartly.

" What for ? " asked Fly, politely.

" Is it not written," said the old man, solemnly, " that in that day all the trees of the field shall clap their hands ? "

" But what about ? " persisted Fly

" The voice said, ' Cry ! ' " said Bijah, shrilly ; "and I said, 'What shall I cry ? ' " He lifted his petition to the Legislature of the State of Massachusetts in his shaking hand, and fixed his bleared eyes over it upon Fly's pretty, frightened face. " What shall I cry ? *' And thou saidst in thine heart, I shall be a lady forever ; so that thou didst not lay these things to thy heart, neither didst remember the latter end of it !*' "

" O dear ! " said Fly, and rippled away.

" A Hebrew prophet and a canary-bird," thought Perley, when she heard of it.

Fly rippled out into the hall, where the stir and stop seemed to have centred. The hostess was there, talking to Sip Garth in a low tone. Dirk Burdock was there, having found Sip, he said, half-way over ; and a young Irish girl whom Sip had with her, a fine-featured little creature, with heavy sodden circles about her eyes and mouth.

She was sorry to be so late, Sip was saying, "But Maggie'd set her heart so on coming, you see; and there she lay and fainted, and I have n't been able to bring her round enough to get over here till this minute. Her folks was all away, and I could n't seem to leave her; and she did so set her heart on coming! She has been carried in a faint out of the mill four times to-day — out into the air, and a dash of water — and back again; and down again. The thermometer has stood at 115° in our room to-day. It has n't been below 110° not since last Saturday. It's 125° in the dressing-room. There's men in the dressing-room with the blood all gathered black about their faces, just from heat; they look like men in a fit; they're all purple. You'd ought to see the clothes we wear! — drenched like fine folks' bathing-clothes. I could wring mine out. We call it the lake of fire, — our room. That's all I could think of since Sunday: the Last Day and the lake with all the folks in it. I have n't been in such a coolness not since I was here last time, Miss Kelso. It's most as bad as hell to be mill-folks in July!"

"A blowzy, red-faced girl," Miss Van Doozle thought, when the reader came in.

" My Lords ! " began the red-faced reader, " I impart to you a novelty. The human race exists " . . . .

" We have nothing so popular," whispered Miss Kelso, " as that girl's readings and recitations. They ring well."

" An unappreciated Siddons, perhaps ? " The pale Van Doozle eyes assumed the homœopathic trituration of a sarcasm. The Van Doozle eyes were not used to Sip exactly.

"I have thought that there might be greater than Siddons in Sip," replied Miss Kelso, musingly ; " but not altogether of the Siddons sort, I admit."

Sip followed Miss Kelso, in the breaking up of the evening, after the books and the ices were out of the way. They had some plan about the little Irish girl already ; a week's rest at least. There was that family on the Shore Line ; and the hush of the sea; where they took such care of poor Bert Bush. If Catty were well, Sip would take her down.

" I know the girl. She must be got away till

this drought's over.   She'll work till the breath is out of her, but she'll work; has a brother in an insane asylum, and likes to pay his board. Maggie's obstinate as death about such things. You'd ought to see her pushing back her hair and laughing out, when she come out of those faints to-day, and at it again, for all anybody could say.   You would n't think that she'd ever take to Jim, would you?   But got over it, I guess. Had a hard time, though.   Look here !   I found a piece in a newspaper yesterday, and cut it out to show to you."

Sip handed to Miss Kelso, with a smile, a slip from one of the leading city dailies, reading thus : —

"What is generally written about Lorenzo factory-girls is sensational and pure nonsense.   They are described as an overworked class, rung up, rung out, rung in ; as going to their labors worn, dispirited, and jaded ; as dreading to meet their task-masters in those stifling rooms, where they have cultivated breathing as a fine art ; as coming home from their thraldom happy but for thoughts of the resumption of their toil on the morrow.   The fact is, sympathy has been offered

where it was not needed. The officers of the mills
and the girls themselves will tell you the tasks
are not exhaustive. No one gets so tired that
she cannot enjoy the evening, every thought
of work dismissed. Her employment is such that
constant attention is not demanded. She may
frequently sit thinking of the past or planning
for the future. She earns nearly four dollars per
week, beside her board. The pleasantest relations subsist between her and her overseer, who
is frequently the depositary of her funds, who
perhaps goes with her to buy her wedding or
household outfit, who is her counsellor and pro-
tector. Her step is not inelastic, but firm. . . . .
The mills are high studded, well ventilated, and
scrupulously clean. The girls are healthy and well
looking, and men and women, who have worked
daily for twenty or thirty years, are still in un-
diminished enjoyment of sound lungs and limbs."

"I never was in Lorenzo," said Sip, drily, as
Perley folded the slip, "but mills are mills. I'd
like to see the fellow that wrote that."

Fly and her friends had sifted into the library,
while Miss Kelso's guests were thinning.

"This, I suppose," Mrs. Silver was sadly saying, " is but a specimen of our poor dear Perley's life."

" You speak as if she were dead and buried, mamma," said Fly, making a dazzling little heap of herself upon a cricketful of pansies.

" So she is," affirmed Mrs. Silver, plaintively, — " so she is, my dear, as far as Society is concerned. I have been struck this evening by the thought, what a loss to Society ! Why, Miss Kenna, I am told that this superb house has been more like a hospital or a set of public soup-rooms for six months past, than it has like the retiring and secluded home of a young lady. Those people overrun it. They are made welcome to it at all hours and under all circumstances. She invites them to tea, my dear ! They sit down at her very table with her. I have known her to bring out Mirabeau from town to furnish their music for them. Would you credit it ? Mirabeau ! In the spring she bought a Bierstadt. I was with her at the time. ' I have friends in Five Falls who have never seen a Bierstadt,' she said. Now what do you call that ? *I* call it morbid," nodded the lady, making soft gestures with her soft hands, — " morbid !"

"I don't suppose anybody knows the money that she has put into her libraries, and her model tenements, and all that, either," mused Fly, from her cricket.

"It does well enough in that Mr. Garrick," proceeded Mrs. Silver, in a gentle bubble of despair; "I don't object to fanatical benevolence in a man like him. It is natural, of course. He is self-made entirely; twenty years ago might have come to Miss Kelso's evenings himself, you know. It is excusable in him, though awkward in the firm, as I had reason to know, when he started to build that chapel. Now there is another of poor Perley's freaks. What does she do but leave Dr. Dremaine's, where she had at least the dearest of rectors and the best pew-list in Five Falls, on the ground that the mill-people do not frequent Dr. Dremaine's, and take a pew in the chapel herself! They have a young preacher there fresh from a seminary, and Perley and the mill-girls will sit in a row together and hear him! Now that *may* be Christianity," adds Mrs. Silver, in a burst of heroism, "but *I* call it morbidness, sheer morbidness!"

"But these people are very fond of Perley, mamma," urged Fly, lifting some honest trouble in her face out of the pretty shine that she made in the dim library.

"They ought to be!" said Mrs. Silver, with unwonted sharpness.

Now Fly, in her own mind, had meant to find out something about that ; she went after the Hugo reader, it just occurring to her, and took her into a corner before everybody was gone.

She made a great glitter of herself here too ; she could not help it, in her shirred lace and garnets. Sip looked her over, smiling as she would at a pretty kitten. Sip was more gentle in her judgments of "that kind of folks" than she used to be.

"What do we think of *her ?*" Sip's fitful face flushed. "How can I tell you what we think of her ? There 's those of us here, young girls of us," Nynee Mell's blue ribbons, just before them, were fluttering through the door, " that she has saved from being what you would n't see in here to-night. There 's little children here that would be little devils, unless it was for her. There 's men of us with rum to fight, and boys in prison, and debts to

pay, and hearts like hell, and never a friend in
this world or the other but her. There's others
of us, that — that — God bless her!" broke off
Sip, bringing her clenched little hands together,
— "God bless her, and the ground she treads on,
and the air she breathes, and the sky that is over
her, and the friends that love her, and the walls
of her grand house, and every dollar of her
money, and every wish she wishes, and all the
prayers she prays — but I cannot tell you, young
lady, what we think of *her!*"

"But Society," sighed Mrs. Silver, — "Society
has rights which every lady is bound to respect;
poor Perley forgets her duties to Society. Where
we used to meet her in our circle three times, we
meet her once now."

"Once of Perley is equal to three times of
most people," considered Fly, appearing with
Maverick (who had slipped in as the "evening"
slipped out) from some lovers' corner. "And she
does n't rust, you must own, mamma; and seems
to enjoy herself so, besides."

"I have understood," observed the elder Miss
Van Doozle, "that she has been heard to say

that she could never spend an evening in an ordinary drawing-room party happily again."

This, in fact, was a report very common about Miss Kelso at one time. Those well acquainted with her and with her movements in Five Falls will remember it.

" Poor Perley " herself came in just in time to hear it then.

" I always forgave the falsity of that, for the suggestiveness of it," she said, laughing.

" A thoughtful set of guests you have here," said Fly. " We have been finding fault with you all the evening."

" That is what I expected."

" So we supposed. Perley ! "

" Well, my dear ? "

" Are you happy ? "

" Quite happy, Fly."

" I should be so miserable ! " said Fly, with a shade of the honest trouble still on her pretty face.

" I have been saying," began Mrs. Silver, " that Society is a great loser by your philanthropy, Perley."

Perley lighted there.

"Society !" she said, "I feel as if I had but just begun to go into society !"

"But, on your theories," said Kenna Van Doozle, with a clumsy smile of hers, "we shall have our cooks up stairs playing whist with us, by and by."

"And if we did ?" quietly. "But Miss Van Doozle, I am not a reformer ; I have n't come to the cooks yet ; I am only a feeler. The world gets into the dark once in a while, you know ; throws out a few of us for groping purposes."

"Kenna and I, for instance, being spots on the wings ?" asked Fly.

"Naturalists insist that the butterfly will pause and study its own wings, wrapt in — "

"O Maverick !"

"Admiration," finished Maverick.

"But one must feel by something," persisted Fly, "guess or measure. It is all very beautiful in you, Perley. But it seems to me such a venture. I should be frightened out of it a dozen times over."

Perley took a little book out of a rack upon one of the tables, where Mr. Mell's ice-cream saucer yet lay unremoved, — Isaac Taylor in bevelled board.

" Here," she said, " is enough to feel by, even if I feel my way to your cook, Miss Kenna."

" ' *To insure, therefore, its large purpose of good-will to man, the law of Christ spreads out its claims very far beyond the circle of mere pity or natural kindness, and in absolute and peremptory terms demands for the use of the poor, the igno-rant, the wretched, and demands from every one who names the name of Christ, the whole residue of talent, wealth, time, that may remain after primary claims have been satisfied.*' "

CHAPTER XII.

MAPLE LEAVES.

AN incident connected with Miss Kelso's experiments in Five Falls, valuable chiefly
as indicative of the experimenter, and rather as a
hint than as history, occurred in the ripening
autumn. It has been urged upon me to find
place for it, although it is fragmentary and
incomplete.

A distant sea-swell of a strike was faintly
audible in Hayle and Kelso.

Hayle and Kelso were in trouble. Standfast
Brothers, of Town, solid as rock and old as
memory, had gone down ; gone as suddenly and
blackly as Smashem & Co. of yesterday, and
gone with a clutch on Five Falls cotton, under
which Five Falls shook dizzily.

The serene face of the senior partner took, for
the first time since 1857, an anxious, or, it might
rather be called, an annoyed groove. All the

manufacturing panics of the war had fanned it placidly, but Standfast Brothers were down, and behold, the earth reeled and the foundations thereof.

Two things, therefore, resulted. The progress of the new mill was checked, and a notice of reduction of wages went to the hands.

The sea-swell murmured.

Hayle and Kelso heard nothing.

The sea-swell growled.

Hayle and Kelso never so much as turned the head.

The sea-swell splashed out a few delegates and a request, respectful enough, for consultation and compromise.

" We will shut down the mills first ! " said young Mr. Hayle between his teeth.

So the swell broke with a roar the next " Lord's day."

The groove grew a little jagged across the Senior's face. A strike, it is well known, is by no means necessarily an undesirable thing. Stock accumulates. The market quickens. You keep your finger on its pulse. You repair your machinery and bide your time. A thousand people, living from hand to mouth, may be under your finger, empty-handed. What so easy as a little stir of the finger now and then? *You* are not hungry meanwhile; *your* daughter has her winter clothes. You sit and file handcuffs playfully, against that day when your "hands" shall have gone hungry long enough. No more striking presently! Meantime, you may amuse yourself.

There is something noteworthy about this term "strike." A head would think and outwit us. A heart shall beat and move us. The "hands" can only struggle and strike us, — foolishly too, and madly, here and there, and desperately, being ill-trained hands, never at so much as a boxing-school, and gashing each other principally in the contest.

There had been strikes in Hayle and Kelso which had not caused a ruffle upon the Senior's gentlemanly, smooth brow or pleasant smile; but just now a strike was unfortunate.

" *Very* unfortunate," said Mr. Hayle in the counting-room on pay-day, in the noise of the breaking swell.

The Company were all upon the ground, silent and disturbed. There was a heavy crowd at the gates, and the sound of the overseers' voices in altercation with them, made its way in jerks to the counting-room.

By a chance Miss Kelso was in the counting-room ; had been over to put Mill's " Liberty " into the library, and had been detained by the gathering crowd.

She was uneasy like the rest ; was in and out, taking her own measure of the danger.

" There is nothing to be done," said Mr. Garrick, anxiously, the last time that she came into the little gloomy room where they were sitting. It was beginning to rain, and the windows, through which growing spots of lowering faces could be seen darkening the streets, were spattered and dirty. " There is nothing to do about it. If they will, they will. Had you better stay here ? We may have a noisy time of it."

" There is one thing to do," said the young lady, decidedly, " only one. I wish, Mr. Garrick, that you had never shut me out of this firm. I belonged here ! You do not one of you know now what it is for your own interest to do ! "

Mr. Hayle signified, smiling across his groove of anxiety, that she was at liberty, of course, to offer any valuable suggestion with which she might be prepared for such an emergency.

"And fold my hands for a romantic woman after it. However, that does not alter the fact; there is just one thing to do to prevent the most serious strike known in Five Falls yet. I know those men better than you do."

"We know them well enough," said Maverick, with a polite sneer. "This is a specimen of 'intelligent labor,' a fair one! These fellows are like a horse blind in one eye; they will run against a barn to get away from a barrel. Loose the rein, and there's mischief immediately. You may invite them to supper to the end of their days, Miss Kelso; but when you are in a genuine difficulty, they will turn against you just as they are doing now. There's neither gratitude nor common business sense among them. There's neither trust nor honor. They have no confidence in their employers, and no foresight for themselves. They would ruin us altogether for fifty cents a week. A parcel of children with the blessed addition of a few American citizens at their head!"

"I was about to propose," said Perley, quietly,

"that their employers should exhibit some trust or confidence in *them*. I want Mr. Garrick to go out and tell them *why* we must reduce their wages."

"Truly a young lady's suggestion," said the Senior.

"It is none of their business," said Maverick, "why we reduce their wages."

Stephen Garrick said nothing.

"Such a course was never taken in the company," said the Senior.

"And never ought to be," said the Junior. "It is an unsuitable position for an employer to take, — unsuitable! And disastrous as a precedent. Next thing we know, we should have them regulating the salary of our clerks and the size of our invoices. Outside of the fancy of a co-operative economist, such a principle would be im—— What a noise they 're making!"

"Every minute is precious," exclaimed Perley, rising nervously. "I tell you I know those men! They will trust Mr. Stephen Garrick, if he treats them like reasonable beings before it is too late!"

The counting-room door slammed there, behind

a messenger from the clerk. Things looked badly, he said ; the Spinners' Union had evidently been at work ; there were a few brickbats about, and rum enough to float a schooner ; and an ugly kind of *setness* all around ; we were in for it, he thought, now. Were there any orders ?

No, no orders.

The counting-room door slammed again, and the noise outside dashed against the sound with a little spurt of defiance.

" It would be a most uncommon course to take," said the Senior, uneasily ; " but the emergency is great, and perhaps if Mr. Garrick felt inclined to undertake such an extraordinary — "

Miss Kelso overrated his chances of success, Mr. Garrick said, but she did not overrate the importance of somebody's doing something. He was willing to make the attempt.

The counting-room door slammed once more ; the spurt died down ; the swell reared its head, writhing a little to see what would happen.

Mr. Garrick took his hat off, and stood in the door.

It was an ugly crowd, with a disheartening " setness " about it. He wished, when he looked it over, that he had not come ; but stood with his hat off, smiling.

He was smiling still when he came back to the counting-room.

" Well ? " asked Perley.

" For an unpopular master — "

" O hush ! " said Perley.

" For an unpopular master," repeated Mr. Garrick, " I did as well as I expected. In fact, just what I expected all the time has happened. Listen ! "

He held the door open. A cry came in from outside, —

" *Ask the young leddy !* "

" You see, you should have gone in the first place," said the unpopular master, patiently. " The rest of us are good for little, without your indorsement."

" *Call the young leddy ! Let's hear what the young leddy says to't ! The young leddy ! The young leddy !* "

The demand came in at the counting-room door just as the " young leddy " went out.

The people parted for her right and left. She stood in the mud, in the rain, among them.

They made room for her, just as the dark day would have made room for a sunbeam. The drunkest fellows, some of them, slunk to the circumference of the circle that had closed about her. Oaths and brickbats seemed to have been sucked out to sea by a sudden tide of respectability. It has been said by those who witnessed it that it was a scene worth seeing.

" She just stood in the mud and the rain," said Sip Garth, in telling the story. " If we 'd all been in her fine parlors, we would n't have been stiller. There was a kind of a shame and a sense came to us, to see her standing so quiet in the rain. The fellow that opened his lips for a roughness before her would ha' been kicked into the gutter, I can tell you. It was just like her. There 's never mud nor rain amongst us, but you look, and there she is ! That day there seemed to be a shining to her. We were all worked up and angered ; and she stood so white and still. There was a minute that she looked at us, and she looked — why, she looked as if she 'd be poor folks herself, if only she could say how sorry she was for us. Then she blazed out at us ! ' Did Mr. Garrick ever tell any man of us a word but honest truth?' she wanted to know. 'And has n't he proved himself a friend to every soul of you that needed friendliness?' says she. 'And when he told you that he must reduce your wages, you should n't have sent for me!' says she. But then she talks to us about the trouble that the Company was in, and a foolishness creeps round amongst us, as if we wished we were at home. It's not that they so much disbelieved Mr. Garrick," said Sip, "but when *she* said she could n't afford to pay 'em, they believed *that*."

"I don't understand about these things," said Reuben Mell, slowly stepping out from the crowd. "It's very perplexing to me. It does n't mean a dollar's worth less of horses and carriages, and grand parties to the Company, such a trouble as this don't seem to. And it means as *we* go without our breakfast so's the children sha'n't be hungry; and it means as when our shoes are wore out, we know no more than a babby in its cradle where the next pair is to come from. That's what reduction o' wages means to *us*. I don't understand the matter myself, but I'm free to say that we'll not doubt as the young leddy does.

I 'll take the young leddy's word for it, this time, for one."

Mr. Mell, with this, peaceably stepped up and took the reduction from the counter, and peaceably went home with it.

There was a little writhing of the flood-tide at this, and then an ebb.

Miss Kelso came out of it, and left it to bubble by itself for a while.

Within half an hour it had ebbed away, leaving only a few weeds of small boys and a fellow too drunk to float in sight of the mill-gate.

Until at least next " Lord's day," there would be no strike in Hayle and Kelso.

By that time Mr. Garrick hoped that we should be upon our feet again.

Mr. Garrick walked home with Miss Kelso in the autumn rain.

Unfortunately for the weed of a fellow stranded in the mill-yard, they passed and recognized him. It was the overseer, Irish Jim. Next morning he received his notice. They had borne with him too long, and warned him too often, Mr. Garrick insisted. Go he should, and go he did.

But Mr. Garrick walked home with Miss Kelso in the autumn rain.

They passed between the cotton-house and the old boiler, in going out. Dirk Burdock had stepped through just before them, trying to overtake Sip in the distance, hurrying home. Either this circumstance or a mood of the mill-master's own recalled to his mind his midnight talk with the young watchman on that spot, and what Dirk had said of its being a " churchly place." It was a dreary, dingy place now, in the gray storm-light, prosaic and extremely rusty. He held the lady's cloak back from the boiler in passing by.

His hand had but brushed the hem of her garment, but it trembled visibly. He touched a priestess in a water-proof. Fire from heaven fell before his eyes upon the yellow boiler. Such a " churchliness " struck the mill-yard, that the man would have lifted his hat, but considered that he would take cold, and so kept it on like a sensible fellow.

Of course he loved her. How should he help it ? Anybody but Perley would have thought of it, long ago.

Yet, oddly enough, nobody had thought of it. Occasionally one meets people, though they are rather apt to be men than women, who seem to go mailed through life in a gossip-proof armor. Perley Kelso is one of them. Rumor winks and blinks and shuts its eyes upon her. Your unpleasant stories, " had upon authority," pass her by unscathed. This young lady's life had been a peculiar, rather a public one, for now nearly two years, and in its most vital interests Stephen Garrick had stood heart and soul and hand in hand with her. Yet her calm eyes turned upon him that autumn afternoon as placidly as they did upon the old boiler. When she saw that tremble of the hand, she said : " You are cold ? It is growing chilly. The counting-room was close."

How could man help it ? Of course he loved her. He had seen the shining of her rare, fine face in such strange places ! In sick-rooms and in the house of mourning he had learned to listen for the stealing, strong sweetness of her young voice. They had met by death-beds and over graves. They had burrowed into mysteries of misery and sin, in God's name, together. Wherever people were cold, hungry, friendless, desolate, in danger, in despair, she struck across his path. Wherever there was a soul for which no man cared, he found her footprints. Wherever there was a life to be lifted from miasmas to heights, he saw the waving of her confident white hand. If ever there were earnest work, solemn work, solitary work, mistrusted work, work misunderstood, neglected, discouraging, hopeless, thankless, — Christ's work, to be done, he faced her.

Now, among several hundred factory-operatives, it naturally happened that he had thus faced her not infrequently.

The woman's life had become a service in a temple, and he had lighted the candles for her. One would miss it, perhaps, to worship in the dark ? The man asked himself the question, turning his face stiffly against the autumn storm.

There had been no sun since yesterday. The sky was locked with a surcharged cloud. A fine, swift rain blurred the outlines of the river-banks and hills.

" And yet," he said, " the day seems to be full of sun. Do you notice ? There is light about us everywhere."

" It is from the hickories and maples," said Perley.

Ripened leaves streaked and dotted their path, wreathed blazing arms about the pine groves, smouldered over the fields, flung themselves scorched into the water, flared across the dam, and lighted the little cascades luridly. The singular effect of dying trees on a dead day was at its richest. One could not believe that the sun did not shine.

"An unreal light," said Stephen Garrick, hardly, "and ugly. We should find it cold to live by."

"I had not thought of that," said Perley, smiling; "I rather like it."

Her face, as she lifted it to his, seemed to warm itself at its own calm eyes; slowly, perhaps, as if the truant day had tried to leave a chill upon it, but thoroughly and brightly.

Garrick turned, and looked it over and over and through and through, — the lifted haunting face!

What a face it was! His own turned sharply gray.

"I see no room for me there!" he said, and stopped short where he stood.

No; he was right. There was no room. The

womanly, calm face leaped with quick color, then drifted pale as his own.

" Let us walk on," said Garrick, with a twang in his voice.

They walked on nervously. Neither spoke just then. They walked on, under and through a solid arch of the unreal sunshine, which a phalanx of maples made in meeting over their heads.

" I had hoped," said Stephen Garrick then, between his breath, " that I had — a chance. I have been — stupid, perhaps. A man is so slow to feel that he has — no chance. I have not played at love like — many men. There has been such an awfulness," said Stephen Garrick, passing his hand confusedly over his eyes, — " such an awfulness about the ground I have seen you tread upon. Most men love women in parlors and on play-days ; they can sing them little songs, they can tie up flowers for them, they can dance and touch their hands. I — I have had no way in which to love you. We have done such awful work together. In it, through it, by it, because of it, I loved you. I think there 's something — in the love — that is like the work. It has struck me under a ledge

of granite, I believe.   Miss Kelso, it would come
up — hard."

His hand dropped against his side, very slowly,
but the blue nails clenched the flesh from its
palm.

What did the woman mean?   What should he
do with the sight, sound, touch of her; the rustle
of her dress, the ripple of her sweet breath, the
impenetrable calm of her grieving eyes?

He felt himself suddenly lifted and swung from
the centre of his controlled, common, regula-
ted, and regulating days.   Five Falls operatives
ceased to appear absorbing as objects of life.
How go dribbling ideal Christian culture through
highways and hedges, if a man sat and starved on
husks himself, before the loaded board?   The
salvation of the world troubled him yesterday.
To-day there was only this woman in it.

They two, in the mock light of dying leaves,
they two only and together, stood, the Alpha and
Omega, in the name of nature and in the sight
of God.

" I have loved you," said the man, trembling
heavily, " so long !   My life has not been like
that of — many people.   I have taken it — hard

and slowly. I have loved you slowly, and — hard. You ought to love me. Before God, I say you ought to love me!"

"The fact is — " said Perley, in her sensible, every-day voice.

Stephen Garrick drew breath and straightened himself. His blanched face quivered and set into its accustomed angles. His shut fingers opened, and he cleared his throat. He struck to his orbit. Ah! Where had he been? Most too old a man for that! See how he had let the rain drip on her. He grasped his umbrella. He could go to a Mission meeting now. All the women in the world might shake their beautiful heads at him under yellow maple-trecs in an autumn rain!

"The fact is?" he gravely asked.

"The fact is," repeated Perley, "that I have no time to think of love and marriage, Mr. Garrick. That is a business, a trade, by itself to women. I have too much else to do. As nearly as I can understand myself, that is the statc of the case. I cannot spare the time for it."

And yet, as nearly as she understood herself, she might have loved this man. The dial of her young love and loss cast a little shadow in her sun to-day. She felt old before her time. All the glamour that draws men and women together had escaped her somehow. Possible wifehood was no longer an alluring dream. Only its pro- saic and undesirable aspects presented them- selves to her mind. No bounding impulse cried within her: That is happiness! There is rest! But only: It were unreasonable; it is unwise.

And yet she might have loved the man. In all the world, she felt as if he only came within calling distance of her life. Out of all the world, she would have named him as the knightly soul that hers delighted to honor.

Might have loved him? *Did* she love him? Garrick's hungry eyes pierced the lifted face again over and over, through and through. If not in this world, in another, perhaps? In any? Somewhere? Somehow?

" I cannot tell," said the woman, as if she had been called; " I do not need you now. Women talk of loneliness. I am not lonely. They are sick and homeless. I am neither. They are miserable. I am happy. They grow old. I am not afraid of growing old. They have nothing to do. If I had ten lives, I could fill them! No, I do not need you, Stephen Garrick."

" Besides," she added, half smiling, half sighing, " I believe that I have been a silent partner long enough. If I married you, sir, I should invest in life, and you would conduct it. I suspect that I have a preference for a business of my own. Perhaps that is a part of the trouble."

They had reached the house, and turned, faces against the scattering rain, to look down at the darkening river, and the nestling that the town made against the hill. The streets were full; and the people, through the distance and the rain, had a lean look, passing to and fro before the dark, locked mills.

Perley Kelso, with a curious, slow gesture, stretched her arms out toward them, with a face which a man would remember to his dying day.

" Shall they call," she said, " and I not answer? If they cried, should not I hear?"

" Mr. Garrick!" She faced him suddenly on the dripping lawn. " If a man who loves a woman can take the right hand of fellowship from her, I wish you would take it from me!"

She held out her full strong hand. The rain

dripped on it from an elm-tree overhead. Stephen Garrick gently brushed the few drops, as if they had been tears, away, and, after a moment's hesitation, took it.

If not in this world in another, perhaps ? In any ? Somewhere ? Somehow ?

" I shall wait for you," said the man. Perhaps he will. A few souls can.

CHAPTER XIII.

A FEVERISH PATIENT.

THE Pompeian statues in Hayle and Kelso were on exhibition in a cleared and burnished condition for nearly a week last spring.

That is to say, Hayle and Kelso were off work, for high water. It will be well remembered how serious the season's freshets were, and that Five Falls had her full share of drenching.

The river had been but two days on the gallop before the operatives, wandering through their holidays in their best clothes, began to knot into little skeins about the banks, watching the leap that the current made over the dam.

By the third day the new mill was considered in danger, and diked a little.

By the fourth day heavy wagons were forbidden the county bridge.

The skeins upon the banks interwound and thickened. Five Falls became a gallery. Sun-break had flung back the curtain from a picture which hundreds crept up on tiptoe to see.

Between the silent, thronged banks and the mute, unclouded sky, the river writhed like a thing that was tombed alive. The spatter of the cascades had become smooth humps, like a camel's. The great pulse of the dam beat horribly. The river ran after it, plunged at it, would run full and forever. It looked as hopeless as sin, and as long as eternity. You gazed and despaired. There was always more, more, more. There was no chain for its bounding. There was no peace to its cries. No sepulchre could stifle it, no death still it. You held out your hands and cried for mercy to it.

Beautiful whirlpools of green light licked the base of the stone river-walls. Flecks of foam were picked up in the fields. People stood for hours in the spray, clinging to the iron railings by the dam, deafened and drenched, to watch the sinuous trail of the under-tints of malachite and gold and umber that swung through. As one looked, the awful oncoming of the upper waters ceased to be a terror, ceased, or seemed to cease, to be a fact. Mightiness of motion became repose. The dam lay like a mass of veined agate before the eyes, as solid as the gates of the city whose builder and maker is God ; of the city in which sad things shall become joy, dark things light, stained things pure, old things new.

The evening and the morning were the fifth day. Between their solemn passing, Sip and Catty sat alone in the little damp, stone house.

The air was full of the booming of the flood, and Catty laid her head upon Sip's knee, listening, as if she heard it. The wind was high and blew a kind of froth of noise in gusts against the closed windows and doors ; but never laid finger's weight upon the steady, deadly underflow of sound that filled the night. A dark night. Sip, going to the window, from whence she could dimly see the sparks of alarm-lights and the shadows of watchmen on the endangered bridge, felt a little displeasure with the night. It was noisy and confused her. It was wild and disturbed her. The crowds still lingered on the banks, where the green whirlpools had grown black, and where the tints of malachite and gold and umber, swinging on their bright arms through the dam, had become purple and gray and ghastliness, and wrapped the stone piers in dark files, as if they had been mourners at a mighty funeral. Cries of excitement or fear cut the regular thud of the water, now and then, and there was unwonted light about the dikes of the new mill, and on the railway crossing, which had been loaded with the heaviest freight at command, in anticipation of the possible ruin and attack of the upper bridge.

The water was still rising, and the wind. An undefined report had risen with them, through the day, of runaway lumber up the stream. Five Falls was awake and uneasy.

"I don't wonder," thought Sip, coming back from the window. "It's a kind of night that I can't make out. Can you, Catty?"

It was a night that Catty could hear, or thought she could, and this pleased her.

"It is like wheels," she said, having never heard but those two things, the machinery in the mills and this thunder. It carried her round and round, she signified, making circles with her fingers in the air.

She got up presently and walked with the fancy in circles about the little kitchen. It seemed to perplex her that she always came back to her starting-point.

"I thought I was going to get out," she said, stretching out her arms.

" Don't!" said Sip, uneasily, covering her eyes. Catty looked so ugly when she took fancies! She never could bear them ; begged her to come back again and put her head upon her knee.

" But where shall I stop ?" persisted Catty. " I can't go round and go round. Who will stop me, Sip ?"

" Never mind," said Sip. " There, there!" All the stone house was full of the boom of the river. The two girls sat down again, it seemed, in the heart of it. Sip took Catty's hands. She was glad to have her at home to-night. She kissed her finger-tips and her cropped, coarse hair.

" Last night," said Catty, suddenly, " I stayed at home."

" So you did, dear."

" And another night, besides."

" Many other nights," said Sip, encouragingly. Did that make Sip happy ? Catty asked.

Very, very happy.

For love's sake ?

For love's sake, dear.

"I'll stay at home to-morrow night," Catty nodded sharply, — "I'll stay at home to-morrow night, for love's sake."

In the middle of the night, Sip, with a sense of disturbance or alarm, waked suddenly. The little closet bedroom was dark and close. A great shadow in the kitchen wrapped her pictured dreamer, and his long, unresting dream. It was so dark, that she could fairly touch, she thought, the solemn sound that filled the house. It took waves like the very flood itself. If she put her hand out over the edge of the bed, she felt an actual chill from it. There seemed to be nothing but that noise in all the world.

Except Catty, sitting up straight in bed, awake and talkative.

"What is it?" asked Sip, sitting up too.

In the dead dark, Catty put out her hands. In the dead dark Sip answered them.

"Sip," said Catty, "who was it?"

"Who was what, dear?"

"Who was it that made this?" touching her ears.

"Him that made this awful noise," said Sip.

"And this?" brushing her eyes.

"Him that made this awful dark," said Sip.

"And this?" She put her fingers to her mute, rough lips.

"Him that learned the wind to cry at nights," said Sip.

"Did he do it for love's sake?" asked Catty. "I can't find out. Did he do it for love's sake, Sip?"

"For — love's — sake?" said Sip, slowly. "I suppose he did. I pray to Heaven that he did. When I'm on my knees, I know he did."

"If it was for love's sake," said Catty, "I'll go to sleep again."

So the evening and the morning were the fifth day of the great freshets at Five Falls.

Catty woke early and helped Sip to get breakfast. She was very happy, though the coffee burned, and laughed discordantly when Sip made griddle-cakes for her of the Indian meal. Sip could not eat her own griddle-cakes for pleasure at this. She walked up and down the room with her hands behind her, kissing Catty's finger-tips and her ragged hair.

The Pompeian statues came to the face of the day; the crowds upon the river-brinks formed again, thickened, doubled ; the bright-armed malachite and umber leaped again dizzily down the dams.

Still the pulse of the river rose. The county bridge shrunk and shivered in fits to it. The river had the appearance of having an attack of fever and ague.

The timber alarm, in the wearing on of the day, waxed and grew.

Five thousand feet of timber, in the upper floods, had broken loose, and were on their way down stream.

Ten thousand feet.

Twenty.

Five hundred thousand.

A million feet of logs, in the upper floods, had broken their chains, and would be at Five Falls before night.

Catty was sitting alone in the stone house, in the slope of the afternoon. She had been out with Sip, half the day, "to see the flood" ; lifting her listening face against the spray, with pathetic pleasure ; holding out her hands sometimes, they said, as if to measure the sweep of the sounding water ; nodding to herself about it, with her dull laugh.

Sip would be back at dusk. Catty had promised, coming home a little tired, to sit still and wait for her ; would not venture out again among the crowd ; would go to sleep perhaps ; would be a good girl, at any rate ; stroked Sip's face a little as she went away. Sip kissed her, and, when she had shut the door, came back and kissed her again. A little shopping up town, and an errand at Miss Kelso's, and perhaps another look at the flood, would not delay her very long ; and Catty had kept her promises lately. Sip bade her good by with a light heart, and shut the door again.

Catty sat still for a while after the door was shut. Then she slept awhile. Afterwards she sat still for a while again. She got up and walked about the kitchen. She sat down on the kitchen floor. She nodded and talked to herself. Sip might have been gone an hour ; she might have been gone a week ; Catty did not feel sure which ; she lost her hold of time when she sat alone ; she put her fingers down on the floor and counted them, guessing at how long Sip had been away.

Her fingers, when she put them on the floor, splashed into something cold.

Had the water-pail tipped over ? If it had, it

must have been very full. Catty discovered that
she was sitting in a puddle of water; that
water gurgled over her feet; that water rippled
about the legs of the stove; that a gentle bubble of water filled the room.

She crawled, dripping, up, and made her way
to the door. As she opened it, she let in a swash
about her ankles.

She spattered across the entry to find the Irish
woman who rented the other tenement; she had
gone, like the rest of the world, to see the flood,
it seemed; Catty received no answer to her uncouth calls; she was alone in the house.

This disturbed her. She felt puzzled about
the water; alarmed, because she could neither see
nor hear the reason of it; annoyed at the cold
crawling that it made about her ankles, and
anxious for Sip to come and explain it.

She went to the front door and opened that.
A rush, like a tiny tide, met her. She stooped
and put her hand out, over the step. It dipped
into a pool of rising water.

Catty shrank back and shut the door. The
noise like wheels was plain to her. It waited for
her outside of that door. It struck like claws

upon her locked ears. It frightened her. She would not for the world open the door to it. She drew the bolt hard, in a childish fright, and sat down again in the slow gurgle on the kitchen floor.

Suddenly it occurred to her that she might go and find Sip. But Sip would not be in the noise. Where would she be?

Catty pushed herself along on the floor, pushing out of the way of the water as she reflected. That was how another thing occurred to her.

.The farther that she pushed herself the thinner the gurgle grew. In the closet bedroom it was scarcely wet.

At this side of the house she lost, or thought she lost, the noise. It must be at this side of the house that she should find Sip. Sip had often lost *her* out of the closet bedroom. She remembered, with a laugh, how many times she had climbed out of that little cupboard window after Sip was asleep. She felt her way to it eagerly. It was shut and buttoned. She pushed it, slamming, back, climbed to the high sill, and let herself drop.

Catty might have remained in the closet bedroom, had she but known it, high and dry. The stone house received a thorough soaking, but not a dangerous one. The water sucked in for a while at the locked front door, played drearily about the empty kitchen, mopped the entry floor, set the Irish woman's bread-pan and coal-hod afloat, and dawdled away again down the steps; the result, it seemed, of a savage and transient shiver on the part of that fitful invalid, the river.

The county bridge, in fact, was as good as gone. The transient shiver in the lower floods had been caused by the sinking of a pier.

It had been a fine sight. Masses of men, women, and children hung, chained like galley-slaves, to either bank, intent and expectant on it. Foot and horse forsook the bridge. Police guarded it.

A red sunset sprang up and stared at it. An avalanche of dead-white spray chewed the malachite and umber. Curious, lurid colors bounded up where they sank, and bruised and beat themselves against the fallen and the falling piers.

The gorgeous peril of the tinted water, and the gorgeous safety of the tinted sky, struck against each other fancifully. There seemed a rescue in the one for the ruin of the other. One was sure that the drowned colors held up their arms again, secure, inviolate, kindled, living, in the great resurrection of the watching heavens.

It must have been not far from the moment when Catty dropped from the cupboard window, that, on the beautiful madness of the river, up where the baby souls of the cascades had transmigrated into camels, a long, low, brown streak appeared.

It appeared at first sight to lie quite still. At second sight, it undulated heavily, like a huge boa. At the third, it coiled and plunged.

" The logs ! The logs ! The logs are here ! "

The cry ran round the banks. Maverick Hayle sat down on a stone and looked at his new mill stupidly. Passers cleared the railway crossing. People ran about and shouted. They climbed rocks and trees to look. The guards on the bridge disappeared. The smooth outlines of the boa grew jagged. The timber leaped and tangled in sweeping down. All through its wounded arches, the heavy bridge creaked and cried.

The people on the banks cried too, from sheer excitement.

" The logs, the logs, the logs ! The bridge ! "

" Look on the bridge ! Look *there !* Good God ! How did she get there ? *On the bridge ! Woman on the bridge !* "

Past the frightened guards, past the occupied eyes of a thousand people, on the bridge, over the bridge, not twelve feet from the sunken piers, stood a girl with low forehead, and dropping lip, and long, outstretching hands.

" Catty ! Catty ! O Catty, Catty, Catty ! "

The uncouth name rang with a terrible cry. It cleft the crowd like a knife. They parted before it, here and there and everywhere, letting a ghastly girl plunge through.

" O Catty, Catty, Catty ! For love's sake, stop ! For dear love's sake ! "

It was too late for dear love to touch her. Its piteous call she could not hear. Its wrung face she could not see. Her poor, puzzled lips moved as if to argue with it, but made no sound.

Type of the world from which she sprang, — the world of exhausted and corrupted body, of exhausted and corrupted brain, of exhausted and corrupted soul, the world of the laboring poor as man has made it, and as Christ has died for it, of a world deaf, dumb, blind, doomed, stepping

confidently to its own destruction before our eyes,
— Catty stood for a moment still, a little perplexed, it seemed, feeling about her patiently in
the spray-sown, lighted air.

One beck of a human hand would save her ;
but she could not see it. One cry would turn
her ; but her ears were sealed.

Still, in the great dream of dying, as in the
long dream of life, this miserable creature listened
for what she never heard, and spoke that which
no man understood.

" She 's making signs to me," groaned Sip ;
" she 's making signs to call my name ! "

Then Perley Kelso put both arms about her.
Then the solid shore staggered suddenly. Then
a ragged shadow loomed across the dam. Then
there was a shock, and thunder.

Then some one covered her eyes, close.

When she opened them, timber was tearing by.
Spray was in her face. Dirk was beside her on
his knees, and men had their hats off.

On the empty ruin of the sliced bridge, two
logs had caught and hung, black against the color
of the water and the color of the sky. They
had caught transversely, and hung like a cross.

CHAPTER XIV.

SWEPT AND GARNISHED.

IT was Dirk who had covered Sip's eyes when the timber struck the bridge.

She did not think of it at the time, but remembered it afterwards.

She remembered it when he came that evening to the door of the lonely, sodden house, after Miss Kelso had gone, asking how she was, but refusing to enter lest, he said, he should be "one too many." She liked that. They did not want him — she and Catty — that night. This thing, in the solitude of the dripping house, had surprised her. God in heaven did not seem to have separated her and Catty, after all. The *silence* of death was spared her. Catty's living love had made no sound ; her dead love made none either. A singular comfort came to Sip, almost with the striking of her sorrow. She and Catty could not be parted like two speaking people.

Passed into the great world of signs, the deaf-mute, dead, grew grandly eloquent. The ring of the flood was her solemn kiss. The sunshine on the kitchen floor to-morrow would be her dear good-morning. Clouds and shadows and springing green gave her speech forever. The winds of long nights were language for her. Ah, the ways, the ways which Catty could find to speak to her!

Sip walked about the room with dry, burning eyes. She could not cry. She felt exultant, excited. The thing which she greatly feared had come upon her. The worst that ever could hurt her and Catty was over. And now how privileged and rich she was! What ways! How many ways! Only she and Catty knew. How glad she was now that Catty had never talked like other people!

This curious mood — if it should be called a mood — lasted, evenly, till the poor, disfigured heap found one day in the ebbing of the flood flung upright against a rock, a mile below the dam, with its long hands outstretched, spelling awful dumb words, had been brought to the stone house and carried away again, and left until the day when the lips of the dumb shall be unsealed, to spell its untranslated message through a tangle of myrtle into the smoky factory air.

After that she shrank suddenly, like a waked somnambulist, and went sick to bed.

One day she got up and went to work again.

That was the day that Dirk Burdock had watched for, had grown impatient about, seized impetuously when it came.

It had been a pleasant day, with a grave sunlight and a quiet sky. Sip took a grave and pleasant face out into it. She wore a grave and pleasant smile when the young watchman's eager step overtook her, where the rusty boiler (made rustier than ever by the flood, and since removed) had stood beside the cotton-house.

" I 'm glad to see you out again, Sip," said the young man, awkwardly, striding out of step with her, and falling back with a jerk.

" Yes," said Sip, " it is quite time I should be at work again."

" It 's a pleasant day," said Dirk.

" A very pleasant day," said Sip.

" Been to see the new mill since the repairs ?" asked Dirk, as if struck by a bright thought. Now Dirk had vowed within himself, that, whatever else he said to Sip, he would say nothing about the flood. He had an idea that it might make her cry. He had another, that it was about time for her to forget it. He had another still, somewhat to the effect that he was the man to make her forget. In the face of these three ideas, Dirk could have bitten his tongue out for his question. However, Sip did not cry, neither did she seem to have forgotten the flood, neither did she seem anxious to forget it or avoid it.

She said, Yes, smiling, that she had walked by on her way to work this morning. There must have been a good deal of damage done ?

" A sight," said Dirk, with a sigh of relief. " They say the young man lost the most out o' that affair."

" Young Hayle ?"

" Yes ; though they was all involved, I suppose, for that matter, — her among 'em. But she never bothered her head about it at the time o' 't. She was all taken up with — "

" I know," Sip ran on, gently, when poor Dirk stuck in despair. " I do not think she *thought* of

anything else but Catty and me. It was like her,
— like her."

"She must have lost," said Dirk, reviving
again ; "I thought the fall lectures would be
broke off, but it seems they ain't."

Sip said nothing ; did not seem inclined to
talk, and the two young people turned a couple
of corners on the way to the stone house in
thoughtful silence. They were almost too young
to be so thoughtful and so silent ; more especially
the young man, growing nervous, and taking
furtive, anxious glances at the girl's face.

It was an inscrutable face.

Sip had shut her lips close ; she looked straight
ahead ; the brown, dull tints of her cheeks and
temples came out like a curtain, and folded all
young colors and flushes and tremors, all hope
and fear, all longing or purpose, need or fulness
in her, out of sight. She only looked straight on
and waited for Dirk to speak.

She quite knew that and what he would speak.
When he began, presently, with a quivering face,
"Well, Sip, I don't see that I'm getting on
any in the mills, after all," she was neither
surprised nor off her guard. She was not yet

twenty-three, but she was too old to be put off her guard by a young man with a quivering face. If she had a thing to do, she meant to do it ; put her hands together in that way she had, bent at the knuckles, resolutely.

"No," she said, "no ; you'll never get any farther, Dirk."

"But I meant to," said Dirk, hotly. "I thought I should ! Mebbe you think it's me that's the trouble, not the getting on ! "

"Perhaps there *is* a trouble about you," said Sip, honestly ; "I don't know ; and I don't much care whether there is or not. But I think most of the trouble is in the getting on. Mills ain't made to get on in. It ain't easy, I know, Dirk. It ain't. It's the *staying put* of 'em, that's the worst of 'em. *Don't* I know ? It's the staying put that's the matter with most o' folks in the world, it seems to me. For we *are* the most o' folks, — us that stay put, you know."

"Are we ? " said Dirk, a little puzzled by Sip's social speculations. "But I'm getting steady pay now, Sip, at any rate ; and I've a steady chance. Garrick's a friend o' mine, I believe, and has showed himself friendly.   He'll keep me the watch, at least, — Mr. Garrick. I might be worse off than on watch, Sip."

"O yes," said Sip; "you 've got a good place, Dirk."

"With a chance," repeated Dirk.

"With a chance? Maybe," answered Sip.

"And now," said Dirk, trembling suddenly, "what with the place and the chance — maybe, and the pay and the steadiness, sure, I 've been thinking, Sip, as the time had come to ask you — "

"Don't !" said Sip.

All young colors and flushes and tremors, hopes and fears, longing and need, broke now out of the brown curtain of Sip's face. In the instant she was a very lonely, very miserable little girl, not by any means over twenty-three, and the young man had eyes so cruelly kind! But she said : "Don't, Dirk! O please, don't !"

"Well!" said Dirk. He stopped and drew breath as if she had shot him.

They had come to the stone house now, and Sip began walking back and forth in front of it.

"But I was going to ask you to be my wife !" said Dirk. "It 's so long that I have n't dared to ask you, and now you say don't! Don't? But I will; I'll ask at any rate. Sip, will you marry me? There! I should choke if I did n't ask. You may say what you please."

"I *can't* say what I please," said Sip, in a low voice, walking faster.

"I don't know what's to hinder," said Dirk, in an injured tone; "I always knew I was n't half fit for you, and I always knew you'd ought to have a man that could get on. But considering the steadiness and the chance, and that I — I set such a sight by you, Sip, and sometimes I've thought you — liked me well enough," concluded Dirk, candidly.

"I like you, Dirk," said Sip, slowly, "well enough."

"Well enough to be my wife?"

"Well enough to be your wife."

"Then I should n't think," observed Dirk, simply, and with a brightening face, "that you'd find it very hard saying what you please."

"Maybe I should n't," said Sip, "if I could be your wife; but I can't."

Her bent hands fell apart weakly; she did not look at Dirk; she fixed her eyes on a little clump of dock-weed at her feet, beside the fence ; she looked sick and faint.

"I'll not marry you," said the girl feebly ; "I'll not marry anybody. Maybe it is n't the way a girl had ought to feel when she likes a young fellow," added Sip, with a kind of patient aged bitterness crawling into her eyes. "But we don't live down here so 's to make girls grow up like girls should, it seems to me. Things as would n't trouble rich folks troubles us. There's things that troubles me. I'll never marry anybody, Dirk. I'll never bring a child into the world to work in the mills ; and if I'd ought not to say it, I can't help it, for it's the truth, and the reason, and I've said it to God on my knees a many and a many times. I've said it before Catty died, and I've said it more than ever since, and I'll say it till I die. I'll never bring children into this world to be factory children, and to be factory boys and girls, and to be factory men and women, and to see the sights I've seen, and to bear the things I've borne, and to run the risks I've run, and to grow up as I've grown up, and to stop where I've stopped, — never. I've heard tell of slaves before the war that would n't be fathers and mothers of children to be slaves like them. That 's the way I feel, and that 's the way I mean to feel. I won't be the mother of a child to go and live my life over again. I 'll never marry anybody."

" But they need n't be factory people," urged Dirk, with a mystified face. " There 's trades and — other things."

" I know, I know," Sip shook her head, — "I know all about that. They 'd never get out of the mills. It 's from generation to generation. It could n't be helped. I know. It 's in the blood."

" But other folks don't take it so," urged Dirk, after a disconsolate pause. " Other folks marry, and have their homes and the comfort of 'em. Other folks, if they love a man, 'll be his wife someways or nuther."

" Sometimes," said Sip, " I seem to think that that I 'm not other folks. Things come to me someways that other folks don't understand nor care for." She crushed the dock-weed to a wounded mass, and dug her foot into the ground, and stamped upon it.

" I 've made up my mind, Dirk. It 's no use talking. It — it hurts me," with a tender motion of the restless foot against the bruised, rough leaves of the weed which she was covering up with sand. " I 'd rather not talk any more, Dirk. There 's other girls. Some other girl will do."

" I 'll have no other girl if I can't have you !" said poor Dirk, turning away. " I never could set such a sight by another girl as I 've set by you. If you don't marry, Sip, no more 'll I."

Sip smiled, but did not speak.

" Upon my word, I won't ! " cried Dirk. " You think I 'm one of other folks, I guess. You wait and see. I 've loved you true. If ever man loved a girl, I 've loved you true. If I can't have you, I 'll have nobody !"

But Sip only smiled.

She went into the house after Dirk had gone, weakly. The flushing tremors in her face had set into a dead color, and her hands came together again at the knuckles.

The Irish woman was away, and the house was lonely and still. The kitchen fire was out. She went out into the little shed for kindlings, thinking that she would make a cup of tea directly, she felt so weak.

When she got there, she sat down on the

chopping-block, and covered her face, her feet hanging listlessly against the axe. She wished that she need never lift her head nor look about again. She wished that when the Irish woman came home she should just step into the little shed and find her dead. What a close little warm sheltered shed it was! All the world outside of it seemed emptied, swept, and garnished. She felt as if her life had just been through a "house-cleaning." It was clean and washed, and proper and right, and as it should be, and drearily in order forever. Now it was time to sit down in it.

Sip had what Mr. Mill calls a "large share of human nature," and she loved Dirk, and she led a lonely life. She was neither a heroine, nor a saint, nor a fanatic, sitting out there in the little wood-shed on the chopping-block.

"I don't see why I couldn't have had *that*, leastways," she cried between her hands. "I haven't ever had much else. I don't see why *that* should go too."

But she did see. In about ten minutes she saw clearly enough to get up from the chopping-block, and go in and make her cup of tea.

CHAPTER XV.

A PREACHER AND A SERMON.

SHE saw clearly enough in time to be a very happy woman.

Perley Kelso, at least, was thinking so, when she went the other day with young Mrs. Hayle to hear one of her street sermons.

Sip had " set up for a preacher," after all ; she hardly knew how ; nobody knew exactly how ; it had come about, happened ; taken rather the form of a destiny than a plan.

The change had fallen upon her since Catty's passing " out of sight."   She was apt to speak of Catty so.   She was not dead nor lost.   She listened still and spoke.   She only could not see her.

" But she talks," said Sip under her breath, — "she talks to me.   There's things she'd have me say.   That was how I first went to the meetings. I'd never cared about meetings.   I'd never been religious nor good. But Catty had such things to say! and when I saw the people's faces, lifted up and listening, and when I talked and talked, it all came to me one night like this. Do you see? Like this. I was up to the Mission reading a little hymn I know, and the lights were on the people's faces, and in a minute it was like this. *God had things to say.* I'd been talking Catty's words. *God had words.* I cannot tell you how it was; but I stood right up and said them; and ever since there's been more than I could say."

"What is there about the girl that can attract so many people?" asked Mrs. Maverick Hayle, standing on tiptoe beside Perley on the outer edge of Sip's audience, and turning her wide eyes on it, like a child at a menagerie. "There are old men here, and old women. There's everybody here. The girl looks too young to instruct them."

She must judge for herself what there was about her, Miss Kelso said; it had been always so; since she started her first neighborhood meeting in the Irish woman's kitchen at the stone house, she had found listeners enough; they were too many for tenement accommodations after a while, and so the thing grew.

Sometimes she used the chapel. Sometimes she preferred a doorstep like this, and the open air.

"I undertook to help her at the first," said Miss Kelso, smiling, "but I was only *among* them at best ; Sip is *of* them ; she understands them and they understand her ; so I left her to her work, and I keep to my own. Hush ! Here she is ; can you see ? Just over there on the upper step."

They were in a little court, a miserable place, breaking out like a wart from one of the foulest alleys in Five Falls ; a place such as Sip was more apt than not to choose for her "sermons." The little court was sheltered, however, and comparatively quiet. There may have been fifty people in it.

"Everybody," as Mrs. Hayle said, — old Bijah, with heavy crutches, sitting on a barrel, and offering his services as prompter now and then, out of a petition to the Legislature of the State of Massachusetts ; Dib Docket, grown into long curls and a brass necklace ; pretty little Irish Maggie, with her thin cheek upon her hand ; Mr. Mell, frowningly attentive ; the young watchman, and his young wife in blue ribbons, making a Scotch picture of herself up against the old court pump; all Sip's friends, and strangers who drifted in, from curiosity, or idleness, or that sheer misery which has an instinct always for such crowds.

Sip was used now to the Scotch picture, quite. She had expected it, was ready for it. Dirk was one of "other folks," in spite of himself. She had understood that from the first. She did not mind it very much. She framed the picture in with "God's words," with a kind of solemn joy. Dirk was happy. She liked to see it, know it, while she talked. She was glad that Nynee inclined to come with him so often to hear her.

Sip came out on the doorstep and stood for a moment with her hands folded down before her, and her keen eyes taking the measure of every face, it seemed, in the little court.

There was nothing saintly about Sip. No halo struck through the little court upon her doorstep. Florence Nightingale or the Quaker Dinah would not have liked her. She was just a little rough, brown girl, bringing her hands together at the knuckles and talking fast.

"But such a curious preacher!" said Mrs. Maverick Hayle.

The little preacher had a wandering style, as most such preachers have. Such a style can no more be caught on the point of a pen than the rustle of crisp leaves or the aroma of dropping nuts. There was a syntax in Sip's brown face and bent hands and poor dress and awkward motions. There were correctness and perspicuity about that old doorstep. The muddy little court was an appeal, the square of sky above her head a peroration. In that little court Sip was eloquent. Here on the parlor sofa, in clean cuffs and your slippers, she harangues you.

"Look here," she was saying, "you men and women, and you boys and girls, that have come to hear me! You say that you are poor and miserable. I've heard you. You say you're worked and drove and slaved, and up early and down late, and hurried and worried and fretted, and too hot and too cold, and too cross and too poor, to care about religion. I know. I'm worked and drove, and up and down, and hurried and worried and fretted, and hot and cold, and cross and poor myself. I know about that.

Religion will do for rich folks.   That's what you say, — I know.   I've said it a many times myself.   Curse the rich folks and their religion ! — that's what you say.   I know.   Have n't I said it a many times myself ?

"Now see here !   O you men and women, and you boys and girls, can't you *see ?*   It ain't a rich folks' religion that I 've brought to talk to you.   Rich religion ain't for you and ain't for me. We 're poor folks, and we want a poor folks' religion.   We must have a poor folks' religion or none at all.   We know that.

"Now listen to me !   O you men and women, and you girls and boys, listen to what I 've got to tell you.   The religion of Jesus Christ the Son of God Almighty is the only poor folks' religion in all the world.   Folks have tried it many times. They 've got up pious names and pious fights. There have been wars and rumors of wars, and living and dying, and books written, and money spent, and blood shed for other religions, but there 's never been any poor folks' religion but that of Jesus Christ the Son of God Almighty. . . . .

"O listen to me !   You go on your wicked

ways, and you drink, and fight, and swear, and
you live in sinful shames, and you bring your
little children up to shameful sins, and when
Jesus Christ the Son of God Almighty does you
the favor to ask you for your wicked hearts, you
hold up your faces before him, and you say,
' We 're poor folks, Lord. We 're up early, and
we 're down late, and we 're droved and slaved,
and rich folks are hard on us. The mill-masters
drive their fine horses, Lord, and we walk and
work till we 're worn out. There 's a man with
a million dollars, Lord, and we have n't laid by
fifty yet against a rainy day !' Then you grow
learned and wise, and you shake your heads, and
you say, ' Capital has all the ease, Lord, and
labor has all the rubs ; and things ain't as they
should be ; and it can't be expected of us to be
religious in such a state of affairs.' And you say,
' I 'm at work all day and nights, I 'm tired ' ; or,
' I 'm at work all the week, and of a Sunday I
must sleep ; I can't be praying ' ; and so you say,
' I pray thee, Lord, have me excused !' and so
you go your wicked ways.

" O listen to me ! This is what he says, ' *I*
was up, and down, and drove, and slaved, and

13 *

hurried, myself,' he says, 'I was too hot, and too cold, and worried, and anxious, and *I* saw rich folks take their ease, and *I* was poor like you,' he says.

"O you men and women, and you boys and girls, listen to him! Never you mind about me any longer, listen to HIM!

"He won't be hard on you. Don't you suppose he knows how the lives you live are hard enough without that heaped against them? Don't you suppose he *knows* how the world is all a tangle, and how the great and the small, and the wise and the foolish, and the fine and the miserable, and the good and the bad, are all snarled in and out about it? And does n't he know how long it is unwinding, and how the small and the foolish and the bad and the miserable places stick in his hands? And don't you suppose he *knows* what places they are to be born in and to die in, and to inherit unto the third and fourth generations of us, like the color of our hair, or the look about our mouths?

"I tell you, he knows, he knows! I tell you, he knows where the fault is, and where the knot is, and who's to blame, and who's to suffer.

And I tell you he knows there 'll never be any way but his way to unsnarl us all.

" Folks may make laws, but laws won't do it. Kings and congresses may put their heads together, but they 'll have their trouble for nothing. Governments and churches may finger us over, but we 'll only snarl the more.

" Rich and poor, big or little, there 's no way under heaven for us to get out of our twist, but Christ's way.

" O you men and women, and you girls and boys, look in your own hearts and see what way that is. That way is in the heart. I can't see it. I can't touch it. I can't mark it and line it for you. Look. Mind that you don't look at the rich folks' ways ! Mind that you don't stop to say, It 's their way to do this, and that, and the other, that they 'd never do nor think on. Perhaps it is. But that 's none of your business, when the Lord Jesus Christ the Son of God Almighty does you the favor to ask for *you*, and *your* heart, and *your* ways, to gather 'em up into his poor cut hands and hold them, and to bow his poor hurt face down over them and bless them !

"O you men and women, and you boys and girls, Christ's way is a patient way, it is a pure way, it is a way that cares more for another world than for this one, and more to be holy than to be happy, and more for other folks than for itself. It 's a long way and a winding way, but it 's a good way and a true way, and there 's comfort in it, and there 's joy at the end of it, and there 's *Christ all over it*, and I pray God to lead you in it, every one, forever.

"Christ in heaven!" said Sip then, bending her lighted, dark face, "thou hast been Christ on earth. That helps us. That makes us brave to hunt for thee. We are poor folks, Christ, and we 've got a load of poor folks' sorrows, and of poor folks' foolishness, and of poor folks' fears, and of poor folks' wickedness, and we 've got nowheres else to take it. Here it is. Lord Christ, we seem to feel as if it belonged to thee. We seem to feel as if we was thy folks. We seem to know that thou dost understand us, someways, better than the most of people. Be our Saviour, Lord Christ, for thine own name's sake."

Miss Kelso and Mrs. Hayle left the little

preacher still speaking God's words — and Catty's, and stole away before the breaking up of her audience. They walked in silence for a few minutes up the street.

" They listened to her," said Fly then, musingly. " On the whole, I don't know that I wonder. They looked as if they needed it,"

" There are few things that they do not need," said Perley, quietly. " We do not quite understand that, I think, — we who never need. It is a hungry world, Fly."

" Yes ? " said Fly, placidly perplexed ; " I don't know much about the world, Perley."

Perley was silent. She was wondering what good it would do — either the world or Fly — if she did.

" Kenna Van Doozle was asking the other day," said Fly, suddenly, " whether you still went about among these people at all hours of the day and evening, as you used, alone. I should be so timid, Perley ! And then, do you always find it quite proper ? "

" I have no reason to feel afraid of my friends in Five Falls at any hour," said Miss Kelso, reservedly. There seemed such a gulf between her and this pretty, good-natured little lady. Proper ! Why try to pass the impassable ? Fly might stay where she was.

" And yet," sighed Mrs. Maverick Hayle, " this dreary work seems to suit you through and through. That is what troubles me about it."

Perley Kelso's healthy, happy face took the quiver of a smile. The fine, rare face ! The womanly, wonderful face ! Fly was right. It was a " suited " face. It begged for nothing. It was opulent and warm. Life brimmed over at it.

Stephen Garrick, on the opposite side of the road, climbed the hill alone. It was a late November day ; a day of cleared heavens and bared trees. Yet he looked about for bright maples, and felt as if he walked under a sealed sky, and in an unreal light of dying leaves.

THE END.

Cambridge : Electrotyped and Printed by Welch, Bigelow, & Co.

"The Tenth of January"

THE TENTH OF JANUARY.

THE city of Lawrence is unique in its way.

For simooms that scorch you and tempests that freeze; for sand-heaps and sand-hillocks and sand-roads; for men digging sand, for women shaking off sand, for minute boys crawling in sand; for sand in the church-slips and the gingerbread-windows, for sand in your eyes, your nose, your mouth, down your neck, up your sleeves, under your *chignon*, down your throat; for unexpected corners where tornadoes lie in wait; for "bleak, uncomforted" sidewalks, where they chase you, dog you, confront you, strangle you, twist you, blind you, turn your umbrella wrong side out; for "dimmykhrats" and bad ice-cream; for unutterable circus-bills and religious tea-parties; for uncleared ruins, and mills that spring up in a night; for jaded faces and busy feet; for an air of youth and incompleteness at which you laugh, and a consciousness of growth and greatness which you respect, — it —

I believe, when I commenced that sentence, I intended to say that it would be difficult to find Lawrence's equal.

Of the twenty-five thousand souls who inhabit that city, ten thousand are operatives in the factories. Of these ten thousand two thirds are girls.

These pages are written as one sets a bit of marble to mark a mound. I linger over them as we linger beside the grave of one who sleeps well ; half sadly, half gladly, — more gladly than sadly, — but hushed.

The time to see Lawrence is when the mills open or close. So languidly the dull-colored, inexpectant crowd wind in ! So briskly they come bounding out ! Factory faces have a look of their own, — not only their common dinginess, and a general air of being in a hurry to find the wash-bowl, but an appearance of restlessness, — often of envious restlessness, not habitual in most departments of " healthy labor." Watch them closely : you can read their histories at a venture. A widow this, in the dusty black, with she can scarcely remember how many mouths to feed at home. Worse than widowed that one : she has put her baby out to board, — and humane people know what that means, — to keep the little thing beyond its besotted father's reach. There is a group who have "just come over." A child's face here, old before its time. That girl — she climbs five flights of stairs twice a day — will climb no more stairs for herself or another by the time the clover-leaves are green. " The best thing about one's grave is that it will be level," she was heard once to say. Somebody muses a little here, — she is to be married this winter. There is a face just behind her whose fixed eyes repel and attract you ; there may be more love than guilt in them, more despair than either.

Had you stood in some unobserved corner of Essex Street, at four o'clock one Saturday afternoon towards the last of November, 1859, watching the impatient stream pour out of the Pemberton Mill, eager with a saddening eagerness for its few holiday hours, you would have observed one girl who did not bound.

She was slightly built, and undersized ; her neck and shoulders were closely muffled, though the day was mild ; she wore a faded scarlet hood which heightened the pallor of what must at best have been a pallid face. It was a sickly face, shaded off with purple shadows, but with a certain wiry nervous strength about the muscles of the mouth and chin : it would have been a womanly, pleasant mouth, had it not been crossed by a white scar, which attracted more of one's attention than either the womanliness or pleasantness. Her eyes had light long lashes, and shone through them steadily.

You would have noticed as well, had you been used to analyzing crowds, another face, — the two were side by side, — dimpled with pink and white flushes, and framed with bright black hair. One would laugh at this girl and love her, scold her and pity her, caress her and pray for her, — then forget her perhaps.

The girls from behind called after her : " Del ! Del Ivory ! look over there ! "

Pretty Del turned her head. She had just flung a smile at a young clerk who was petting his mustache in a shop-window, and the smile lingered.

One of the factory boys was walking alone across the Common in his factory clothes.

" Why, there 's Dick ! Sene, do you see ? "

Sene's scarred mouth moved slightly, but she made no reply. She had seen him five minutes ago.

One never knows exactly whether to laugh or cry over them, catching their chatter as they file past the show-windows of the long, showy street.

" Look a' that pink silk with the figures on it ! "

" I 've seen them as is betther nor that in the ould counthree. — Patsy Malorrn, let alon' hangin' onto the shawl of me ! "

" That 's Mary Foster getting out of that carriage with the two white horses, — she that lives in the brown house with the cupilo."

" Look at her dress trailin' after her. I 'd like my dresses trailin' after me."

" Well, may they be good, — these rich folks ! "

" That 's so. I 'd be good if I was rich ; would n't you, Moll ? "

" You 'd keep growing wilder than ever, if you went to hell, Meg Match : yes you would, because my teacher said so."

" So, then, he would n't marry her, after all ; and she — "

" Going to the circus to-night, Bess ? "

" I can't help crying, Jenny. You don't *know* how my head aches ! It aches, and it aches, and it seems as if it would never stop aching. I wish — I wish I was dead, Jenny ! "

They separated at last, going each her own way, — pretty Del Ivory to her boarding-place by the canal, her companion walking home alone.

This girl, Asenath Martyn, when left to herself, fell into a contented dream not common to girls who have reached her age, — especially girls who have seen the phases of life which she had seen. Yet few of the faces in the streets that led her home were more gravely lined. She puzzled one at the first glance, and at the second. An artist, meeting her musing on a canal-bridge one day, went home and painted a May-flower budding in February.

It was a damp, unwholesome place, the street in which she lived, cut short by a broken fence, a sudden steep, and the water ; filled with children, — they ran from the gutters after her, as she passed, — and filled to the brim ; it tipped now and then, like an over-full soup-plate, and spilled out two or three through the break in the fence.

Down in the corner, sharp upon the water, the east-winds broke about a little yellow house, where no children played ; an old man's face watched at a window, and a nasturtium-vine crawled in the garden. The broken panes of glass about the place were well mended, and a clever little gate, extemporized from a

wild grape-vine, swung at the entrance. It was not
an old man's work.

Asenath went in with expectant eyes; they took in
the room at a glance, and fell.

" Dick has n't come, father ? "

" Come and gone child; did n't want any supper,
he said. Your 're an hour before time, Senath."

" Yes. Did n't want any supper, you say ? I don't
see why not."

" No more do I, but it 's none of our concern as I
knows on; very like the pickles hurt him for dinner;
Dick never had an o'er-strong stomach, as you might
say. But you don't tell me how it m' happen you 're
let out at four o'clock, Senath," half complaining.

" O, something broke in the machinery, father;
you know you would n't understand if I told you
what."

He looked up from his bench, — he cobbled shoes
there in the corner on his strongest days, — and after
her as she turned quickly away and up stairs to change
her dress. She was never exactly cross with her
father; but her words rang impatiently sometimes.

She came down presently, transformed, as only
factory-girls are transformed, by the simple little toilet
she had been making; her thin, soft hair knotted
smoothly, the tips of her fingers rosy from the water,
her pale neck well toned by her gray stuff dress and
cape ; — Asenath always wore a cape: there was one
of crimson flannel, with a hood, that she had meant

to wear to-night ; she had thought about it coming home from the mill ; she was apt to wear it on Saturdays and Sundays ; Dick had more time at home. Going up stairs to-night, she had thrown it away into a drawer, and shut the drawer with a snap ; then opened it softly, and cried a little ; but she had not taken it out.

As she moved silently about the room, setting the supper-table for two, crossing and recrossing the broad belt of sunlight that fell upon the floor, it was easy to read the sad story of the little hooded capes.

They might have been graceful shoulders. The hand which had scarred her face had rounded and bent them, — her own mother's hand.

Of a bottle always on the shelf ; of brutal scowls where smiles should be ; of days when she wandered dinnerless and supperless in the streets through loathing of her home ; of nights when she sat out in the snow-drifts through terror of her home ; of a broken jug one day, a blow, a fall, then numbness, and the silence of the grave, — she had her distant memories ; of waking on a sunny afternoon, in bed, with a little cracked glass upon the opposite wall ; of creeping out and up to it in her night-dress ; of the ghastly twisted thing that looked back at her. Through the open window she heard the children laughing and leaping in the sweet summer air. She crawled into bed and shut her eyes. She remembered stealing out at last, after many days, to the grocery round the corner for

3   D

a pound of coffee. " Humpback! humpback!" cried the children, — the very children who could leap and laugh.

One day she and little Del Ivory made mud-houses after school.

" I 'm going to have a house of my own, when I 'm grown up," said pretty Del; "I shall have a red carpet and some curtains; my husband will buy me a piano."

" So will mine, I guess," said Sene, simply.

" *Yours!*" Del shook back her curls; "who do you suppose would ever marry *you?*"

One night there was a knocking at the door, and a hideous, sodden thing borne in upon a plank. The crowded street, tired of tipping out little children, had tipped her mother staggering through the broken fence. At the funeral she heard some one say, "How glad Sene must be!"

Since that, life had meant three things, — her father, the mills, and Richard Cross.

" You 're a bit put out that the young fellow did n't stay to supper, — eh, Senath?" the old man said, laying down his boot.

" Put out! Why should I be? His time is his own. It 's likely to be the Union that took him out, — such a fine day for the Union! I 'm sure I never expected him to go to walk with me *every* Saturday afternoon. I 'm not a fool to tie him up to the notions of a crippled girl. Supper is ready, father."

But her voice rasped bitterly. Life's pleasures were so new and late and important to her, poor thing! It went hard to miss the least of them. Very happy people will not understand exactly how hard.

Old Martyn took off his leather apron with a troubled face, and, as he passed his daughter, gently laid his tremulous, stained hand upon her head. He felt her least uneasiness, it would seem, as a chameleon feels a cloud upon the sun.

She turned her face softly and kissed him. But she did not smile.

She had planned a little for this holiday supper; saving three mellow-cheeked Louise Bonnes — expensive pears just then — to add to their bread and molasses. She brought them out from the closet, and watched her father eat them.

" Going out again Senath ? " he asked, seeing that she went for her hat and shawl, " and not a mouthful have you eaten ! Find your old father dull company hey ? Well, well ! "

She said something about needing the air; the mill was hot; she should soon be back; she spoke tenderly and she spoke truly, but she went out into the windy sunset with her little trouble, and forgot him. The old man, left alone, sat for a while with his head sunk upon his breast. She was all he had in the world, — this one little crippled girl that the world had dealt hardly with. She loved him; but he was not, probably would never be, to her exactly what she was to

him. Usually he forgot this. Sometimes he quite
understood it, as to-night.

Asenath, with the purpose only of avoiding Dick,
and of finding a still spot where she might think her
thoughts undisturbed, wandered away over the eastern
bridge, and down to the river's brink. It was a moody
place ; such a one as only apathetic or healthy natures
(I wonder if that is tautology !) can healthfully yield
to. The bank sloped steeply ; a fringe of stunted
aspens and willows sprang from the frozen sand : it
was a sickening, airless place in summer, — it was
damp and desolate now. There was a sluggish wash
of water under foot, and a stretch of dreary flats behind. Belated locomotives shrieked to each other
across the river, and the wind bore down the current
the roar and rage of the dam. Shadows werè beginning to skulk under the huge brown bridge. The
silent mills stared up and down and over the streams
with a blank, unvarying stare. An oriflamme of scarlet
burned in the west, flickered dully in the dirty, curd-
ling water, flared against the windows of the Pemberton, which quivered and dripped, Asenath thought, as
if with blood.

She sat down on a gray stone, wrapped in her gray
shawl, curtained about by the aspens from the eye of
passers on the bridge. She had a fancy for this place
when things went ill with her. She had always
borne her troubles alone, but she must be alone to
bear them.

She knew very well that she was tired and nervous that afternoon, and that, if she could reason quietly about this little neglect of Dick's, it would cease to annoy her. Indeed, why should she be annoyed? Had he not done everything for her, been everything to her, for two long, sweet years? She dropped her head with a shy smile. She was never tired of living over these two years. She took positive pleasure in recalling the wretchedness in which they found her, for the sake of their dear relief. Many a time, sitting with her happy face hidden in his arms, she had laughed softly, to remember the day on which he came to her. It was at twilight, and she was tired. Her reels had troubled her all the afternoon; the overseer was cross; the day was hot and long. Somebody on the way home had said in passing her: "Look at that girl! I'd kill myself if I looked like that": it was in a whisper, but she heard it. All life looked hot and long; the reels would always be out of order; the overseer would never be kind. Her temples would always throb, and her back would ache. People would always say, "Look at that girl!"

"Can you direct me to — " She looked up; she had been sitting on the door-step with her face in her hands. Dick stood there with his cap off. He forgot that he was to inquire the way to Newbury Street, when he saw the tears on her shrunken cheeks. Dick could never bear to see a woman suffer.

"I would n't cry," he said simply, sitting down

beside her. Telling a girl not to cry is an infallible
recipe for keeping her at it. What could the child
do, but sob as if her heart would break? Of course
he had the whole story in ten minutes, she his in another ten. It was common and short enough: — a
"Down-East" boy, fresh from his father's farm,
hunting for work and board, — a bit homesick here in
the strange, unhomelike city, it might be, and glad of
some one to say so to. .

What more natural than that, when her father came
out and was pleased with the lad, there should be no
more talk of Newbury Street; that the little yellow
house should become his home ; that he should swing
the fantastic gate, and plant the nasturtiums ; that his
life should grow to be one with hers and the old man's,
his future and theirs unite unconsciously ?

She remembered — it was not exactly pleasant,
somehow, to remember it to-night — just the look of
his face when they came into the house that summer
evening, and he for the first time saw what she was,
her cape having fallen off, in the full lamplight. His
kindly blue eyes widened with shocked surprise, and
fell ; when he raised them, a pity like a mother's had
crept into them ; it broadened and brightened as time
slid by, but it never left them.

So you see, after that, life unfolded in a burst of
little surprises for Asenath. If she came home very
tired, some one said, "I am sorry." If she wore a
pink ribbon, she heard a whisper, "It suits you." If

she sang a little song, she knew that somebody listened.

"I did not know the world was like this!" cried the girl.

After a time there came a night that he chanced to be out late, — they had planned an arithmetic lesson together, which he had forgotten, — and she sat grieving by the kitchen fire.

"You missed me so much then?" he said regretfully, standing with his hand upon her chair. She was trying to shell some corn; she dropped the pan, and the yellow kernels rolled away on the floor.

"What should I have if I did n't have you?" she said, and caught her breath.

The young man paced to the window and back again. The firelight touched her shoulders, and the sad, white scar.

"You shall have me always, Asenath," he made answer. He took her face within his hands and kissed it; and so they shelled the corn together, and nothing more was said about it.

He had spoken this last spring of their marriage; but the girl, like all girls, was shyly silent, and he had not urged it.

Asenath started from her pleasant dreaming just as the oriflamme was furling into gray, suddenly conscious that she was not alone. Below her, quite on the brink of the water, a girl was sitting, — a girl with a bright plaid shawl, and a nodding red feather in her hat. Her head was bent, and her hair fell against a profile cut in pink-and-white.

" Del is too pretty to be here alone so late," thought Asenath, smiling tenderly. Good-natured Del was kind to her in a certain way, and she rather loved the girl. She rose to speak to her, but concluded, on a second glance through the aspens, that Miss Ivory was quite able to take care of herself.

Del was sitting on an old log that jutted into the stream, dabbling in the water with the tips of her feet. (Had she lived on The Avenue she could not have been more particular about her shoemaker.) Some one — it was too dark to see distinctly — stood beside her, his eyes upon her face. Asenath could hear nothing, but she needed to hear nothing to know how the young fellow's eyes drank in the co-quettish picture. Besides, it was an old story. Del counted her rejected lovers by the score.

" It 's no wonder," she thought in her honest way, standing still to watch them with a sense of puzzled pleasure much like that with which she watched the print-windows, — " it 's no wonder they love her. I 'd love her if I was a man : so pretty ! so pretty ! She 's just good for nothing, Del is ; — would let the kitchen fire go out, and would n't mend the baby's aprons ; but I 'd love her all the same ; marry her, probably, and be sorry all my life."

Pretty Del ! Poor Del ! Asenath wondered whether she wished that she were like her ; she could not quite make out ; it would be pleasant to sit on a log and look like that ; it would be more pleasant to be watched as Del was watched just now : it struck her suddenly that Dick had never looked like this at her.

The hum of their voices ceased while she stood there with her eyes upon them ; Del turned her head away with a sudden movement, and the young man left her, apparently without bow or farewell, sprang up the bank at a bound, and crushed the undergrowth with quick, uneasy strides.

Asenath, with some vague idea that it would not be honorable to see his face, — poor fellow ! — shrank back into the aspens and the shadow.

He towered tall in the twilight as he passed her, and a dull, umber gleam, the last of the sunset, struck him from the west.

Struck it out into her sight, — the haggard struggling face, — Richard Cross's face.

Of course you knew it from the beginning, but remember that the girl did not.   She might have known it, perhaps, but she had not.

Asenath stood up, sat down again.

She had a distinct consciousness, for the moment, of seeing herself crouched down there under the aspens and the shadow, a humpbacked white creature, with distorted face and wide eyes.   She remembered a picture she had somewhere seen of a little chattering goblin in a graveyard, and was struck with the resemblance. Distinctly, too, she heard herself saying, with a laugh,

3 *

she thought, " I might have known it ; I might have known."

Then the blood came through her heart with a hot rush, and she saw Del on the log, smoothing the red feather of her hat. She heard a man's step, too, that rang over the bridge, passed the toll-house, grew faint, grew fainter, died in the sand by the Everett Mill.

Richard's face ! Richard's face, looking — God help her ! — as it had never looked at her ; struggling — God pity him ! — as it had never struggled for her.

She shut her hands. into each other, and sat still a little while. A faint hope came to her then perhaps, after all ; her face lightened grayly, and she crept down the bank to Del.

" I won't be a fool," she said, " I 'll make sure, — I 'll make as sure as death."

" Well, where did *you* drop down from, Sene ? " said Del, with a guilty start.

" From over the bridge, to be sure. Did you think I swam, or flew, or blew ? "

" You came on me so sudden ! " said Del, petulantly ; " you nearly frightened the wits out of me. You did n't meet anybody on the bridge ? " with a quick look.

" Let me see." Asenath considered gravely. " There was one small boy making faces, and two — no, three — dogs, I believe ; that was all."

" Oh ! "

Del looked relieved, but fell silent.

" You 're sober, Del. Been sending off a lover, as usual ? "

" I don't know anything about its being usual," answered Del, in an aggrieved, coquettish way, " but there 's been somebody here that liked me well enough."

" You like him, maybe ? It 's time you liked somebody, Del."

Del curled the red feather about her fingers, and put her hat on over her eyes, then a little cry broke from her, half sob, half anger.

" I might, perhaps, — I don't know. He 's good. I think he 'd let me have a parlor and a door-bell. But he 's going to marry somebody else, you see. I sha' n't tell you his name, so you need n't ask."

Asenath looked out straight upon the water. A dead leaf that had been caught in an eddy attracted her attention ; it tossed about for a minute, then a tiny whirlpool sucked it down.

" I was n't going to ask ; it 's nothing to me, of course. He does n't care for her then, — this other girl ? "

" Not so much as he does for me. He did n't mean to tell me, but he said that I — that I looked so — pretty, it came right out. But there ! I must n't tell you any more."

Del began to be frightened ; she looked up sideways at Asenath's quiet face. " I won't say another word," and so chattered on, growing a little cross ; Asenath

need not look so still, and sure of herself, — a mere
humpbacked fright!

"He 'll never break his engagement, not even for
me; he 's sorry for her, and all that. I think it 's too
bad. He 's handsome. He makes me feel like saying
my prayers, too, he 's so good! Besides, I want to be
married. I hate the mill. I hate to work. I 'd
rather be taken care of, — a sight rather. I feel bad
enough about it to cry."

Two tears rolled over her cheeks, and fell on the
soft plaid shawl. Del wiped them away carefully
with her rounded fingers.

Asenath turned and looked at this Del Ivory long
and steadily through the dusk. The pretty, shallow
thing! The worthless, bewildering thing!

A fierce contempt for her pink-and-white, and tears
and eyelashes and attitudes, came upon her; then a
sudden sickening jealousy that turned her faint where
she sat.

What did God mean, — Asenath believed in God,
having so little else to believe in, — what did he mean,
when he had blessed the girl all her happy life with
such wealth of beauty, by filling her careless hands
with this one best, last gift? Why, the child could
not hold such golden love! She would throw it away
by and by. What a waste it was!

Not that she had these words for her thought, but
she had the thought distinctly through her dizzy pain.

"So there 's nothing to do about it," said Del, pinning her shawl. "We can't have anything to say to each other, — unless anybody should die, or anything ; and of course I 'm not wicked enough to think of *that*. — Sene ! Sene ! what are you doing ? "

Sene had risen slowly, stood upon the log, caught at an aspen-top, and swung out with it its whole length above the water. The slight tree writhed and quivered about the roots. Sene looked down and moved her marred lips without sound.

Del screamed and wrung her hands. It was an ugly sight !

" O don't, Sene, *don't !* You 'll drown yourself ! you will be drowned ! you will be — O, what a start you gave me ! What *were* you doing, Senath Martyn ? "

Sene swung slowly back, and sat down.

" Amusing myself a little ; — well, unless somebody died, you said ? But I believe I won't talk any more to-night. My head aches. Go home, Del."

Del muttered a weak protest at leaving her there alone ; but, with her bright face clouded and uncomfortable, went.

Asenath turned her head to listen for the last rustle of her dress, then folded her arms, and, with her eyes upon the sluggish current, sat still.

An hour and a half later, an Andover farmer, driving home across the bridge, observed on the river's edge — a shadow cut within a shadow — the outline of a woman's figure, sitting perfectly still with folded arms. He reined up and looked down; but it sat quite still.

"Hallo there!" he called; "you'll fall in if you don't look out!" for the wind was strong, and it blew against the figure; but it did not move nor make reply. The Andover farmer looked over his shoulder with the sudden recollection of a ghost-story which he had charged his grandchildren not to believe last week, cracked his whip, and rumbled on.

Asenath began to understand by and by that she was cold, so climbed the bank, made her way over the windy flats, the railroad, and the western bridge confusedly with an idea of going home. She turned aside by the toll-gate. The keeper came out to see what she was doing, but she kept out of his sight behind the great willow and his little blue house, — the blue house with the green blinds and red moulding. The dam thundered that night, the wind and the water being high. She made her way up above it, and looked in. She had never seen it so black and smooth there. As she listened to the roar, she remembered something that she had read — was it in the Bible or the Ledger? — about seven thunders uttering their voices.

"He's sorry for her, and all that," they said.

A dead bough shot down the current while she stood there, went over and down, and out of sight, throwing up its little branches like helpless hands.

It fell in with a thought of Asenath's, perhaps; at

any rate she did not like the looks of it, and went home.

Over the bridge, and the canal, and the lighted streets, the falls called after her: " He 's sorry for her, and all that." The curtain was drawn aside when she came home, and she saw her father through the window, sitting alone, with his gray head bent.

It occurred to her that she had often left him alone, — poor old father! It occurred to her, also, that she understood now what it was to be alone. Had she forgotten him in these two comforted, companioned years?

She came in weakly, and looked about.

" Dick 's in, and gone to bed," said the old man, answering her look. " You 're tired, Senath."

" I am tired, father."

She sunk upon the floor, — the heat of the room made her a little faint, — and laid her head upon his knee ; oddly enough, she noticed that the patch on it had given way, — wondered how many days it had been so, — whether he had felt ragged and neglected while she was busy about that blue neck-tie for Dick. She put her hand up and smoothed the corners of the rent.

" You shall be mended up to-morrow, poor father ! "

He smiled, pleased like a child to be remembered. She looked up at him, — at his gray hair and shrivelled face, at his blackened hands and bent shoulders, and dusty, ill-kept coat. What would it be like, if the days brought her nothing but him ?

" Something 's the matter with my little gal ? Tell father, can't ye ? "

Her face flushed hot, as if she had done him wrong. She crept up into his arms, and put her hands behind his rough old neck.

" Would you kiss me, father ? You don't think I 'm too ugly to kiss, maybe, — you ? "

She felt better after that. She had not gone to sleep now for many a night unkissed; it had seemed hard at first.

When she had gone half-way up stairs, Dick came to the door of his room on the first floor, and called her. He held the little kerosene lamp over his head; his face was grave and pale.

" I have n't said good night, Sene."

She made no reply.

" Asenath, good night."

She stayed her steps upon the stairs without turning her head. Her father had kissed her to-night. Was not that enough ?

" Why, Sene, what 's the matter with you ? "

Dick mounted the stairs, and touched his lips to her forehead with a gently compassionate smile.

She fled from him with a cry like the cry of a suffocated creature, shut her door, and locked it with a ringing clang.

" She 's walked too far, and got a little nervous," said Dick, screwing up his lamp ; " poor thing ! "

Then he went into his room to look at Del's photograph awhile before he burned it up ; for he meant to burn it up.

Asenath, when she had locked her door, put her lamp before the looking-glass and tore off her gray cape ; tore it off so savagely that the button snapped and rolled away, — two little crystal semicircles like tears upon the floor.

There was no collar about the neck of her dress, and this heightened the plainness and the pallor of her face. She shrank instinctively at the first sight of herself, and opened the drawer where the crimson cape was folded, but shut it resolutely.

" I 'll see the worst of it," she said with pinched lips. She turned herself about and about before the glass, letting the cruel light gloat over her shoulders, letting the sickly shadows grow purple on her face. Then she put her elbows on the table and her chin into her hands, and so, for a motionless half-hour, studied the unrounded, uncolored, unlightened face that stared back at her ; her eyes darkening at its eyes, her hair touching its hair, her breath dimming the outline of its repulsive mouth.

By and by she dropped her head into her hands. The poor, mistaken face ! She felt as if she would like to blot it out of the world, as her tears used to blot out the wrong sums upon her slate. It had been so happy ! But he was sorry for it, and all that. Why did a good God make such faces ?

She slipped upon her knees, bewildered.

" He *can't* mean any harm nohow," she said, speaking fast, and knelt there and said it over till she felt sure of it.

Then she thought of Del once more, — of her colors and sinuous springs, and little cries and chatter.

After a time she found that she was growing faint, and so stole down into the kitchen for some food. She stayed a minute to warm her feet. The fire was red and the clock was ticking. It seemed to her home-like and comfortable, and she seemed to herself very homeless and lonely; so she sat down on the floor, with her head in a chair, and cried as hard as she ought to have done four hours ago.

She climbed into bed about one o'clock, having decided, in a dull way, to give Dick up to-morrow.

But when to-morrow came he was up with a bright face, and built the kitchen fire for her, and brought in all the water, and helped her fry the potatoes, and whistled a little about the house, and worried at her paleness, and so she said nothing about it.

" I 'll wait till night," she planned, making ready for the mill.

" O, I can't !" she cried at night. So other mornings came, and other nights.

I am quite aware that, according to all romantic precedents, this conduct was preposterous in Asenath. Floracita, in the novel, never so far forgets the whole duty of a heroine as to struggle, waver, doubt, delay. It is proud and proper to free the young fellow;

proudly and properly she frees him; "suffers in silence "— till she marries another man; and (having had a convenient opportunity to refuse the original lover) overwhelms the reflective reader with a sense of poetic justice and the eternal fitness of things.

But I am not writing a novel, and, as the biographer of this simple factory girl, am offered few advantages.

Asenath was no heroine, you see. Such heroic elements as were in her — none could tell exactly what they were, or whether there were any: she was one of those people in whom it is easy to be quite mistaken; — her life had not been one to develop. She might have a certain pride of her own, under given circumstances; but plants grown in a cellar will turn to the sun at any cost; how could she go back into her dark?

As for the other man to marry, he was out of the question. Then, none love with the tenacity of the unhappy; no life is so lavish of itself as the denied life: to him that hath not shall be given, — and Asenath loved this Richard Cross.

It might be altogether the grand and suitable thing to say to him, " I will not be your wife." It might be that she would thus regain a strong shade of lost self-respect. It might be that she would make him happy, and give pleasure to Del. It might be that the two young people would be her " friends," and love her in a way.

But all this meant that Dick must go out of her life.

Practically, she must make up her mind to build the fires, and pump the water, and mend the windows alone. In dreary fact, he would not listen when she sung ; would not say, " You are tired, Sene " ; would never kiss away an undried tear. There would be nobody to notice the crimson cape, nobody to make blue neck-ties for; none for whom to save the Bonnes de Jersey, or to take sweet, tired steps, or make dear, dreamy plans. To be sure, there was her father ; but fathers do not count for much in a time like this on which Sene had fallen.

That Del Ivy was — Del Ivory, added intricacies to the question. It was a very unpoetic but undoubted fact that Asenath could in no way so insure Dick's unhappiness as to pave the way to his marriage with the woman whom he loved. There would be a few merry months, then slow worry and disappointment ; pretty Del accepted at last, not as the crown of his young life, but as its silent burden and misery. Poor Dick ! good Dick ! Who deserved more wealth of wifely sacrifice ? Asenath, thinking this, crimsoned with pain and shame. A streak of good common sense in the girl told her — though she half scorned herself for the conviction — that even a crippled woman who should bear all things and hope all things for his sake might blot out the memory of this rounded Del ; that, no matter what the motive with which he married her, he would end by loving his wife like other people.

She watched him sometimes in the evenings, as he turned his kind eyes after her over the library book which he was reading.

" I know I could make him happy ! I *know* I could ! " she muttered fiercely to herself.

November blew into December, December congealed into January, while she kept her silence. Dick, in his honorable heart, seeing that she suffered, wearied himself with plans to make her eyes shine ; brought her two pails of water instead of one, never forgot the fire, helped her home from the mill. She saw him meet Del Ivory once upon Essex Street with a grave and silent bow ; he never spoke with her now. He meant to pay the debt he owed her down to the uttermost farthing ; that grew plain. Did she try to speak her wretched secret, he suffocated her with kindness, struck her dumb with tender words.

She used to analyze her life in those days, considering what it would be without him. To be up by half past five o'clock in the chill of all the winter mornings, to build the fire and cook the breakfast and sweep the floor, to hurry away, faint and weak, over the raw, slippery streets, to climb at half past six the endless stairs and stand at the endless loom, and hear the endless wheels go buzzing round, to sicken in the oily smells, and deafen at the remorseless noise, and weary of the rough girl swearing at the other end of the pass ; to eat her cold dinner from a little cold tin pail out on the stairs in the three-quarters-of-an-hour recess ; to come exhausted home at half past six at night, and get the supper, and brush up about the shoemaker's bench, and be too weak to eat; to sit with aching shoulders and make the button-holes of her best dress, or darn her father's stockings, till nine o'clock; to hear no bounding step or cheery whistle about the house; to creep into bed and lie there trying not to think, and wishing that so she might creep into her grave, — this not for one winter, but for all the winters, — how should *you* like it, you young girls, with whom time runs like a story?

The very fact that her employers dealt honorably by her; that she was fairly paid, and promptly, for her wearing toil; that the limit of endurance was consulted in the temperature of the room, and her need of rest in an occasional holiday, — perhaps, after all, in the mood she was in, did not make this factory life more easy. She would have found it rather a relief to have somebody to complain of, — wherein she was like the rest of us, I fancy.

But at last there came a day — it chanced to be the ninth of January — when Asenath went away alone at noon, and sat where Merrimack sung his songs to her. She hid her face upon her knees, and listened and thought her own thoughts, till they and the slow torment of the winter seemed greater than she could bear. So, passing her hands confusedly over her forehead, she said at last aloud, "That 's what God means, Asenath Martyn!" and went back to work with a purpose in her eyes.

She "asked out" a little earlier than usual, and went slowly home. Dick was there before her; he had been taking a half-holiday. He had made the tea and toasted the bread for a little surprise. He came up and said, "Why, Sene, your hands are cold!" and warmed them for her in his own.

After tea she asked him, would he walk out with her for a little while? and he in wonder went.

The streets were brightly lighted, and the moon was up. The ice cracked crisp under their feet. Sleighs, with two riders in each, shot merrily by. People were laughing in groups before the shop-windows. In the glare of a jeweller's counter somebody was buying a wedding-ring, and a girl with red cheeks was looking hard the other way.

"Let's get away," said Asenath, — "get away from here!"

They chose by tacit consent that favorite road of hers over the eastern bridge. Their steps had a hollow, lonely ring on the frosted wood; she was glad when the softness of the snow in the road received them. She looked back once at the water, wrinkled into thin ice on the edge for a foot or two, then open and black and still.

"What are you doing?" asked Dick. She said that she was wondering how cold it was, and Dick laughed at her.

They strolled on in silence for perhaps a mile of the desolate road.

" Well, this is social ! " said Dick at length ; " how much farther do you want to go? I believe you 'd walk to Reading if nobody stopped you ! "

She was taking slow, regular steps like an automaton, and looking straight before her.

" How much farther ? Oh ! " She stopped and looked about her.

A wide young forest spread away at their feet, to the right and to the left. There was ice on the tiny oaks and miniature pines ; it glittered sharply under the moon ; the light upon the snow was blue ; cold roads wound away through it, deserted ; little piles of dead leaves shivered ; a fine keen spray ran along the tops of the drifts ; inky shadows lurked and dodged about the undergrowth ; in the broad spaces the snow glared ; the lighted mills, a zone of fire, blazed from east to west ; the skies were bare, and the wind was up, and Merrimack in the distance chanted solemnly.

" Dick," said Asenath, " this is a dreadful place ! Take me home."

But when he would have turned, she held him back with a sudden cry, and stood still.

" I meant to tell you — I meant to say — Dick ! I was going to say — "

But she did not say it.   She opened her lips to speak once and again, but no sound came from them.

" Sene ! why, Sene, what ails you ? "

He turned, and took her in his arms.

" Poor Sene ! "

He kissed her, feeling sorry for her unknown trouble. He wondered why she sobbed. He kissed her again. She broke from him, and away with a great bound upon the snow.

" You make it so hard ! You 've no right to make it so hard ! It ain't as if you loved me, Dick ! I know I 'm not like other girls ! Go home and let me be ! "

But Dick drew her arm through his, and led her gravely away. " I like you well enough, Asenath," he said, with that motherly pity in his eyes; " I 've always liked you. So don't let us have any more of this."

So Asenath said nothing more.

The sleek black river beckoned to her across the snow as they went home. A thought came to her as she passed the bridge, — it is a curious study what wicked thoughts will come to good people ! — she found herself considering the advisability of leaping the low brown parapet; and if it would not be like Dick to go over after her; if there would be a chance for them, even should he swim from the banks; how soon the icy current would paralyze him; how sweet it would be to chill to death there in his arms; how all this wavering and pain would be over; how Del would look when they dragged them out down below the machine-shop !

" Sene, are you cold ? " asked puzzled Dick. She was warmly wrapped in her little squirrel furs ; but he

4

felt her quivering upon his arm, like one in an ague, all the way home.

About eleven o'clock that night her father waked from an exciting dream concerning the best method of blacking patent-leather; Sene stood beside his bed with her gray shawl thrown over her night-dress.

" Father, suppose some time there should be only you and me — "

" Well, well, Sene," said the old man sleepily, — " very well."

" I 'd try to be a good girl! Could you love me enough to make up ? "

He told her indistinctly that she always was a good girl; she never had a whipping from the day her mother died. She turned away impatiently; then cried out and fell upon her knees.

" Father, father! I 'm in a great trouble. I have n't got any mother, any friend, anybody. Nobody helps me! Nobody knows. I 've been thinking such things — O, such wicked things — up in my room ! Then I got afraid of myself. You 're good. You love me. I want you to put your hand on my head and say, ' God bless you, child, and show you how.' "

Bewildered, he put his hand upon her unbound hair, and said: " God bless you, child, and show you how ! "

Asenath looked at the old withered hand a moment, as it lay beside her on the bed, kissed it, and went away.

There was a scarlet sunrise the next morning. A pale pink flush stole through a hole in the curtain, and fell across Asenath's sleeping face, and lay there like a crown. It woke her, and she threw on her dress, and sat down for a while on the window-sill, to watch the coming-on of the day.

The silent city steeped and bathed itself in rose-tints; the river ran red, and the snow crimsoned on the distant New Hampshire hills; Pemberton, mute and cold, frowned across the disk of the climbing sun, and dripped, as she had seen it drip before, with blood.

The day broke softly, the snow melted, the wind blew warm from the river. The factory-bell chimed cheerily, and a few sleepers, in safe, luxurious beds, were wakened by hearing the girls sing on their way to work.

Asenath came down with a quiet face. In her communing with the sunrise helpful things had been spoken to her. Somehow, she knew not how, the peace of the day was creeping into her heart. For some reason, she knew not why, the torment and unrest of the night were gone. There was a future to be settled, but she would not trouble herself about that just now. There was breakfast to get; and the sun shone, and a snow-bird was chirping outside of the door. She noticed how the tea-kettle hummed, and how well the new curtain, with the castle and waterfall on it, fitted the window. She thought that she would scour the closet at night, and surprise her father by finishing those list slippers. She kissed him when she had tied on the red hood, and said good-by to Dick, and told them just where to find the squash-pie for dinner.

When she had closed the twisted gate, and taken a step or two upon the snow, she came thoughtfully back. Her father was on his bench, mending one of Meg Match's shoes. She pushed it gently out of his hands, sat down upon his lap, and stroked the shaggy hair away from his forehead.

" Father ! "

" Well, what now, Sene ? — what now ? "

" Sometimes I believe I 've forgotten you a bit, you know. I think we 're going to be happier after this. That 's all."

She went out singing, and he heard the gate shut again with a click.

Sene was a little dizzy that morning, — the constant palpitation of the floors always made her dizzy after a wakeful night, — and so her colored cotton threads danced out of place, and troubled her.

Del Ivory, working beside her, said, " How the mill shakes! What 's going on ? "

" It 's the new machinery they 're h'isting in," observed the overseer, carelessly. " Great improvement, but heavy, very heavy; they calc'late on getting it all into place to-day; you 'd better be tending to your frame, Miss Ivory."

As the day wore on, the quiet of Asenath's morning

deepened. Round and round with the pulleys over her head she wound her thoughts of Dick. In and out with her black and dun-colored threads she spun her future. Pretty Del, just behind her, was twisting a pattern like a rainbow. She noticed this, and smiled.

"Never mind!" she thought, "I guess God knows."

Was He ready "to bless her, and show her how"? She wondered. If, indeed, it were best that she should never be Dick's wife, it seemed to her that He would help her about it. She had been a coward last night; her blood leaped in her veins with shame at the memory of it. Did He understand? Did He not know how she loved Dick, and how hard it was to lose him?

However that might be, she began to feel at rest about herself. A curious apathy about means and ways and decisions took possession of her. A bounding sense that a way of escape was provided from all her troubles, such as she had when her mother died, came upon her.

Years before, an unknown workman in South Boston, casting an iron pillar upon its core, had suffered it to "float" a little, a very little more, till the thin, unequal side cooled to the measure of an eighth of an inch. That man had provided Asenath's way of escape.

She went out at noon with her luncheon, and found a place upon the stairs, away from the rest, and sat there awhile, with her eyes upon the river, thinking.

She could not help wondering a little, after all, why God need to have made her so unlike the rest of his fair handiwork. Del came bounding by, and nodded at her carelessly. Two young Irish girls, sisters, - - the beauties of the mill, — magnificently colored creatures, — were singing a little love-song together, while they tied on their hats to go home.

" There *are* such pretty things in the world!" thought poor Sene.

Did anybody speak to her after the girls were gone? Into her heart these words fell suddenly, " *He* hath no form nor comeliness. *His* visage was so marred more than any man."

They clung to her fancy all the afternoon. She liked the sound of them. She wove them in with her black and dun colored threads.

The wind began at last to blow chilly up the staircases, and in at the cracks; the melted drifts out under the walls to harden; the sun dipped above the dam; the mill dimmed slowly; shadows crept down between the frames.

" It 's time for lights," said Meg Match, and swore a little at her spools.

Sene, in the pauses of her thinking, heard snatches of the girls' talk.

" Going to ask out to-morrow, Meg ? "

" Guess so, yes; me and Bob Smith we thought we 'd go to Boston, and come up in the theatre train."

" Del lvory, I want the pattern of your zouave."

" Did I go to church ? No, you don't catch me ! If I slave all the week, I 'll do what I please on Sunday."

" Hush-sh ! There 's the boss looking over here ! "

" Kathleen Donnavon, be still with your ghost-stories. There 's one thing in the world I never will hear about, and that 's dead people."

" Del," said Senc, " I think to-morrow — "

She stopped. Something strange had happened to her frame ; it jarred, buzzed, snapped ; the threads untwisted and flew out of place.

" Curious ! " she said, and looked up.

Looked up to see her overseer turn wildly, clap his hands to his head, and fall ; to hear a shriek from Del that froze her blood ; to see the solid ceiling gape above her ; to see the walls and windows stagger ; to see iron pillars reel, and vast machinery throw up its helpless, giant arms, and a tangle of human faces blanch and writhe !

She sprang as the floor sunk. As pillar after pillar gave way, she bounded up an inclined plane, with the gulf yawning after her. It gained upon her, leaped at her, caught her ; beyond were the stairs and an open door ; she threw out her arms, and struggled on with hands and knees, tripped in the gearing, and saw, as she fell, a square, oaken beam above her yield and crash ; it was of a fresh red color ; she dimly wondered why, — as she felt her hands slip, her knees slide, support, time, place, and reason, go utterly out.

"*At ten minutes before five, on Tuesday, the tenth of January, the Pemberton Mill, all hands being at the time on duty, fell to the ground.*"

So the record flashed over the telegraph wires, sprang into large type in the newspapers, passed from lip to lip, a nine days' wonder, gave place to the successful candidate, and the muttering South, and was forgotten.

Who shall say what it was to the seven hundred and fifty souls who were buried in the ruins ? What to the eighty-eight who died that death of exquisite agony ? What to the wrecks of men and women who endure unto this day a life that is worse than death ? What to that architect and engineer who, when the fatal pillars were first delivered to them for inspection, had found one broken under their eyes, yet accepted the contract, and built with them a mill whose thin walls and wide, unsupported stretches might have tottered over massive columns and on flawless ore ?

One that we love may go upon battle-ground, and we are ready for the worst: we have said our goodbys ; our hearts wait and pray : it is his life, not his death, which is the surprise. But that he should go out to his safe, daily, commonplace occupations, unnoticed and uncaressed, — scolded a little, perhaps, because he leaves the door open, and tells us how cross

we are this morning ; and they bring him up the steps
by and by, a mangled mass· of death and horror, —
that is hard.

Old Martyn, working at Meg Match's shoes, — she
was never to wear those shoes, poor Meg ! — heard, at
ten minutes before five, what he thought to be the
rumble of an earthquake under his very feet, and
stood with bated breath, waiting for the crash.   As
nothing further appeared to happen, he took his stick
and limped out into the street.

A vast crowd surged through it from end to end.
Women with white lips were counting the mills, —
Pacific, Atlantic, Washington, — Pemberton ? Where
was Pemberton ?

Where Pemberton had winked its many eyes last
night, and hummed with its iron lips this noon, a
cloud of dust, black, silent, horrible, puffed a hundred
feet into the air.

Asenath opened her eyes after a time. Beautiful
green and purple lights had been dancing about her,
but she had had no thoughts. It occurred to her now
that she must have been struck upon the head. The
church-clocks were striking eight. A bonfire which
had been built at a distance, to light the citizens in
the work of rescue, cast a little gleam in through the
débris across her two hands, which lay clasped together at her side. One of her fingers, she saw, was
gone ; it was the finger which held Dick's little engagement ring. The red beam lay across her fore-

4 *   F

head, and drops dripped from it upon her eyes. Her feet, still tangled in the gearing which had tripped her, were buried beneath a pile of bricks.

A broad piece of flooring, that had fallen slantwise, roofed her in, and saved her from the mass of iron-work overhead, which would have crushed the breath out of Titans. Fragments of looms, shafts, and pillars were in heaps about. Some one whom she could not see was dying just behind her. A little girl who worked in her room — a mere child — was crying, be-tween her groans, for her mother. Del Ivory sat in a little open space, cushioned about with reels of cotton ; she had a shallow gash upon her cheek; she was wringing her hands. They were at work from the outside, sawing entrances through the labyrinth of planks. A dead woman lay close by, and Sene saw them draw her out. It was Meg Match. One of the pretty Irish girls was crushed quite out of sight; only one hand was free ; she moved it feebly. They could hear her calling for Jimmy Mahoney, Jimmy Maho-ney ! and would they be sure and give him back the handkerchief? Poor Jimmy Mahoney ! By and by she called no more ; and in a little while the hand was still. On the other side of the slanted flooring some one prayed aloud. She had a little baby at home. She was asking God to take care of it for her. " For Christ's sake," she said. Sene listened long for the Amen, but it was never spoken. Beyond, they dug a man out from under a dead body, unhurt. He crawled to his feet, and broke into furious blasphemies.

As consciousness came fully, agony grew. Sene shut her lips and folded her bleeding hands together, and uttered no cry. Del did screaming enough for two, she thought. She pondered things calmly as the night deepened, and the words that the workers outside were saying came brokenly to her. Her hurt, she knew, was not unto death ; but it must be cared for before very long ; how far could she support this slow bleeding away ? And what were the chances that they could hew their way to her without crushing her ?

She thought of her father, of Dick ; of the bright little kitchen and supper-table set for three ; of the song that she had sung in the flush of the morning. Life — even her life — grew sweet, now that it was slipping from her.

Del cried presently, that they were cutting them out. The glare of the bonfires struck through an opening ; saws and axes flashed ; voices grew distinct.

" They never can get at me," said Sene. " I must be able to crawl. If you could get some of those bricks off of my feet, Del ! "

Del took off two or three in a frightened way ; then, seeing the blood on them, sat down and cried.

A Scotch girl, with one arm shattered, crept up and removed the pile, then fainted.

The opening broadened, brightened ; the sweet

night-wind blew in; the safe night-sky shone through. Sene's heart leaped within her. Out in the wind and under the sky she should stand again, after all! Back in the little kitchen, where the sun shone, and she could sing a song, there would yet be a place for her. She worked her head from under the beam, and raised herself upon her elbow.

At that moment she heard a cry:

" Fire ! *fire !* GOD ALMIGHTY HELP THEM, — THE RUINS ARE ON FIRE ! "

A man working over the *débris* from the outside had taken the notion — it being rather dark just there — to carry a lantern with him.

" For God's sake," a voice cried from the crowd, " don't stay there with that light ! "

But before the words had died upon the air, it was the dreadful fate of the man with the lantern to let it fall, — and it broke upon the ruined mass.

That was at nine o'clock. What there was to see from then till morning could never be told or forgotten.

A network twenty feet high, of rods and girders, of beams, pillars, stairways, gearing, roofing, ceiling, walling ; wrecks of looms, shafts, twisters, pulleys, bobbins, mules, locked and interwoven ; wrecks of human creatures wedged in ; a face that you know turned up at you from some pit which twenty-four hours' hewing could not open ; a voice that you know crying after you from God knows where ; a mass of long, fair hair visible here, a foot there, three fingers of a hand over there; the snow bright-red under foot ; charred limbs and headless trunks tossed about ; strong men carrying covered things by you, at sight of which other strong men have fainted ; the little yellow jet that flared up, and died in smoke, and flared again, leaped out, licked the cotton-bales, tasted the oiled machinery, crunched the netted wood, danced on the heaped-up stone, threw its cruel arms high into the night, roared for joy at helpless firemen, and swallowed wreck, death, and life together out of your sight, — the lurid thing stands alone in the gallery of tragedy.

" Del," said Sene, presently, " I smell the smoke." And in a little while, " How red it is growing away over there at the left ! "

To lie here and watch the hideous redness crawling after her, springing at her ! — it had seemed greater than reason could bear, at first.

Now it did not trouble her. She grew a little faint, and her thoughts wandered. She put her head down upon her arm, and shut her eyes. Dreamily she heard them saying a dreadful thing outside, about one of the overseers ; at the alarm of fire he had cut his throat, and before the flames touched him he was taken out. Dreamily she heard Del cry that the shaft behind the heap of reels was growing hot. Dreamily she saw a tiny puff of smoke struggle through the cracks of a broken fly-frame.

They were working to save her, with rigid, stern faces. A plank snapped, a rod yielded; they drew out the Scotch girl; her hair was singed; then a man with blood upon his face and wrists held down his arms.

"There's time for one more! God save the rest of ye, — I can't!"

Del sprang; then stopped, — even Del, — stopped ashamed, and looked back at the cripple.

Asenath at this sat up erect. The latent heroism in her awoke. All her thoughts grew clear and bright. The tangled skein of her perplexed and troubled winter unwound suddenly. This, then, was the way. It was better so. God had provided himself a lamb for the burnt-offering.

So she said, " Go, Del, and tell him I sent you with my dear love, and that it's all right."

And Del at the first word went.

Sene sat and watched them draw her out; it was a slow process; the loose sleeve of her factory sack was scorched.

Somebody at work outside turned suddenly and caught her. It was Dick. The love which he had fought so long broke free of barrier in that hour. He kissed her pink arm where the burnt sleeve fell off. He uttered a cry at the blood upon her face. She turned faint with the sense of safety; and, with a face as white as her own, he bore her away in his arms to the hospital, over the crimson snow.

Asenath looked out through the glare and smoke with parched lips. For a scratch upon the girl's smooth cheek, he had quite forgotten her. They had left her, tombed alive here in this furnace, and gone their happy way. Yet it gave her a curious sense of relief and triumph. If this were all that she could be to him, the thing which she had done was right, quite right. God must have known. She turned away, and shut her eyes again.

When she opened them, neither Dick, nor Del, nor crimsoned snow, nor sky, were there; only the smoke writhing up a pillar of blood-red flame.

The child who had called for her mother began to sob out that she was afraid to die alone.

"Come here, Molly," said Sene. "Can you crawl around?"

Molly crawled around.

"Put your head in my lap, and your arms about my waist, and I will put my hands in yours, — so. There! I guess that 's better."

But they had not given them up yet. In the still unburnt rubbish at the right, some one had wrenched an opening within a foot of Sene's face. They clawed at the solid iron pintles, like savage things. A fireman fainted in the glow.

"Give it up!" cried the crowd from behind. "It can't be done! Fall back!" — then hushed, awestruck.

An old man was crawling along upon his hands and

knees over the heated bricks. He was a very old man. His gray hair blew about in the wind.

"I want my little gal!" he said. "Can't anybody tell me where to find my little gal?"

A rough-looking young fellow pointed in perfect silence through the smoke.

"I'll have her out yet. I'm an old man, but I can help. She's my little gal, ye see. Hand me that there dipper of water; it'll keep her from choking, may be. Now! Keep cheery, Sene! Your old father'll get ye out. Keep up good heart, child! That's it!"

"It's no use, father. Don't feel bad, father. I don't mind it very much."

He hacked at the timber; he tried to laugh; he bewildered himself with cheerful words.

"No more ye need n't, Senath, for it'll be over in a minute. Don't be downcast yet! We'll have ye safe at home before ye know it. Drink a little more water, — do now! They'll get at ye now, sure!"

But above the crackle and the roar a woman's voice rang out like a bell: —

"We 're going home, to die no more."

A child's notes quavered in the chorus. From sealed and unseen graves, white young lips swelled the glad refrain, —

"We 're going, going home."

The crawling smoke turned yellow, turned red.

Voice after voice broke and hushed utterly. One only sang on like silver. It flung defiance down at death. It chimed into the lurid sky without a tremor. For one stood beside her in the furnace, and his form was like unto the form of the Son of God. Their eyes met. Why should not Asenath sing?

"Senath!" cried the old man out upon the burning bricks; he was scorched now, from his gray hair to his patched boots.

The answer came triumphantly, —

"To die no more, no more, no more!"

"Sene! little Sene!"

But some one pulled him back.

Afterword

AFTERWORD

Mari Jo Buhle and Florence Howe

"Whether for self-support, or for the pure employment's sake, the search for work—for successful work, for congenial work," Elizabeth Stuart Phelps wrote in 1867, "is at the bottom of half the feminine miseries of the world."[1] In her autobiography, written nearly thirty years later, Phelps describes herself as "proud . . . that I have always been a working woman, and always had to be." "When the first little story appeared in 'Harper's Magazine,' " she continues, "it occurred to me, with a throb of pleasure greater than I supposed then that life could hold, that I could take care of myself, and from that day to this I have done so."[2]

Phelps was that rare creature, a writer whose books and articles earned enough to support her comfortably, and, after age forty-four, her young husband as well. Her life and her art mirror the conflicts, failures, and achievements of women in the nineteenth century and presage women's lives today. To read her fiction is to find strong female characters who not only work in mills or as medical doctors, but, on occasion, refuse matrimony, or, entering it, are allowed to outlive their fictional husbands and return to work. Most prophetically, in *The Silent*

Partner, women in search of work attempt to cross not only the forbidden boundaries of gender, but, perhaps more significant for the future, the still more rigid boundaries of social class.

THE WORKING LIFE

Though Elizabeth Stuart Phelps was an important and prolific writer in her own day, and though she has been dead more than seventy years, there is still no standard biography of her. The known facts of her life are few; those who would catch a glimpse of the person have only *Chapters from a Life*, an autobiography Phelps wrote when she was in her fifties, which, in the manner of nineteenth-century autobiography, omits at least as much as it includes. We learn mainly of the passion she felt for her mother, the cool respect for her father, and, following the record of the early years of her life, we visit the persons she knew, the pantheon of nineteenth-century literary life: Harriet Beecher Stowe, Henry Wadsworth Longfellow, Oliver Wendell Holmes, Lucy Larcom, Lydia Maria Child, and others. Most important for the modern reader, the volume closes with an *apologia* for the literary life.[3]

There is no discussion in the autobiography of the young Phelps's relationships with women or men, of why she did not marry at a younger age, or of why she married, at forty-four, a man seventeen years her junior, who needed to be nursed back to health, and who did not stay with her for long, but who came and went through the remaining years of her life. That part of Phelps's own life is still hidden from view. But it is possible to build a portrait from the autobiography and from other writing, of the public Phelps who lived a productive life as a working woman.[4]

Born in 1844, Phelps began to write before she was twenty, modeling her life on her mother's. Elizabeth Stuart Phelps *senior* died giving birth to her third child, leaving behind this eight-year-old daughter, whom she had christened Mary, and a younger son. "Mary" promptly changed her name to "Elizabeth"; and, as she later wrote, ". . . It was impossible to be her daughter and not to write."[5] Her first published piece appeared in *Harper's* when she was still in her teens. Her first novel, *The Gates Ajar*, written in her early twenties in an unheated room in which she wore her mother's fur cape across her shoulders, was published to immediate acclaim when she was twenty-four. *The Gates Ajar* was quickly translated into fourteen languages. Of all books published in the nineteenth century, only *Uncle Tom's Cabin* sold more copies.

In the forty-two years between the publication of *The Gates Ajar* (1869) and her death in 1911, Phelps published fifty-six volumes of fiction, poetry, reminiscences, advice, theology, and drama, as well as some two hundred uncollected shorter pieces. Her life and her writing span almost the whole of the period now known as the "century of struggle." She was four years old when Elizabeth Cady Stanton and others met in a little church in Seneca Falls, New York, to ratify the "Declaration of Sentiments" that established the agenda for the nineteenth-century women's movement. That agenda, though she would not have described it as such, reflected the major concerns of Phelps's fiction: the right of women to equal educational opportunity, to satisfying and decent-paying work, and to political equality in the ballot box.

In her autobiography, Phelps explains that in the years before and during the Civil War, she was not interested "at all in any especial movement for the peculiar needs of women as a class." "I was reared," she continues, "in circles which did not concern themselves with those whom we should probably have called agitators. I was taught the old ideas of womanhood, in the old way, and had not to any important extent begun to resent them."[6] To some extent, the life glimpsed in the autobiography belies that self-description, for Phelps portrays herself as a growing girl who was a solitary figure, resenting the noisy company of four younger brothers, and an ambitious girl, whose father was so insensitive to her longings for achievement as to be unwilling even to provide her with a heated room of her own. She does not remember taking any interest in the first rounds of the women's rights

campaigns that swept New England during the 1850s. In
the early sixties, before reaching adulthood, she joined a
group of women who aimed to rescue "fallen women"—
the "indigent" and "friendless" of Abbot Hill, a factory
town near Andover, Massachusetts—from a life of degradation. In this philanthropic work, she was behaving
in a manner appropriate to a daughter of her social class.[7]

The Civil War dislodged Phelps from her conven-
tional moorings. Personal grief for a dear friend killed in
battle in 1862 grew into a pervasive sympathy for the
hundreds of thousands of bereaved women who suffered
with her—"the helpless, outnumbering, unconsulted
women; they whom war trampled down, without a choice
or protest; the patient, limited, domestic women, who
thought little, but loved much, and loving, had lost all—
to them I would have spoken."[8] Phelps had begun to re-
alize that, like the poor factory women of Abbot Hill who
succumbed to temptation because they had so few alternatives, the great mass of American women were simi-
larly powerless to participate directly in the affairs governing their lives. Phelps wrote *The Gates Ajar* to comfort
these women, to offer them a spiritual relief from the
Calvinist "chains of rusty iron, eating into raw hearts."[9]
This novel, a mixture of Christian fantasy and youthful
daring, was a *cause célèbre*. Flattered by the acclaim and
surprised by the sales, she seems to have withstood the
hostile attacks, especially—but not only—from the clergy.

The novel has since been neglected by critics—its wit and humor have not been noted, nor has Phelps's feminist consciousness been praised.

The Gates Ajar was finished by 1866, and published in late 1868 (though dated 1869). During that period, Phelps had moved on to another task: loosening the earthly chains that bound women to powerlessness. Her second novel, *Hedged In*, published in 1870, virtually sanctified the innocent victims of man's lust and society's scorn. Several stories, including "The Tenth of January," focused on the poor women of Abbot Hill, documenting their limited opportunities for wages and illustrating their vulnerability to sexual abuse. In addition, Phelps wrote a weekly column in 1871 for *The Independent*, an influential religious journal, in which her most consistent subject was the right of women to determine their own lives and especially to earn their own living.

Thus, by the early seventies, Phelps's compassion for the downtrodden, her special empathy with women "thrown on [their] own resources," grew into a profound realization that all women, rich and poor, were bound by a system of dependence on men. In 1871, she named the Woman Question "the most important question God had ever asked the world since he asked 'What think ye of Christ' on Calvary."[10] As a successful young writer, Phelps could be influential. She chose to turn away from the fantasy of a world in which women might draw their own pictures of a perfect heaven as sustenance against the unfriendly world they could not control, especially the world of war. Phelps turned from fantasy to the realism of factory life.

That she was able to do this in her mid-twenties, to write first "The Tenth of January" (1868) and then *The Silent Partner* (1871), is a measure of the depth of her social conscience and her feminist consciousness. The images of women in these novels, not surprisingly, come out of her own experience, and especially out of the perception of her mother and of other women whose lives she knew in Andover, including Harriet Beecher Stowe, with whose daughter Phelps went to school.

Phelps's greatest novel, *The Story of Avis* (1879), is a full portrayal of her mother's life—as a painter, as a wife (her marriage occurs half-way through the four-hundred-page novel), and mother; and, with a sharp reversal of the actual life, the novel concludes with the ambiguous expectations for work of the widow still surrounded by children. It is a brilliant, evocative, and complex portrait of a strong woman, swept from her moorings by marriage and childbearing, and it is also what Christine Stansell has called "a devastating analysis of the nature of heterosexuality."[11] In her autobiography, Phelps describes her mother as having "the tact and power" with which to achieve "the difficult reconciliation between genius and domestic life." In other words, her mother's children did not suffer, and, Phelps suggests, her father did not suffer. Who then suffered?

> Her last book and her last baby came together, and killed her. She lived one of those rich and piteous lives such as only gifted women know; torn by the civil war of the dual nature which can be given to women only. It was as natural for her daughter to write as to breathe; but it was impossible for her daughter to forget that a woman of intellectual power could be the most successful of mothers.[12]

The "reconciliation" could be achieved only at the greatest human cost of life itself.

Whether or not this was a direct lesson to the daughter who never bore children we will, of course, never know. But the knowledge of this mother, and the awareness that grew as the child matured—"that a mother can be strong and still be sweet, and sweet although she is strong"[13]—provided the daughter with an understanding of womanhood that was key to her fiction. She could write to Longfellow a year after the publication of *Avis*, "I believe more solemnly than I know how to say, in feminine *strength*." "Always," she continues, "I find the deepest tenderness in the strongest woman; there, too, the largest self-sacrifice, and the most faithful friend. A woman of force without tenderness is not strong but brittle."[14]

Phelps's fiction implicitly argues the case for women's right to define the character and potential of women. By describing women *as she knew them*, by using her own sensations and perceptions, including fantasies, and her own feelings and experiences, including those she deliberately, in the manner of a fictional reporter, set out to have, Phelps provides us with a world startlingly different from those drawn by her male contemporaries. Women in fiction by male writers in the nineteenth century either die or marry at the ends of novels—or they manage both at once. In those nineteenth-century American novels most celebrated today as "art," moreover, women are entirely absent, or they are sinful sufferers like Hester Prynne. But in Phelps's fiction, her readers were able to view the rich and varied fictional portraits of women in action. For women readers, these portraits sustained and encouraged: they said, "Women can lead productive and independent lives."[15]

THE LIVES OF MANY WOMEN

Elizabeth Stuart Phelps mirrored in her own life a major ideological transformation in progress among other nineteenth-century American women. A spirit of benevolence, a special concern for poor women, had called hundreds of Christian women into organized activities during the decades preceding the Civil War. The war itself seemed to mark a two-fold turning point. This developing social consciousness intensified, and at the same time a growing bloc of activists moved to articulate a far-reaching historical interpretation of woman's fate linked directly to the rising industrial order. By the late 1860s, many thousands of women had emerged as a discernible entity in American society, one that grew rapidly into the first mass women's movement in history. By the end of the century "equal wages for equal work" would serve not merely as strategic demand but also as a platform for broader principles. Women who claimed the right of fair treatment in the marketplace signaled their intention to become educated and to enter all areas of employment accessible to men. In an age when descriptive journalism and fiction provided entertainment for the literate majority, Phelps captured this nascent sensibility. Her stories and novels, which reached a contemporary popular audience, demand a knowledge of this context now distant from today's readers.

At the heart of the matter was the significant impact of the industrial revolution, especially as increasing numbers of women left their homes to join the growing ranks of wage-earners. As early as the 1820s, the sage entrepreneurs of the first mills knew they could depend upon a ready population of young women to speed the production of cotton textiles, and so they recruited vigorously among the teenagers of the New England countryside, luring them away from the protection of their families by promises of good wages and useful labor. By the 1830s young women constituted a major portion of the industrial work force in such burgeoning mill towns as Waltham and Lowell in Massachusetts and Pawtucket in Rhode Island. With much less fanfare, the old commercial cities also attracted a sizable body of young workers. Boston, which lacked the industrial employments of its neighboring mill towns, nevertheless enjoyed a prospering clothing trade with openings for women skilled with their needles. By 1837 the Massachusetts "Tables of Industry" recorded nearly 2,500 women engaged in the manufacture of garments in that great city, although many more who finished goods in their homes often went uncounted. Retail establishments, an expanding market for domestic servants, and a host of light manufacturers brought thousands of women into the growing mass of wage-earners.[16]

Within a short time, abuses overshadowed opportunities. The fact that women received less than half the wages paid to men in similar jobs distressed many who had hoped to live decently on their earnings. Worse, working conditions soon began to deteriorate as competition among manufacturers drove wages down and the speed of labor up. As early as 1834 the Lowell mill operatives staged a series of protests. Earning less than $1.25 per week in a city where a room could not be rented for under $1.00 per week, Boston seamstresses took steps toward forming a union in their trade. The economic crisis of 1837, forcing thousands from their jobs, proved yet more devastating, so that even the recovery of the 1840s could not dispel the heart-rending tragedy of "she who has seen better days."[17]

Groups of middle-class women responded in various ways to the hardships and inequities suffered by working women. Active in charities sponsored by the Protestant churches, many built upon their experiences with the poor of their communities, while redesigning programs to serve wage-earning women in particular. Exchanges for women's work appeared as early as the 1830s, in which poor women might offer their goods directly to women consumers, thus bypassing profit-hungry capitalist businessmen and receiving a steadier if not always higher wage for their labor. Sewing schools were opened by the dozens, with classes for improving the skills of common seamstresses. Day nurseries for the children of working mothers, temporary homes for newcomers to the city, infirmaries for the sick and disabled, relief agencies for the unemployed, employment bureaus to assist women searching for work, and homes for "fallen women" were among the various institutions organized by middle-class women.[18]

What began as philanthropy, an approved avocation for middle-class women, sometimes took on larger purposes. In Boston, for example, the Needle Woman's Friend Society, formed in 1847, aimed to pay seamstresses a just wage for their labor and managed, for a time, to provide a meager living to approximately sixty or seventy poor women each week. The society's managers insisted that they nurtured no charitable intentions but rather aimed "to elevate the conditions of our sex, and to do it in the way which shall best conduct self-respect as well as physical comfort."[19] They issued formal protests against the paltry wages paid by local clothing manufacturers and demanded the opening of a greater variety of employment to women. Equal opportunity and equal wages for equal work, the managers averred, would help alleviate the "army of evils" to which wage-earning women were unfairly subjected. Meanwhile, their own humble society served as a mediator, "a common group, where 'the rich and the poor may meet together,' " to benefit mutually from aid given and received.[20]

In some cases middle-class women began to draw broader lessons from their benevolent activities and identified a bond with their less fortunate peers. It was not uncommon for a woman to look into the eyes of her beleaguered sister and see there the reflection of her own potentially precarious situation. Dependent upon her father or husband, she claimed few resources she could legally call her own; death or desertion posed a comparable threat to her security and status. She knew, too, that on the relief rolls of her own benevolent society were friends and neighbors reduced, often quite suddenly, to destitution. At this point, she not infrequently drew the necessary conclusion.[21]

In 1860 woman's rights advocate Caroline Healey Dall underscored this insight in a lengthy text, *Woman's Right to Labor*. Pulling together a series of popular lectures delivered over the previous year, Dall surveyed the steady growth of the female wage-earning population and catalogued some of the most blatant forms of discrimination and injustice. She addressed middle-class women, imploring them to take up the cause of the "perishing class," to understand that economic injury to one group is, ultimately, injury to all women. She hoped "to drive the reality of the wretchedness home: *I wanted* the women to whom I spoke to feel for those 'in bonds as bound with them.' "[22]

The Civil War quickened this impulse, for the plight of working-class women was especially severe. Wages fluctuated as wildly as the prices of food and rent. While the changeover to wartime production, along with the draft of young men into the army, drew additional women into employment, especially in the rapidly expanding garment and clerical trades, it brought increased hardships to others. The loss of male breadwinners sent mothers and young children scrambling after menial, low-paying jobs. In their various societies, middle-class women were overwhelmed by the situation of the most desperate. They came to understand more fully how difficult it was for a woman to earn a livelihood for her family and even for herself, and also how unfair it was to pay men higher wages while women often carried the major burden of a family's financial support. This first-hand daily observation of so many women in distress not only deepened sympathies for the "under-class" but allowed a select group to gain yet additional insights into the economic order.[23]

Equally important, the wartime emergency had a direct impact on the lives of middle-class women. While many men were occupied with military or government affairs, wives and daughters were drawn into complex programs to ease the social upheaval caused by the war. Unprecedented demands were placed upon legions of women who took up, some for the first time, volunteer work in Northern relief agencies and hospitals. Women became affiliated with the United States Sanitary Commission, the federal government's mammoth relief agency, and conducted a great share of its labor, held fairs to raise the necessary funds for supplies, and cared for the injured. They handled the cases not only of disabled soldiers but of the seemingly more numerous women and children left poverty-stricken by the financial hard times of the era.

Although the horror of war left a permanent scar on the spirits of many, some women grew in self-esteem through their various contributions and the public acclaim they earned for valuable service. Women came to understand that they themselves were as capable as men of conducting the affairs of the community and state, and they demanded the right to participate more fully. Moreover, a sizable number expected to turn skills gained in voluntary service into credentials for paid positions in the growing professional work force.[24]

Thus, by the war's end, thousands of middle-class women had experienced an awakening similar to Elizabeth Stuart Phelps's. The suffering endured by women in a war in which they had no say, in a wartime economy in which women were the principal victims, made the injustices of the social order all the more glaring. Women who, like Phelps, had once drawn back from the militant woman's rights campaigns of the 1850s, and had limited their activities to benevolent work among poor women, now acted upon their enlarged perspective and ascended to the front ranks of a burgeoning women's movement, a movement committed not only to political equality but also to opening the doors of advancement to women into the public sphere. The right to earn just wages, to work under humane conditions, to labor freely in an occupation of one's choice—these issues now came to the fore as the basic principles of a grand movement aspiring to unite women across class lines in common struggle.

Phelps herself participated only briefly in social reform after the Civil War, amidst a flurry of temperance evangelism, but she served the rising women's movement with her pen. Her "idea of literary art" centered upon the duty of the writer "to portray the most important . . . aspects of the world he lived in."[25] For Phelps, this imperative clearly demanded focusing on women's lives in the emerging industrial order, as in the tragedy she drew from life in "The Tenth of January" and in the more imaginative, hopeful resolution of *The Silent Partner*. As historian Walter Fuller Taylor has remarked, Phelps must be regarded as "the first American novelist to treat the social problems of the Machine Age seriously and at length."[26] Writing before the naturalistic or realistic novel had taken hold, she utilized and revised a form rooted in the genre of mid-century fiction and appropriate for her intended audience.

The vision offered in *The Silent Partner* represents the culmination of a stage in feminist political development. Writing for a generation of activists, Phelps located the dynamic of the Woman Question within a specific historical context, namely, the emergence of industrial capitalism. She offered one of the first studies of its impact on women at once divided by social class, yet joined by a common state of economic dependence. Working decades before empirical, "scientific" analysis came into vogue, she went remarkably far in sketching the rudiments of a materialist perspective on sex roles. Although later writers would benefit intellectually from the forging of socialist and labor movements in the second half of the century and offer more realistic appraisals of social class, none would capture better the aspirations of women to redress their own situation. *The Silent Partner* may thus be viewed historically as a parable about the possibilities for liberation as women confront the ravages of nascent industrial capitalism.

"THE TENTH OF JANUARY" AND
THE SILENT PARTNER

In "The Tenth of January" and *The Silent Partner*, the conception of strong women, of deep tenderness—the deep tenderness we identify with "mothering"—appears without marriage or childbearing, and in a social setting distant from Phelps's Andover upbringing, and yet out of her own experience. Andover was three and one-half miles from Lawrence, Massachusetts, the home of four large textile mills, one of which, the Pemberton mill, literally collapsed onto the seven hundred and fifty workers in its midst, burying eighty-eight of them alive, and, through the additional accident of a fire begun by one of those attempting to rescue victims that night, burning many others alive.

In *Chapters from a Life* Phelps recalls this incident, which occurred when she was fifteen years old. "My brother," she writes, "being of the privileged sex, was sent over to see the scene; but I was not allowed to go."[27] From Andover Phelps could see the "red and awful glare," and in the days that followed, she writes,

> With blanching cheeks we listened to the whispers that told us how the mill-girls, caught in the ruins beyond hope of escape, began to sing . . . their young souls took courage from the familiar sound of one another's voices. They sang the hymns and

songs which they had learned in the schools and churches. No
classical strains, no "music for music's sake," ascended from that
furnace; no ditty of love or frolic; but the plain religious outcries
of the people: "Heaven is my home," "Jesus, lover of my soul,"
and "Shall we gather at the river?" Voice after voice dropped.
The fire raced on. A few brave girls sang still,—

> *"Shall we gather at the river, . . .*
> *There to walk and worship ever?"*[28]

This was in 1860. In 1861, *Life in the Iron Mills*, by
Rebecca Harding Davis, was published anonymously in
the *Atlantic*, and it is clear enough not only that Phelps
read it at some point, but that it encouraged her to write
a story about that mill accident she had been forbidden
to witness.

In 1868, Phelps published "The Tenth of January"
in the *Atlantic*. To write this story, she did what we would
call "research" or "investigative reporting": she visited the
scene itself, interviewed workers and relatives, and read
all the accounts she could find of the event as well as
later analyses of responsibility. The story she wrote falls
in a direct line between *Life in the Iron Mills* and *The
Silent Partner*. Asenath, called Sene, the hero of "The
Tenth of January," is, like Deborah in Davis's story, a
hunchbacked young woman. She is scarred across her face
as well as her shoulders as a result of beatings by an al-
coholic mother. In Phelps's story, heterosexual love, not
expected by and long denied to this misshapen creature
(and of course denied absolutely in Davis's work), comes
in the form of a kind man who for two years is her be-

trothed, wholly loyal to her, at least until he is aroused
by a beautiful woman who works beside Sene at the mill.
By accident, Sene discovers that Dick loves Del, and
though she considers committing suicide and then tries to
give Dick up in martyrdom, she is unable to do either.
Finally, the day before the fatal mill accident, she knows
she will be able to act. The accident, in fact, allows her
to act out her convictions, and also allows the reader to
judge the hitherto quite decent Dick as a shallow and
heartless fellow, since he goes off with the slightly
wounded Del, rather than help rescue the seriously
wounded Sene, who dies because no one can get to her
before the fire does. Only her pitiful old father tries to
save her and fails.

Despite the industrial accident, the point of the story
is the competition between two women, one beautiful,
the other ugly, for a man. While the germ is present in
Life in the Iron Mills, here Phelps has placed the hunchbacked woman at her story's center in order to portray
vividly a young woman's desire to be loved despite her
self-loathing and her awareness that others cannot bear
to look at her.

When this story was published, Phelps records in her
autobiography that she received her "first recognition . . .
from literary people."[29] If one can take her at her word
in the autobiography, rewards of that sort were very important to her. Hence, it is not surprising that she spent
the next two years on *The Silent Partner*, trying to explore

the lives of working-class people more fully and more realistically, and asking new questions about women and work, as well as feminist questions about the possibility of combining marriage and work. It is important to reiterate that these two works are youthful. "The Tenth of January" was published when Phelps was twenty-four; *The Silent Partner* when she was twenty-seven. They represent Phelps's effort to come to terms with two principal facts of her youthful consciousness: that she was treated differently from her brother because of gender; and that, as a female person, she was treated differently from "mill-girls" because of social class.

The Silent Partner is about the education of two young women out of silence and into speech. Sip and Perley learn from each other and from looking closely—with both feeling and intellect—at the world around them. What is unique is that the two women come from opposite ends of the social scale; under ordinary conditions, they could not have been friends. But the conditions that Phelps invents for her plot are and are not ordinary.

Both young women are connected to the factory of a mill town outside of Boston; both are motherless, and shortly after the novel opens, they are both also fatherless as well. Their first chance meeting—on the streets of Boston—would have been no more than that, except that the death of Perley Kelso's father makes her "the silent partner" in the mill—in the very town in which Sip Garth works and cares for the last remaining member of her factory-working family, a sixteen-year-old deaf and mute sister. Just as Sip has learned about the world from the people who "own it," so Perley follows that process as well: in the brilliant scene of sexual politics called "A Game of Chess," Perley discusses her legal status as her father's heir with the two men who control the mill and, as significantly, her life. Perley's partners are her fiancé and his father. Their opposition to her desire to be an *active* partner rouses latent feelings: "For the first time in her life, she was inclined to feel ashamed of being a woman."[30] Relatively quickly, Perley decides that she does not "love" her fiancé, and that she would rather spend her life working even as a "silent" partner to ameliorate the living conditions she has opened her eyes, heart, and mind to see, feel, and understand, in order to gain a sense of identity, dignity, and value as a human being.

Sip's education is different. In the course of the novel, she loses what she has seen as her best reason for living— the care of her deaf and mute sister. She has to find another purpose for living, and she cannot find it in Perley's way, for though she is only twenty-three, she thinks she is too old for further education or training. Here the novel is particularly *un*sentimental: Sip will not go to school and live happily ever after in another trade. The factory work is in her blood so deeply that she rejects marriage for fear that her children will find their way into the factory, too. Rather, she becomes at the end of the novel

the person she has unobtrusively been throughout her life
and the novel itself: the community caretaker, especially
with respect to vulnerable young women, but also to others too weak to look after themselves. Early in the novel
she says, as she rescues a young girl from rum and sex, "I
don't set up to be a preacher."[31] But that is exactly where
she ends up, with a strong voice, rich imagery, and a
fierce anger and independence as well as sympathy for
human pain and struggle:

> "Folks may make laws, but laws won't do it. Kings and con-
> gresses may put their heads together, but they'll have their trou-
> ble for nothing. Governments and churches may finger us over,
> but we'll only snarl the more.
>
> "Rich and poor, big or little, there's no way under heaven for
> us to get out of our twist, but Christ's way. . . . That way is in
> the heart. . . ."[32]

Both women refuse marriage—Perley does so twice—
because to accept even the "good" man would be to accept all that goes along with being a "wife," and, in Sip's
case, the possibility of children who would, in her view,
inevitably have to be factory workers. So the two carve
out for themselves what in the late 1860s were prophetic
visions of women's lives. As the novel ends, they are each
alone, but in the company of other women.

Several problems may trouble the modern reader of
this novel, or the literary critic. Is the novel strengthened
or weakened by the flood and the death of Catty, Sip's

young sister, imbued as they are with religious symbol-
ism? Will readers conclude, as does Carolyn Lenz of
Rhode Island College, that an interesting discussion would
follow from Phelps's "use of Christian imagery to question
whether the universe is benevolent, and by the unusual
figure of a deaf and blind Christ figure, who is also a
woman"?[33] Is Sip's evangelism a fit human and literary
conclusion for a woman who sees so clearly through class
differences and the privilege that comes with money and
position? And perhaps most problematic of all: Perley's
ability to foreclose the strike near the novel's end—is that
not a sign of the limited political vision of the young novelist? Perhaps. Certainly, all are arguable questions for
the reader, teacher, and critic.

On the other hand, one could also admire the bold
shift of the traditional nineteenth-century "woman's" plot:
these orphans—Perley and Sip—do not make their way
in the course of the novel to the safe harbor of a marriage
and domestic, submissive bliss. Rather, they move with
conviction and without self-righteousness—Sip's refusal
of Dirk, for example, causes her great pain—to the independence of their own employment.[34] Here is Perley's
way of refusing her second proposal:

> "The fact is that I have no time to think of love and mar-
> riage, Mr. Garrick. That is a business, a trade, by itself to women.
> I have too much else to do. As nearly as I can understand myself,
> that is the state of the case. I cannot spare the time for it."[35]

And yet, Phelps tells us,

> "she might have loved this man. . . . She felt old before her time. All the glamour that draws men and women together had escaped her somehow. Possible wifehood was no longer an alluring dream. Only its prosaic and undesirable aspects presented themselves to her mind."

Perley speaks to this good man once more on the subject. She breaks her silence to sound with striking simplicity the notes of her independence:

> "I do not need you now. Women talk of loneliness. I am not lonely. They are sick and homeless. I am neither. They are miserable. I am happy. They grow old. They have nothing to do. If I had ten lives, I could fill them. . . . Besides, I believe that I have been a silent partner long enough. If I married you, sir, I should invest in life, and you would conduct it. I suspect that I have a preference for a business of my own."[36]

One could write at length about the complex use of the breaking of silences, not only the silences of women, but also of working people about the conditions of their employment. And through the silence and the speech, the sounds—of the wind and the river; of the factory machines themselves; of the voices attempting song above the machines; of the silence when the machine stops so that the body of the child caught in its maw may be released. Even the silence of Beethoven's music in the painting by Lemude enlarges the metaphor, especially since the painting becomes Sip's consolation after Perley gives it to her. The painting speaks to Sip across the gulf of class, as Beethoven's music speaks to many who cross Perley's threshold, even as the voices of Sip and of the child Bub, among others, are meant to speak to the middle-class reader of the novel.

The voices ring true, not only in those striking scenes between Perley and the men who run the factory and would run her life, but in the ones that attempt to break the barrier of social class. When Perley meets eight-year-old Bub Mell, who wants a ten-cent piece in exchange for the glove she had not missed until he appeared on the street with it, Phelps gives Perley the "straight" lines in a dialogue that portrays the lives of factory children forgotten by schools, churches, and middle-class families.

> "I never saw such a little boy as you chew tobacco before," said Perley, gasping.
> "You must be green! I took my fust swag a year and a half ago. We all does. I'm just out, it happens," said Bub, with a candid smile. "That's what I wanted your ten cents for. I smokes too," added Bub, with an air of having tried not to mention it, for modesty's sake, but of being tempted overmuch. "You bet I do! Sometimes it's pipes, and sometimes it's ends. As a gener'l thing, give me a pipe."[37]

For many readers, the most important silence broken by the novel will be the silence between the Perleys and the Sips. Their encounters are unsentimentally portrayed: Sip and Perley are not afraid to say what they think. In their first encounter on the issue of class differences, Sip points out that she usually "hates" Perley's "kind of folks," that, indeed, all working people do hate Perley's kind of folks, not "because they don't care, but because they don't *know;* nor they don't care enough to *know.*"[38] Phelps envisions this friendship between Sip and Perley allowing each of them to garner the strength to redirect her life. Sip gains the confidence to become a public figure. She vindicates the memory of her martyred sister by becoming an evangelist for the mill workers. Through her life, Christianity serves not social control, but social justice, the truth of social solidarity that will ultimately free people. Perley, who has learned that she needs to act on her sense of social responsibility, finds new purpose in the practical work of helping to organize a cooperative, self-help society among the female mill operatives.

In both cases, Phelps's appeal to the reader is to the rational mind as well as to the feeling heart. Pity is *not* enough. Seeing the abominable conditions under which working-class people are forced to live; hearing the lies of the mill owners about the ways in which factories are run, about housing, about the unprotected labor of children; understanding the feelings of factory workers in conflict even with a sympathetic employer—these are the routes for Perley and the middle-class reader both to consciousness and to social reform.

As a woman-centered work, the novel is extraordinary, since its focus is not domestic life and romance, but rather industry and women's vocations. And yet, the "feminine strength" of women, the caring quality that Phelps admired in her mother, is present throughout. As Perley "cares" for Bub and sees him home, and attempts to inquire into the conditions of work for eight-year-olds more generally; as Sip cares for Catty, and for other young women in her purview; and as these women care for each other, Phelps portrays the reality of women as she sees them: the strong caretakers. They are not over-idealized—they break, they weep, they suffer the deprivations of romantic love, and not with unbelievably perfect stoicism. They move with dignity and grace, each to her own rhythm. From silvence on public subjects, the two women move through conversations with each other to find their unique public voices. Except for a handful of novels,[39] we know none like this one in which the silence of women finds voice in public places.

Mari Jo Buhle
Brown University

Florence Howe
*State University of New York
at Old Westbury*

NOTES

[1] Elizabeth Stuart Phelps, "What Shall They Do?" *Harper's* 35 (September 1867): 519–23.

[2] Elizabeth Stuart Phelps (Ward), *Chapters from a Life* (Boston: Houghton Mifflin & Co., 1897), p. 79. To avoid confusion, and since Elizabeth Stuart Phelps published for most of her life as Phelps, we are continuing that usage.

[3] Phelps was frankly didactic in her esthetic purpose. *The Silent Partner* originally carried an epigraph on its title page: " 'Read not to contradict and confute, nor to believe and take for granted, nor to find talk and discourse, but to weigh and consider.' —Bacon." The chapter of her autobiography that focuses on the function of literature is called "Art for Truth's Sake." In that chapter, she writes, "Where 'the taste' is developed at the expense of 'the conscience,' the artist is incomplete" (p. 262). And yet, she would advise against writing tracts: "The moral," she says, "takes care of itself" when artists "portray the struggle," as in Victor Hugo's *Les Miserables* (p. 164). She respects Victor Hugo and other writers particularly because they "portray life as it is . . . steadily and sturdily and always [with] moral responsibility" (p. 263). In this chapter also, she notes, "I am distinctly aware that such sympathies with the moral agitations of our day as have touched me at all, have fed, not famished my literary work" (p. 256).

[4] Before the late 1970s, only one dissertation had been written on Elizabeth Stuart Phelps, by Mary Angela Bennett in 1939. Two have been written recently; one, by Lori Duin Kelly will result in a book entitled *The Life and Works of Elizabeth Stuart Phelps: Victorian Feminist Writer*, to appear in 1983; the other, an unpublished dissertation completed at the University of Iowa in 1979 by Susan Margaret Coultrap-McQuin, is entitled "Elizabeth Stuart Phelps: The Cultural Context of a Nineteenth-Century Professional Writer." We are especially grateful to Professor Coultrap-McQuin for allowing us to read several

of her chapters, and thus to catch a glimpse of Phelps the letter-writer and the complex person awaiting the biographer.

[5] Phelps (Ward), *Chapters from a Life*, p. 15.

[6] Ibid, p. 99.

[7] For a discussion of Phelps's reform activities and their influence on her writing, see Lori Duin Kelly, " 'Oh the Poor Women'—A Study of the Works of Elizabeth Stuart Phelps," unpublished dissertation, University of North Carolina, 1979; and also Coultrap-McQuin, unpublished dissertation, University of Iowa, 1979.

[8] Phelps (Ward), *Chapters from a Life*, p. 98.

[9] Idem.

[10] Elizabeth Stuart Phelps, "The Higher Claim," *The Independent* (October 5, 1871): 1.

[11] Christine Stansell, "Woman: An Issue," *Massachusetts Review* (1972):239.

[12] Phelps (Ward), *Chapters from a Life*, p. 12.

[13] Ibid., p. 15.

[14] Quoted by Coultrap-McQuin, unpublished dissertation, University of Iowa, 1979, p. 75, from a letter that Phelps wrote to Henry Wadsworth Longfellow, August 22, 1878.

[15] In an unpublished essay entitled "The Career Woman Fiction of Elizabeth Stuart Phelps," Susan Ward measures Phelps's ideas about women against the four tenets of the Cult of True Womanhood: piety, purity, domesticity, and obedience. And she finds Phelps, as we have, as not conforming; indeed, as using her power as a writer to undermine at least two of those tenets: domesticity and obedience. She quotes Phelps as writing (in *The Independent* of July 13, 1871, in an essay entitled "The Jist of the Matter"), "The real trouble at the core of this question is the reluctance of men to yield the superiority which they have assumed and acquired by virtue of being the governing class to a class which, at the most which can be said, they have made the foil of their own elevation and the mirror of their own excellencies." Susan Ward concludes, "Phelps called for women's financial independence as a first step toward breaking the 'class rule' " (p. 3).

[16] Helen L. Sumner, *History of Women in Industry in the United States* (New York: Arno Press, 1974; reprint of 1910 ed.), Chapter 3.

For a brief historical overview, see Barbara Mayer Wertheimer, *We Were There: The Story of Working Women in America* (New York: Pantheon Books, 1977), Chapters 5–7.

[17] Philip S. Foner, *Women and the American Labor Movement: From Colonial Times to the Eve of World War I* (New York: The Free Press, 1979). Chapters 3 and 4 detail the early protests by working women.

[18] Keith Melder, *Beginnings of Sisterhood: The American Woman's Rights Movement, 1800–1850* (New York: Schocken Books, 1977), Chapter 3. For a case study of an exchange for women's work, see Susan Porter Benson, "Business Heads and Sympathizing Hearts: The Women of the Providence Employment Society, 1837–1858," *Journal of Social History* 12 (Winter 1978): 302–12.

[19] *Report for the Second Anniversary of the Needle Woman's Friend Society* (Boston, 1849), pp. 3–4.

[20] *Report for the Second Anniversary of the Needle Woman's Friend Society* (Boston, 1850), p. 4.

[21] Barbara J. Berg, *The Remembered Gate: Origins of American Feminism* (New York: Oxford Univ. Press, 1978), describes the development of feminist consciousness within antebellum female reform societies.

[22] Caroline H. Dall, *Woman's Right to Labor; Or, Low Wages and Hard Work* (Boston: Walker, Wise & Co., 1860), p. vii.

[23] Sumner, *History of Women in Industry*, pp. 144–55. For a discussion of feminists' reactions to the plight of working women in the 1860s, see Ellen Carol DuBois, *Feminism and Suffrage: The Emergence of an Independent Women's Movement in America, 1848–1869* (Ithaca, N.Y.: Cornell Univ. Press, 1978), Chapter 4.

[24] For a noteworthy case study, see Mary A. Livermore, *My Story of the War: A Woman's Narrative of Four Years' Personal Experience* (Hartford, Conn.: A. D. Worthington & Co., 1889).

[25] Phelps (Ward), *Chapters from a Life*, p. 265.

[26] Walter Fuller Taylor, *The Economic Novel in America* (Chapel Hill: Univ. of North Carolina Press, 1942), p. 58.

[27] Phelps (Ward), *Chapters from a Life*, p. 91.

[28] Ibid., pp. 90–91.

[29] Ibid., p. 92.

[30] Elizabeth Stuart Phelps, *The Silent Partner* (Boston: James R. Osgood & Co., 1871), p. 59.

[31] Ibid., p. 122.

[32] Ibid., p. 299.

[33] From an unpublished paper delivered at the University of Alabama on July 7, 1979.

[34] Susan Ward, "The Career Woman Fiction." Ward describes the tradition of nineteenth-century novels written by women, and notes that Phelps deliberately broke with that tradition especially on the issue of marriage, but also on the issue of love, since, as Ward says of Phelps's novels, "The love story, when it exists as part of the plot, represents a threat, rather than a salvation, for the heroine" (p. 14).
heroine" (p. 14).

[35] Phelps, *The Silent Partner*, p. 260.

[36] Ibid., pp. 261–62.

[37] Ibid., p. 103.

[38] Ibid., p. 95.

[39] Two such novels are published by The Feminist Press: Agnes Smedley, *Daughter of Earth*, an autobiographical novel about a working-class woman's escape from poverty into political activity; and Elizabeth Robins, *The Convert*, about upper- and working-class women in Britain during the early days of the suffrage movement. In addition, of course, Smedley's *Portraits of Chinese Women in Revolution* portrays a similar transformation among women.

The Feminist Press at The City University of New York offers alternatives in education and in literature. Founded in 1970, this nonprofit, tax-exempt educational and publishing organization works to eliminate stereotypes in books and schools and to provide literature with a broad vision of human potential. The publishing program includes reprints of important works by women, feminist biographies of women, multicultural anthologies, a cross-cultural memoir series, and nonsexist children's books. Curricular materials, bibliographies, directories, and a quarterly journal provide information and support for students and teachers of women's studies. Through publications and projects, The Feminist Press contributes to the rediscovery of the history of women and the emergence of a more humane society.

NEW AND FORTHCOMING BOOKS

The Answer/La Respuesta, including a Selection of Poems, by Sor Juana Ines de la Cruz. Edited by Electa Arenal and Amanda Powell. $35.00 cloth, $12.95 paper.

Changes, a novel by Ama Ata Aidoo. Afterword by Tuzyline Jita Allan. $35.00 cloth, $12.95 paper.

Fault Lines, a memoir by Meena Alexander. $35.00 cloth, $12.95 paper.

Get Smart! What You Should Know (But Won't Learn in Class) about Sexual Harassment and Sexual Discrimination, second edition, by Montana Katz and Veronica Vieland. $35.00 cloth, $12.95 paper.

Proud Man, a novel by Katharine Burdekin. Foreword and afterword by Daphne Patai. $35.00 cloth, $14.95 paper.

The Seasons: Death and Transfiguration, a memoir by Jo Sinclair. $35.00 cloth, $12.95 paper.

Unspeakable Women: Selected Short Stories Written by Italian Women During Fascism, edited by Robin Pickering-Iazzi. $35.00 cloth, $14.95 paper.

Women Composers: The Lost Tradition Found, second edition, by Diane Peacock Jezic. Foreword by Elizabeth Wood. Second edition prepared by Elizabeth Wood. $35.00 cloth, $14.95 paper.

Women Writing in India: 600 B.C. to the Present. Volume I: 600 B.C. to the Early Twentieth Century. Volume II: The Twentieth Century. Edited by Susie Tharu and K. Lalita. Each volume $59.95 cloth, $29.95 paper.

Prices subject to change. Individuals: Send prepaid book orders to The Feminist Press at The City University of New York, 311 East 94 Street, New York, NY 10128. Please include $3.00 postage and handling for the first book, $.75 for each additional. Feminist Press titles are distributed to the trade by Consortium Book Sales & Distribution, (800) 283-3572.